Love & Luck

ALSO BY JENNA EVANS WELCH

Love & Gelato

LOVE & LUCK

JENNA EVANS WELCH

SIMON PULSE
New York Amsterdam/Antwerp London
Toronto Sydney/Melbourne New Delhi

SIMON PULSE
An imprint of Simon & Schuster Children's Publishing Division
1230 Avenue of the Americas, New York, New York 10020
This Simon Pulse paperback edition June 2019

Also available in a Simon Pulse hardcover edition.

Interior designed by Mike Rosamilia
The text of this book was set in Adobe Caslon Pro.
Manufactured in the United States of America
14 16 18 20 19 17 15 13
The Library of Congress has cataloged the hardcover edition as follows:
Library of Congress Cataloging-in-Publication Data
Names: Welch, Jenna Evans.
Title: Love & luck / by Jenna Evans Welch.
Other titles: Love and luck
Description: First Simon Pulse hardcover edition. | New York : Simon Pulse, 2018. |
Summary: In order to fix their shattered sibling relationship—and Addie's broken heart—Addie and Ian take a road trip across Ireland filled with unexpected detours and a stop at a major musical festival.
Identifiers: LCCN 2018024934 | ISBN 9781534401006 (hardcover)
Subjects: | CYAC: Brothers and sisters—Fiction. | Love—Fiction. | Ireland—Fiction.
Classification: LCC PZ7.1.W435 Lq 2018 | DDC [Fic]—dc23
LC record available at https://lccn.loc.gov/2018024934
ISBN 9781534401013 (paperback)
ISBN 9781534401020 (eBook)

To Nora Jane,
the possessor of two exceptionally plucky feet and a one-dimpled smile that lit up my darkness for over a year. This one's for you, baby girl.

Love & Luck

Dear Heartbroken,

What do you picture when you imagine traveling through Ireland? Belting out drinking songs in a dim, noisy pub? Exploring mossy castles? Running barefoot through a field of four-leaf clovers? Or maybe that old Johnny Cash song: *green, green, forty shades of green.*

Whatever you've imagined, my little lovelorn friend, I can emphatically say *you're wrong*. I'm not saying you won't find yourself singing a rousing rendition of "All for Me Grog" at a little tavern in Dublin, or that you won't spend your fair share of afternoons stumbling through waterlogged castle grounds. But I am saying that this trip of yours will undoubtedly be *even better than anything you've imagined*. Don't believe me? Wait until you're standing at the edge of the Cliffs of Moher, your hair being whipped into a single dreadlock, your heart pattering like a drum. Then we'll talk.

I know you're feeling fragile, turtledove, so let me just lay it all out for you. You are about to fall head over heels in love with a place that will not only heal that little heart of yours, but also challenge you in every way imaginable. Time to open your suitcase, your mind, and, most of all, this guidebook, because not only am I an insufferable expert on all things Ireland, but I'm also an insufferable expert on heartbreak. Consider me a two-for-one guide. And don't pretend you don't need me. We both know there are a thousand travel guides on Ireland, and yet you picked up *this* one.

You've come to the right place, love muffin. The Emerald Isle may not be the only place to mend a broken heart, but it is the best.

Trust me.

PS: On a recent, particularly vibrant afternoon in County Clare, Ireland, I counted forty-seven shades of green. So take that, Johnny.

—Introduction to *Ireland for the Heartbroken: An Unconventional Guide to the Emerald Isle, third edition*

Prologue

WORST SUMMER EVER.

That's the thought I went over the side with. Not *I'm falling.* Not *I just shoved my brother off the Cliffs of Moher.* Not even *My aunt is going to kill me for ruining her big day.* Just *Worst summer ever.*

You could say that my priorities weren't in the best shape. And by the bottom of the hill, neither was I.

When I finally rolled to a stop, my designer dress and I had been through at least ten mud puddles, and I was lying in something definitely livestock-related. But cow pies weren't the worst of it. Somewhere along the way I'd hit something—hard—and my lungs were frantically trying to remember what they were supposed to do. *Inhale*, I begged them. *Just inhale.*

Finally, I got a breath. I closed my eyes, forcing myself to slow down and breathe in and out to the count of five like I do whenever I get the wind knocked out of me, which is way more often than the average person.

I have what my soccer coach calls the *aggression factor.* Meaning, whenever we arrive at a school where the players look like Attila the Hun in ponytails, I know I'll be playing the whole game. Getting the wind knocked out of me is kind of a specialty of mine. It's just that usually when it happens, I'm wearing soccer cleats and a jersey, not lipstick and designer heels.

Where's Ian? I rolled to my side, searching for my brother. Like me, he was on his back, his navy-blue jacket half-off, head pointed down the hill toward all the tourist megabuses in the parking lot. But unlike me, he wasn't moving.

At all.

No. I sprang to my knees, panic filming over my vision. My high heels impaled the hem of my dress, and I struggled to untangle myself, scenes from the cheesy CPR movie they made us watch in health class firing through my head. Did I start with mouth to mouth? Chest compressions? Why hadn't I paid attention in health class?

I was about to fling myself at him when his eyes suddenly snapped open.

"Ian?" I whispered.

"Wow," he said wearily, squinting up at the clouds as he wiggled one arm, then the other.

I fell back into a relieved heap, tears spiking my eyes. I may have shoved my brother off the side of a mountain, but I hadn't killed him. That had to count for something.

"Keep moving; eyes up here." I froze. The voice was British and much too close. "Hag's Head is a bit farther. Ooh, and look, there's a wedding going on up top. Everyone see the lovely bride? And . . . oh, my. I think she lost a bridesmaid. A tiny lavender bridesmaid. Hellooooo there, tiny lavender bridesmaid. Are you all right? Looks like you've had a fall."

I whipped around, my body tensed to unleash on whoever had just dubbed me "tiny lavender bridesmaid," but what I saw made me wish I was even tinier. Not only had Ian and I landed a lot closer to the walkway than I'd realized, but a tour guide sporting a cherry-red poncho and a wide-brimmed hat was leading a pack of enraptured tourists right past us. Except none of them were looking at the sweeping landscape or the lovely bride, who happened to be my aunt Mel. They were looking at *me*. All thirty of them.

You'd think they'd never seen a midwedding fistfight before.

Act in control.

I straightened up, shoving my skirt down. "Just a little tumble," I said brightly. *Yikes.* "Tumble" was not a typical part of my vocabulary. And whose robotic happy voice was coming out of my mouth?

The tour guide pointed her umbrella at me. "Did you really just fall down that big hill?"

"Looks like it," I said brightly, the thing I actually wanted to say brimming under the surface. *No. I'm just taking a nap in a manure-coated dress.* I shifted my eyes to Ian. He appeared to be playing dead. Convenient.

"You're sure you're okay?"

This time I injected my voice with a heavy dose of *now please go away.* "I'm sure."

It worked. The guide scowled at me for a moment and then lifted her umbrella, making clucking noises to the group, who begrudgingly shuffled forward like a giant, single-brained centipede. At least that was done with.

"You could have helped me out with the tour group," I called to Ian's motionless form.

He didn't respond. Typical. These days, unless he was cajoling me to come clean to our parents about what had happened this summer, he barely looked at me. Not that I could blame him. *I* could barely look at me, and I was the one who'd messed up in the first place.

A raindrop speckled down on me. Then another. *Really? Now?* I shot a reproachful look at the sky and pulled my elbow in next to my face, cradling my head in my arm as I assessed my options. Apart from seeking shelter in one of the souvenir shops built into the hills like hobbit holes, my only other choice was to hike back up to the wedding party, which included my mother, whose rage was already sweeping the countryside. There was absolutely no way I was going to put myself in the line of fire before I had to.

I listened to the waves smash violently against the cliffs, the wind carrying a few snippets of voices over the top of the hill like the butterfly confetti we'd all thrown a few minutes earlier:

Did you see that?

What happened?

Are they okay?

"I'm not okay!" I yelled, the wind swallowing up my words. I hadn't been okay for exactly one week and three days, which was when Cubby Jones—the boy I'd been sneaking out with all summer, the boy I had been in love with for what amounted to my entire teen life—had decided to crush my heart into a fine powder and then sprinkle it out over the entire football team. *Ian's* football team. No wonder he couldn't stand to look at me.

So no. I was most definitely not okay. And I wasn't going to be okay for a very, very long time.

Maybe ever.

The Wild Atlantic Way

Me again, buttercup. Here to give you an extraordinarily important tip as you enter the planning phase of your journey. Read carefully, because this is one of the few hard-and-fast rules you will find in this entire book. You listening? Here goes. *As a first-time visitor to Ireland, do not, under any circumstances, begin your trip in the capital city of Dublin.*

I know that sounds harsh. I know there's a killer deal to Dublin on that travel website you've been circling like a vulture all week, but hear me out. There are a great many reasons to heed my advice, the main one being this:

Dublin is *seductive as hell.*

I know what you're going to do next, sugar. You're going to argue with me that there isn't anything particularly seductive about hell, to which I would counter that it's an excellent place to meet interesting people, and those fiery lakes? Perfect for soaking away stress.

But let's not get sidetracked.

Bottom line, Dublin is a vacuum cleaner and you are one half of your favorite pair of dangly earrings—the one you've been missing since New Year's. If you get too close to that city, it will suck you up and there will be no hope for unmangled survival. Do I sound like I'm being overly dramatic? Good. Have I used one too many metaphors? Excellent. Because Dublin is dramatic and worthy of metaphor overuse. It's full of interesting museums, and statues with hilariously inappropriate nicknames, and pubs spewing out some of the best music on earth. Everywhere you go, you'll see things you want to do and see and taste.

And therein lies the problem.

Many a well-intentioned traveler has shown up in Dublin with plans to spend a casual day or two before turning their attention to the rest of Ireland. And many a well-intentioned traveler has found themselves, a week later, on their ninetieth lap of Temple Bar, two leprechaun snow globes and a bag full of overpriced T-shirts the only things they have to show for it.

It's a tale as old as time.

My firm recommendation (command?) is that you begin in the west, most particularly, the Wild Atlantic Way. Even more particularly, the Burren and the Cliffs of Moher. We'll get to them next.

HEARTACHE HOMEWORK: *Surprise!* As we traipse across this wild island of ours, I will be doling out little activities designed to engage you with Ireland and baby-step you out from under that crushing load of heartache you're packing around. Assignment one? Keep reading. No, really. *Keep reading.*

—Excerpt from *Ireland for the Heartbroken: An Unconventional Guide to the Emerald Isle, third edition*

"YOU WERE BRAWLING. DURING THE *CEREMONY*." WHENEVER my mom was upset, her voice lowered three octaves and she pointed out things that everyone already knew.

I pulled my gaze away from the thousand shades of green rushing past my window, inhaling to keep myself calm. My dress was bunched up around me in a muddy tutu, and my eyes were swollen drum-tight. Not that I had any room to talk: Ian's eye looked much worse. "Mom, the ceremony was over; we—"

"Wrong side, wrong side!" Archie yelled.

Mom swore, swerving the car over to the left and out of the way of an oncoming tractor while I dug my fingernails into the nearest human flesh, which happened to belong to my oldest brother, Walter.

"Addie, stop!" he yelped, pulling his arm away. "I thought we agreed you weren't going to claw me to death anymore."

"We almost just got into a head-on collision with an oversize piece of farm equipment. It's not like I can control what I do," I snapped, shoving him a few inches to the left. I'd spent the last seventy-two hours crammed between my two largest brothers in every variation of transportation we encountered, and my claustrophobia was hovering around a level nine. Any higher and I was going to start throwing punches. Again.

"Mom, don't listen to them—you're doing great. There were a good three inches between you and that tractor," my other brother Archie said, reaching under the headrest and patting her on the shoulder. He narrowed his blue eyes at me and mouthed, *Don't stress her out*.

Walt and I rolled our eyes at each other. The man at the airport car rental desk had insisted that it would take only an hour, two tops, for my mom to get the hang of driving on the opposite side of the road, but we were more than forty-eight hours in, and every time we got in the car, I got the same sinking feeling that rickety carnival rides always gave me. *Impending doom.* I held the airport car rental man personally responsible for all the emotional and psychological damage I was undoubtedly going home with.

Only Ian, whose perpetual car sickness made him the unspoken victor of the front seat, was unfazed. He rolled down the window, sending a cool burst of cow-scented air into the car, his knee doing the perpetual Ian bounce.

There are two important things to know about Ian. One, he never stops moving. Ever. He's the smallest of my brothers, only a few inches taller than me, but no one ever notices that because his energy fills up whatever room he's in. And two, he has an anger threshold. Levels one through eight? He yells like the rest of us. Nine and above? He goes silent. Like now.

I leaned forward to get another look at his black eye. A slash of mud crossed under his ear, and grass peppered his hair. His eye was really swollen. Why was his eye so swollen already?

Ian gingerly touched the skin under his eye, as if he was thinking the same thing. "Brawling? Come on, Mom. It was just an argument. I don't think anyone even saw." His voice was calm, bored even. He was really trying to convince her.

"'Argument' implies that there wasn't any violence. I saw fists. Which makes it a brawl," Walter added helpfully. "Plus, everyone, look at Ian's eye."

"Do *not* look at my eye," Ian growled, his Zen slipping away.

Everyone glanced at him, including my mom, who immediately started to drift to the opposite side of the road.

"Mom!" Archie yelled.

"I *know*," she snapped, pulling back to the left.

I really hurt Ian. My heart started in on a dangerous free fall, but I yanked it back into place. I had exactly no room for guilt. Not when I was already filled to the brim with remorse, shame, and self-loathing. Plus, Ian *deserved* that black eye. He was the one who kept bringing up Cubby—poking me with Cubby was more like it. Like he had a ball of fire on the end of a stick that he could jab at me whenever he felt like it.

Ian's voice popped into my head—the broken record I'd been listening to for ten days now. *You have to tell Mom before someone else does.*

Hot, itchy anxiety crept up my legs, and I quickly leaned over Archie to unroll the window, sending another rush of air into the car. *Don't think about Cubby. Don't think about school. Just don't think.* I was four thousand miles and ten days out from my junior year—I shouldn't spend my remaining time thinking about the disaster scene I was going back to.

I stared hard out the window, trying to anchor my mind on the scenery. Houses and B and Bs dotted the landscape in charming little clumps, their fresh white exteriors accented with brightly colored doors. Lines of laundry swung back and forth in the Irish drizzle, and cows and sheep were penned so close to the houses, they were almost in the backyards.

I still couldn't believe I was here. When you think destination wedding, you don't think rainy, windswept cliff on the western coast of Ireland, but that's exactly the spot my aunt had chosen. The Cliffs of Moher. Moher, pronounced *more*. As in more wind, more rain, more vertical feet to traverse in a pair of nude high heels. But despite the fact that my brothers had to Sherpa my aunt's new in-laws up to the top, or that all of us had sunk to our ankles in mud by the time *dearly beloved* had been uttered, I completely understood why my aunt had chosen the place.

For one thing, it made for great TV. Aunt Mel's traveling camera crew—a couple of guys in their late twenties with exceptionally well-thought-out facial hair—forced us to do the wedding processional twice, circling in on her as the wind whipped around her art deco dress in a way that should have made her look like the inflatable waving arm guy at a car dealership, but instead made her look willowy and serene. And then once we were all in place, it was all about the view, the overwhelming *grandiosity* of it. Big hunks of soft green ended abruptly in sheer cliffs, dropping straight down into the ocean, where waves threw themselves against the rocks in ecstatic spray.

The cliffs were ancient and romantic, and completely unimpressed with the fact that I'd spent the summer ruining my own life. *Your heart got publicly stomped on?* the cliffs asked. *Big deal. Watch me shatter this next wave into a million diamond fragments.*

For a while there, the view had crowded out every other possible thought. No cameras, no Cubby, no angry brother. It was the first break I'd had from my mind in more than ten days. Until Ian leaned over and whispered, *When are you telling Mom?* and all the anxiety pent up in my chest had exploded. Why couldn't he just let it go?

Walter rolled down his window, creating a cross tunnel of air through the back seat. He sighed happily. "Everyone saw the fight. There was a collective gasp when you went over the edge. I'll bet at least one of the cameramen caught it on film. And then there was that group of tourists. They were talking to you, weren't they?"

The Ian bounce stopped, replaced by angry fist clenching. He whirled on Walter. "Walt, just shut *up*."

"All of you—" my mom started, but then she blanched. "Oh, no."

"What? What is it?" Archie craned his face forward, his shoulders shooting up to his ears. "Roundabout," he said in the exact tone a NASA scientist would announce, *fiery Earth-destroying meteorite*.

I anchored myself onto both my brothers' arms. Walter clutched his seat belt to his chest, and Archie reverted into coach mode, barking out instructions. "Driver stays on the inside of the roundabout. Yield when you enter, not when you're inside. Stay focused, and whatever you do, *don't hit the brakes*. You can do this."

We hit the roundabout as though it were a shark-infested whirlpool, all of us holding our breath except for my mom, who let out a stream of loud profanities, and Ian, who carried on with his regularly programmed fidgeting. When we'd finally cleared it, there was a collective exhale from the back seat, followed by one last expletive from the driver's seat.

"Great job, Mom. If we can handle every roundabout like

that, we'll be golden," Archie said, unhooking my claws from his upper arm.

Walt leaned forward, shaking himself free of me also. "Mom, please stop swearing. You're *awful* at it."

"You can't be awful at swearing," she said shakily.

"You have single-handedly disproven that theory," Walt argued. "There's a science to it; some words go together. You can't just throw them all out at once."

"I'm going to throw *you* all out at once," Mom said.

"See, that's good, Mom," he said. "Maybe stick to the clever quips. At least those make sense."

"It's about context. And respect for the form," Ian added, his voice back to calm. I dug my fingers into my muddy skirt. Now I was confused. Was Ian angry-calm or *calm*-calm?

Archie glared at all of us. "She can use whatever combination of words she wants. Whatever gets us back to the hotel safely. Remember what you practice in your business meditations, Mom. *Go to your powerful place.*"

"Great," Ian groaned. "You've invoked the Catarina."

"There's no reason to bring her into this," I added.

Mom scowled at us dangerously. Thirteen months ago my mom had traded in her yoga pants and oversize T-shirts for a real estate wardrobe and a bunch of *Be the Business, Feel the Business* audio recordings from a local real estate guru named Catarina Hayford. And we couldn't even make fun of her for it, because in one year she had outsold 90 percent of her more seasoned fellow agents, even landing a spot on her agency's billboards. This meant that I could be almost anywhere in Seattle and look up to see her smiling imperiously down on me. And with her new busy schedule, some days it was the only time I saw her at all.

"Remind me why I paid to bring all of you to Ireland," Mom snapped, her voice rising.

Walt piped up. "You didn't pay for it—Aunt Mel did. And besides, if it weren't for Addie and Ian's performance back there, that would have been an unbelievably boring wedding, even with that crazy scenery." He nudged me. "My favorite part was the moment when little sis here decided to shove Ian off the cliff. There was this *deliberateness* to it. Like that scene in *The Princess Bride* when Buttercup shoves Wesley and he's rolling down the hill yelling, 'As yooooou wiiiiiish!'"

"Two things," Ian said, his long hair brushing his shoulder as he looked back. His gaze skipped right over me. "One, great reference, seeing as the Cliffs of Moher is where they filmed the Cliffs of Insanity scenes. And two, did you even *see* what happened?"

Walter drew his breath in sharply. "Why didn't anyone tell me that before we went? You're right. We were totally at the Cliffs of Insanity. We could have done a reenactment—"

"Stop *talking*." I laced my voice with as much menace as I could muster. When Walter got started, he was a human diesel train. Loud and really hard to stop.

"Or what? You'll throw me off a cliff?"

"It was more of a chambered punch," Archie said. "Or maybe a right hook. The technique was actually really good. I was impressed, Addie."

Ian whipped back, and this time his bruised eye stared me down. "She didn't knock me off the cliff. I *slipped*."

"Yeah, right." Walter laughed. "Way to save your ego there, buddy."

I dug my elbows into Walter and Archie's legs, but they both grabbed hold of my arms, locking me into place until I struggled free. "We went down the complete opposite side of the hill. No one was actually in danger."

Walter shook his head. "Lucky break. Auntie Mel would have never forgiven us if you'd ruined her dream wedding by committing *murder*." He whispered *murder* the way the narrator always did in his favorite true crime TV show.

"But could you imagine the ratings on the wedding episode if that happened?" Archie quipped. "HGTV would love you forever. They'd probably give you your own reality show. It would be like international wedding crasher–meets–hired hit man. Or hit woman."

"All of you, *stop*." My mom risked taking her hand off the

steering wheel to massage her right temple. "You know what? I'm pulling over."

"Mom, what are you doing?" I yelled as we bumped off the side of the road, a parade of cars honking behind us. If I had to stay sandwiched in this car for even a minute longer than was completely necessary, I was going to lose it. "There's a whole line of cars behind us. And the shoulder's almost nonexistent."

"Yes, Addie, I know that." She shakily threw the car into park, wrenching us all forward. "This can't wait."

"The fight at the cliffs was one hundred percent Ian's fault." The words screeched—unplanned—out of my mouth, and all three of my brothers turned to stare at me in horror. I had just broken Bennett sibling code rule #1: *Never throw one another under the bus*. Except this Cubby thing was on a whole new level. Maybe old rules didn't apply.

Ian's face tightened in anger. "You're the one who—"

"ENOUGH!" My mom's voice reverberated around the car like a gong. "I don't care *who* started it. I don't care if Addie drenched you with honey and then threw you into a bear den. You're teenagers, practically adults. And I have had it with your arguments. You fell off a hill. In the middle of a wedding."

Bear den? Honey? Mom had a great imagination. Walter started to laugh, but Mom wrenched her neck toward him, and he fell silent. Next she zeroed in on Ian.

"There is one year standing between you and college, and if you think I'm going to put up with how you've been acting, you're wrong. And, Addie, you're sixteen years old and you have all the self-control of a ten-year-old."

"Hey!" I started, but Archie shot his elbow into my ribs, and I doubled over. It was a saving gesture. If I had any chance of surviving this, it was going to involve the subtle art of *keeping quiet*. And Mom was right. As my outburst had just so aptly demonstrated, I did struggle with impulsivity. It got me into trouble a lot.

"You two are so close," Mom said. "The closest of any of you. There were years when I thought that neither of you knew that anyone else existed. What is going on this summer?"

And then suddenly the car was quiet. Horribly quiet. All except for the windshield wipers, which chose this exact moment to become sentient. *This summer, this summer, this summer*, they chanted, sloshing water across the window. Ian's knee slowed, and I felt his stare, heavy on my face. *Tell Mom.*

I raised my eyes to his, my telepathic message just as insistent. *I am not. Telling. Mom.*

"Fine. Don't tell me." Mom slammed her palm down on the steering wheel and we all flinched. "If Dad were here, you know you'd be on the first flight back to Seattle."

Ian and I simultaneously levitated off our seats. "Mom, no! I *have* to go to Italy. I have to go see Lina!" I shouted.

Ian's measured voice filled the car. "Mom, you've got to think this through."

She threw her hand up, deflecting our emotion like one of the backhand shots that ruled her tennis game. "I didn't say you're not going."

"Geez, chill, Addie," Walter whispered. "You almost went headfirst through the windshield."

I sagged back into my seat, panic filtering out of my veins. The only good thing about Aunt Mel's wedding—besides the gorgeous location—was that it had gotten me to Europe, the continent that had stolen my best friend from me at the beginning of the summer.

My aunt had arranged for a postwedding tour of Ireland that was supposed to include all of us, but I'd managed to talk my parents into letting me skip the tour in exchange for a few days in Italy with Lina. I hadn't seen her since she moved to Florence ninety-two days ago to live with her father, Howard, and every single one of those days had felt like a lifetime. Not seeing her was not an option. Especially now, when it was very likely she was the only friend I had left.

Ian slumped forward in relief, twisting the back of his hair into a tight corkscrew. I swore he'd grown his hair out just to give him more fidget options.

"Don't get me wrong," my mom continued. "I should be sending you both back, but we spent way too much on those tickets to Florence, and if I don't have some time away from the two of you and your constant fighting, I'm going to have a breakdown."

A fresh dose of anger hit my system. "Could someone please explain to me *why* Ian's coming with me to Italy?"

"Addie," my mom snapped. Ian shot me a wide-eyed look that said, *Shut up NOW*.

I glared back, our stares connecting. Despite the fact that I definitely should have been *Shutting up NOW,* it was an extremely valid question. Why did he want to come on a trip with me when, by all accounts, he couldn't stand me?

"So here's the deal," my mom said, inserting herself into the middle of our staring match. "Tomorrow morning, Archie, Walter, and I will leave on the tour, and the two of you will continue on to Florence." She spoke slowly, her words lining up like a row of dominoes, and I held my breath, waiting for her to topple the first one.

But . . . she didn't.

After almost ten seconds of silence, I looked up, hope lifting the edges of my voice. "That's it? We just get to go?"

"You're just going to send them to Italy?" Walter asked, sounding as incredulous as I felt. "Aren't you going to, like, punish them?"

"Walter!" Ian and I both yelled.

My mom wrenched herself around again, focusing first on me, then Ian, her spine swiveling seamlessly. At least she was putting all her yoga classes to good use. "You're going to Italy. It will force you two to spend some quality time together," she said, barbing the word "quality." "But there's a catch."

Of course there was. "What?" I asked impatiently, pulling a particularly stabby bobby pin out from its favorite spot in the back of my wilting updo. If it wouldn't completely set him off, I'd stick it in Ian's hair, try to get some of it out of his face.

"Here we go," Ian muttered, just loud enough for me to hear.

Mom paused dramatically, her eyes darting back and forth between us. "Are you both listening?"

"We're listening," I assured her, and Ian's knee bounced receptively. Couldn't he ever just hold still?

"This is your chance to prove to me that you can handle yourselves. If I hear anything bad from Lina's father, and I mean *anything*—if you fight, if you yell, if you so much as look at each other cross-eyed while you're there—both of you are off your teams."

There was a moment of dead air, and then the car exploded. "*What?*" Archie said.

"Whoa, whoa, whoa!" Walter shook his head. "Are you being serious, Mom?"

"We'll be off our teams?" I asked quickly. "Like soccer and football?"

She nodded, a self-satisfied smile spreading like warm butter across her face. She was proud of this one. "Yes. Like soccer and football. And it doesn't even have to be both of you. If one of you messes up, you're both getting punished for it. And there will be absolutely no second chances. One strike, you're out. That's it."

I thought I had no space for fresh panic, but it squeezed in with all the old stuff, turning my chest into an accordion. I leaned forward, putting my hands on the front seats to steady myself. "Mom, you know I have to play soccer this year." My voice was high and stringy, not nearly as reasonable sounding as I'd intended. "If I don't, college scouts won't see me play, and then there's no way I'll get onto a college team. This is the year that matters. This is my *future*."

"Then you'd better not mess up."

Ian's eyes met mine, and I could see the words ping-ponging through his head. *You already messed up, Addie.*

I shot lasers at him. "But—"

"This is in your control. And Ian's. I'm not backing down on this."

As if she needed to add that last part. My parents never backed down on anything. It was one of life's constants: the shortest distance between two points is a line, root beer floats always taste better half-melted, and my parents *never* take back their punishments.

But soccer? That was my way into a good school. Because no matter how hard I tried, my grades were never all that great, which meant I needed to rely on sports to get me into any college with a halfway decent engineering program. It was a long shot, but I had to try.

Plus, *soccer*. I closed my eyes, imagining the smell of the grass, the complicated rhythm of my teammates, the way time disappeared—the rest of life forced to the outer boundaries of the game. It was my place. The only place where I ever truly fit in. And with Lina moving and Ian now hating me, I needed that place more than ever.

Forget future Addie. I needed soccer for present Addie. If I had any chance of surviving post-Cubby life, it was going to be on that soccer field.

Mom tilted her head toward Ian, who was now impersonating a collapsed puppet. "Ian, are you listening?"

"Listening," he responded, his voice oddly resigned. His body language and voice all said *I don't care*, but I knew that couldn't be true. Sports were an even bigger deal to him than they were to me. He was way better at them.

"So you understand that if you *or* Addie do anything wrong, you are off the football team? No second chances, no debating, you're just off?"

"Got it," he said nonchalantly. His hand sank back into his hair, forming a tight knot.

Archie raised one finger in the air. "Not to criticize your wisdom, Mom, but that does seem a tad bit *harsh*. One of them messes up and they're *both* off their—"

"Enough from the peanut gallery," Mom snapped.

"Wait, what?" I startled, the second part of her punishment finally sticking to my brain. "You're saying that if Ian messes up, *I'm* going to be punished for it?"

"Yes. And if you mess up, Ian is going to be punished for it. Think of it as a team sport. One of you blows it, you both lose."

"But, Mom, I have absolutely no control over what Ian does. How is that fair?" I wailed.

"Life isn't fair," my mom vaulted back, a hint of glee in her voice. My parents loved maxims the way other people loved cheese or fine wines.

And how was Ian acting so *chill*? Ever since his first junior football game, where he single-handedly turned the game around and then methodically led them to the championship, football had been Ian's life. Not only was he the starting quarterback on our high school's football team, but he'd already been approached by two different colleges with talks of scholarships. One of them had been right before football camp. No wonder he was acting like he didn't care. He was probably in the process of internal collapse.

You know what Cubby's been doing, right? He's been—Without warning, Ian's words charged into my head, and I had to dive on them before they could gain any ground. I couldn't think about football camp now. Not unless I wanted to go from kind of losing it to *completely* losing it. Not when Italy was on the line.

"Great. We're all in agreement," my mom said to our silence. She turned forward, placing her hands on the steering wheel at a perfect ten and two. "Here's the plan for tonight. When we get back to the hotel, I want everyone to pack up. Walter and Archie, the tour bus leaves at some ungodly hour tomorrow morning, and you need to be ready. Addie and Ian, you are going to change and get cleaned up, and then I am taking you to your aunt's room, where you will apologize profusely and beg for her forgiveness."

"Mom—" I groaned, but she held up a hand.

"Did I say beg? I meant grovel. After that, we're all attending the wedding dinner, where I trust you will all manage to behave like civilized human beings, or at least like mildly trained apes. Then, once we've danced and eaten cake or whatever else my sister wants us to do, we will all go right to bed. And, Addie and Ian, I suggest you both figure out a way to reconcile in a nonviolent manner. Otherwise it's going to be a miserable few days in Italy. I hear that cemetery Lina lives in is pretty small."

"It isn't. It's giant," I blurted out.

"Addie," Ian said, his patience completely spent. "Stop. Talking."

"I just don't get why you—"

"Addie!" the whole car yelled.

I threw myself back into my brothers' meaty shoulders. *Stop talking.* If I wanted to play soccer, I was going to have to keep my focus on two goals: stay on Mom's good side and get along with Ian.

I bit the inside of my lip, Ian's tousled hair on the outskirts of my vision. How had getting along with Ian become a *goal*?

At any other point in our lives, Ian coming to Italy with me would have made perfect sense. He'd always been my partner in adventure. When we were in elementary school, he'd made a game out of finding strange spots around the neighborhood to surprise me with. Once we'd snuck into an abandoned shed full of molding comic books, and another day he'd boosted me up into a massive oak tree littered with initials.

"Field trips," Ian called them. And as we got older, we stuck with the tradition, driver's licenses extending our possibilities. We'd been on one just three weeks earlier.

"Field trip time." As usual, Ian hadn't bothered to knock. He'd just burst into my room, shoving past me at my desk to launch himself onto my unmade bed.

"Not happening. Mom's coworker will be here in an hour, and we will be at dinner," I said, doing my best imitation of Mom. "Also, you're getting my sheets dirty."

I hadn't actually turned around yet, so this was based entirely on speculation. But I knew Ian. Instead of showering and changing like a normal human, Ian almost always jetted straight out of practice the second it was over. The muddy upholstery of our shared car was a testament to that.

I scribbled out my last answer and flipped to a fresh page in my notebook. It offended my very essence to be enrolled in summer school, but I'd barely passed biology, and my parents and I had decided that a second go-around would be a good idea.

Ian flopped around dramatically, making my bedsprings squeak. "Mom is fine with us missing dinner for our important Student Athlete Committee meeting."

"SAC?" I spun around, my chair twisting with me. "Please tell me you did not sign me up for that." SAC was a new and desperate attempt to repair our school's reputation as having the most aggressive (read: mean) spectators in the state.

Ian grinned his signature grin, the one that took over his whole face and let me know that something exciting was about to happen. "Don't worry. I did not sign you up for that. Although if Mom asks, that's where we're going."

I let my pencil clatter onto the desk. "You know they're going to make you do it, though, right? Ms. Hampton said they were going to recruit the school's 'most beloved student athletes,' and I swear she was making googly eyes at you when she said it." I placed my hand over my heart, doing my best impression of her shaky falsetto. *"Ian, you shining star of perfection. Save us from ourselves!"*

He made a gagging face. *"Please, please, please, can we not talk about football? I'll be in the car."* He jumped up and thundered out, leaving a muddy body print splayed out on my white sheets.

"Ian," I groaned, looking at his imprint. But I grabbed my sneakers from under my desk and took off after him. Chasing after Ian never felt like a choice—it was like sleeping or brushing my teeth. It was just what I did.

The Cliffs of Moher

Every time a traveler goes to Ireland and doesn't stop at the Cliffs of Moher, a banshee loses her voice. That's right, sweet pea, a banshee. We are in Ireland after all. Shrieky ghosts abound. And as your tour guide and now friend, I'm required to tell you that one simply does not *go to Ireland and not see the cliffs*. They're nonnegotiable. Required reading. They are the entire point.

Here's why. The cliffs are gorgeous. Breath-stealing, really. But not in the soft, endearing way of a sunset or a wobbly new lamb. They're gorgeous like a storm is gorgeous—one of those raw, tempestuous ones that leave you feeling awed and scared at the same time. Ever been trapped in a car during a particularly brutal thunderstorm? The cliffs are that kind of beautiful. Think drama, rage, and peace all packed up into one stunning package.

I studied the cliffs for years before I figured out their secret—the thing that takes them from merely scenic to life-altering: *they're beautiful because they contradict themselves*. Soft, mossy hills turn to petrifying cliffs. A roiling sea rages against a serene sky. Visitors stand around in a combined state of reverence and exuberance. Before the cliffs I knew that beauty could be delightful and inspiring. After the cliffs I knew that it could also be stark and miserable.

In fact, the cliffs are an *awful* lot like a certain heart I know. You know, the one that has managed to contain both splintering joy and shattering sorrow and still remain exquisitely beautiful?

Not that anyone asked me.

HEARTACHE HOMEWORK: Let's unleash a little rage, shall we, pet? I want you to find something to throw. A rock? An annoying pigeon? Now name it. Give it the identity of the thing that is bothering you the most about this situation, and then let it fly. Sometimes a little rage is good for the system. After that, I want you to take a deep breath. And then another. Notice how the breaths just keep coming? Notice how they just take care of themselves?

—Excerpt from *Ireland for the Heartbroken: An Unconventional Guide to the Emerald Isle, third edition*

"NICE DRESS, SIS. YOU DOING A HOUSE SHOWING LATER?"

I looked up from my book, fully intending to scowl murderously at Archie, but I made it only halfway before my energy fizzled, landing me somewhere between disgust and disdain. After the day I'd had, I just didn't have any murderous left in me.

Archie, being Archie, took my passivity for an invitation and did a sideways trust fall onto the sofa, launching me and the guidebook off in the process.

"Archie, what the hell?" I growled, scrambling back into place and suddenly panicking over the fact that I was holding a book with the word "heartbroken" in the title.

The book had all but jumped into my arms from the shelf of the tiny library off the hotel ballroom. The library was convenient for a lot of reasons. Along with providing a solid view of my still-raging mother, it smelled like a soothing combination of lavender and dust and was packed full of what appeared to be cast-off books from previous hotel guests. In other words, the perfect place to hide out.

Ireland for the Heartbroken had caught my eye immediately. It wasn't much to look at. The cover was decorated with heart-shaped clovers, and a coffee ring obstructed the too-long title. But the cover didn't matter: I was in Ireland, and I was heartbroken. This book was my soul mate.

"What are you reading?" Archie asked as I attempted to stuff the book behind the sofa's cushions.

"*Little House on the Prairie*," I said, spouting off the first thing that came to mind. As a child I'd been slow to reading, but once I picked it up, I'd read those books until they fell apart. "Also, you shouldn't jump on the furniture. I think this sofa's an antique."

"This whole hotel's an antique." He gestured toward the ballroom stuffed with more antique furniture, glittery chandeliers, and precious crystal than I'd ever seen in my entire life.

But even as a pretentious wedding host, Ross Manor definitely had a magical woodland cottage feel to it, thanks to the lush lawn lined with gnarled rosebushes and the freshly plumped pillows that sprouted golden-wrapped chocolates every night before bed. Even the caretakers were adorable—a white-haired wrinkly couple that were constantly in the process of ambushing guests with offers of tea and biscuits. Walter had dubbed them the *garden gnomes*. It fit.

"How much would Dad hate this, by the way?" Archie said.

"I'm so glad he's not here." Earlier this summer, when news of our aunt's engagement had descended on our house like a particularly expensive swarm of bees, my dad had put his foot down fast and firm. *Your sister collects men like other people collect shot glasses. I am not going to another wedding where we spend a week trying to re-create a fairy tale.*

I leaned forward, doing my quarter hourly Mom check. Right now she was walking around the ballroom spiffing up the floral centerpieces that an hour ago Aunt Mel had begun shrieking were starting in on a "slow dance of death." There was obviously no room for slow dances of death. Not when ratings were involved.

Five years ago my aunt Mel started a home design show that had been picked up by HGTV. That meant that on any given afternoon I could plop down on the couch with a couple of strawberry Pop-Tarts and watch her do one of her *Thirty Minutes with Mel* renovations, where she showed viewers how to turn an old pallet into a bookcase using just a screwdriver and a dried-up jar of nail polish. Or at least I think that's what she did. I never seemed to make it all the way through an episode.

Archie tilted his head toward Aunt Mel. "How do you think she tricked this one into marrying her?"

"Clark?" I asked. Our new uncle was standing near the bar, swaying tipsily. Ever since they'd announced their engagement, he'd had the dazed look of a piece of driftwood caught in a persistent current. Par for the course. Uncles number one and two had had that look as well. I'd once heard my dad describe Aunt Mel as a riptide, which made my mom angry and my dad truthful. Mom only got mad when people were telling the truth.

"Probably with her money. And easygoing 'modern eclectic' style," I said, doing an Aunt Mel voice.

"Yeah, but is that really enough? Mom told me she made him lose twenty pounds."

"And shave off his mustache," I added.

"Society should have made him shave off his mustache. It looked like he had a wet rat stuck to his face."

I laughed, my first real laugh in ten days, and it came out creaky, like a door that hadn't been opened in a long time.

Archie flashed me a smile. "Nice to hear that. It's been a while. You've been kind of . . . depressed."

My mood tumbled back down again. He was right. Every time I somehow forgot what junior year was going to be like, Cubby suddenly appeared, landing on my shoulders and sinking my mood a solid three feet. Like now. *How could I have been so stupid?*

"You and Ian do an adequate job of groveling?" Archie asked.

I nodded, grateful for the subject change. "I did. Ian mostly just stood there scowling defiantly."

He groaned. "So in other words, being Ian."

"Exactly." It was just like on the cliffs with the tourists. Me scrambling for an explanation while Ian played dead. At least this time he was upright.

"Speaking of, where is Ian?" Archie asked.

I lifted my chin. "Eight o'clock. Sitting in that throne-looking chair." Ian had come up with the same survival strategy I had: find an out-of-the-way piece of antique furniture to camp out on and pretend you're anywhere other than where you were. Except he'd been texting all night, his face stretched in an expression I could only describe as gleeful.

"Is he *smiling*?" Archie said incredulously. "After everything that happened today? That kid is such a weirdo."

I bit my lip, fighting off my automatic instinct to defend Ian. That's the way our family had always lined up: Ian/Addie versus Walter/Archie. We occasionally formed alliances, but our core allegiances stayed the same. Had I ruined that forever? "He's been grinning at his phone ever since we left the cliffs. Whoever he's texting, it must be good."

"Probably a girl," Archie said.

"Doubt it." Every girl in the world was in love with Ian, but he rarely surfaced long enough to notice them, which left me to fend off all the wannabes who thought that getting close to his little sister was the certain way to his heart. Ha.

Archie plucked at my sleeve. "Seriously, though, sis. This dress. You look like Miss Seattle Real Estate."

This time the glare came without effort. "Come on, Archie. You saw what happened to my dress at the cliffs. I didn't exactly have a lot of options. I had to wear one of Mom's."

"Didn't she have anything less . . . realtory?"

"Um, you've met our mom, haven't you?" I said.

"Briefly. She's the one who's always yelling at us, right? Short hair? Occasionally seen on billboards?"

I shuddered. "We've got to talk her out of those this year."

"Good luck with that. Those billboards are paying my tuition."

"Football is paying your tuition. And Walt's," I pointed out. "And Ian is probably going to be the first college student in history to get paid to play. I'm the only one who's going to need those billboards to help pay for college."

That wasn't self-pity talking; it was truth. My brothers had used up all the *natural athlete* genes, leaving me to do my best with *enthusiastic athlete.* I was good, but not the star. Bad news when your brothers had shrines dedicated to them in the athletics hall.

Archie's face softened. "Hey, don't give up on playing in college so soon. I saw huge improvements in your game last year. You definitely have a shot."

I shrugged. I was in way too wallowy of a mood for a pep talk. "Unless I blow it with Ian."

"You won't. You'll just be with Lina, and Ian will be . . . I don't know. Being Ian."

Being Ian. It was like its own extreme Olympic sport. Music, football, school—all at a higher intensity than everyone else. "Do *you* have any idea why Ian wants to come to Italy with me? Because I don't think he even likes Lina. She lived with us for six months, and he barely even talked to her. Is he just trying to torture me?"

He shrugged. "Little Lina? I'm sure he likes her. She's funny and kind of quirky. Plus, she has all that crazy hair. How long has she been gone again?"

I wanted to say the actual number of days, but I knew that would sound neurotic. "Since the beginning of June."

"And she's staying in Italy permanently?"

My shoulders rounded in on themselves. "Permanent" sounded like a life sentence. "She's staying for the school year. Her dad, Howard, is a serious traveler, so they go all over the place. In October he's taking her and her boyfriend to Paris."

Lina's *boyfriend.* Yet another thing that had changed. Over the past year, Lina had gone through a lot of changes, starting when her mom, Hadley, was diagnosed with pancreatic cancer. A familiar ache ignited in my throat—the one that always flamed up when I thought about Hadley. She had been special, no doubt about it—creative, adventurous, chaotic, and just the right amount of hovering to make you feel cared about but not smothered.

Sometimes I felt like I'd experienced Hadley's loss twice—once for myself and once for Lina. I'd been desperate to drag Lina out of the grief she was floundering in—to the point that I'd made myself sick with worry.

I bit my cheek, fighting back old feelings of helplessness to refocus on Archie and the trip. "It makes way more sense that Ian would choose to visit all the castles and other sites you guys are seeing this week. Aren't you going to the castle where *Braveheart* was filmed?"

Archie perked up, just like I knew he would. Every single one of my brothers could recite that movie by heart. "We are definitely going to the *Braveheart* castle. Walt brought face paint so we can do some reenactments."

Oh, geez. Aunt Mel was going to love that. "See? Ian loves that movie. He used to fall asleep watching it. I think he's coming to Italy just to bug me."

"Maybe he just wanted a little quality time with his sister."

"Right, because he's been spending so much time with me this summer." Archie rolled his eyes, but there was no arguing with my sarcasm. Ian had spent most of the summer locked in his room writing college application essays and driving around on mystery errands, his music blaring. And then I'd gotten involved with Cubby and brought our relationship to a standstill.

Not to mention what happened at football camp.

Suddenly, Archie shifted, his eyes boring into mine. "So, Addie, talk."

There was a serious edge to his voice, and my heart rate climbed to a rickety pace. "About what?"

"What's the deal?"

"With . . . Ian?" I asked uncertainly. *Please tell me he didn't hear.*

Archie shook his head no. My heart clawed its way up to my throat, pushing my voice out in an angry burst. "Well, then I don't know what you're talking about."

"Easy, sis. I'm not the brother you're mad at." He steadied me with his gaze. "I heard what Ian said. Before you pushed him."

My breath caught in my throat, and I scrambled, trying to remember exactly what Ian had said. How much could Archie have pieced together from one whispered conversation? "What did you hear?"

"Are you in some kind of trouble? What does Ian want you to tell Mom and Dad about?"

Archie doesn't know what happened. I flopped back in relief. "I'm not in trouble," I said quickly. So far that was the truth. As long as this thing didn't spread any further than it already had, I was not in trouble. Embarrassed and heartbroken? Yes. In trouble? No. Which was why I was *not* telling my mom.

Archie studied me, his head resting on his hand. "So, what? Does this have something to do with a guy? I'm guessing someone on Ian's team from how pissed off he sounded?"

Was that *incredulity*? My body tensed. "Why, you think it's impossible that a popular football player would like someone like me?" I snapped.

"What? No." He held his hands up defensively, his blue eyes wide. "Addie, I didn't say that at all. Why are you acting so strange?"

Because my heart hurts. Because it actually is *impossible for someone like Cubby to like someone like me.* I kept my eyeballs glued to the green velvet upholstery, scratching my thumbnail against a tear in the seat. Tears burned hot in my eyes. "Did Mom and Walt hear?"

He shook his head. "Mom was secretly negotiating a deal on her phone, and Walt had headphones hidden under his hair. He didn't even know you guys had gone over the side until everyone started freaking out."

At least it was Archie who had heard, and not Walter. Of all my brothers, Archie was the most normal secret keeper, as in he kept most secrets most of the time. It was the other two who were extreme. On the one end was Ian. The second you told him anything, he turned into a human vault—it was the reason I didn't have to worry about him being the one to tell my parents about Cubby. And then there was Walt, the exact opposite. Any time he had a secret to keep, it was like a game of Hot Potato—he just had to throw it somewhere, usually dead center of wherever you *didn't* want it to go.

"If this guy messed with you, I'd be happy to pay him a visit on my way back to campus. Maybe just wait until he's out in the road and do some distracted driving? Back out without looking behind me first? All I need is his name." His tone had gone from his usual laid-back Archie to hyperintense Archie, which was rare.

"*No.* Archie, I do not want you to run over anyone," I said emphatically, just in case his half joke was half-serious.

"You sure?"

"Yes, I'm sure," I wailed. "It's not like it would fix anything."

"It would fix the fact that he's messing with people he shouldn't be messing with."

I put my hands on his shoulders. "Archibald Henry Bennett. Promise me you won't do anything."

"You sure?"

"*Promise* me!" I yelled.

"Fine. I promise."

Oh my hell. Brothers. It was like having a bunch of guard dogs that occasionally turned on you. I was completely exhausted by this conversation. By this whole day. "Well, thanks for the talk, but I could use some time alone," I said, tilting my head ungracefully toward the door. I'd learned long ago that hints get you nowhere with boys—or at least not with the ones I was related to. The more direct the better.

Archie jumped gracefully to his feet and patted me clumsily on the shoulder. "I'm here for you, Addie," he said.

"And I really appreciate it." I tilted my head more aggressively toward the doorway.

"Okay, okay. I'm gone." He jumped up and swaggered out of the room, his to-do list lit up in neon over his head. *Be there for little sister. Check.*

* * *

Once Archie was out of my visual, I grabbed the guidebook and flicked on the library's dusty side lamp. I tried to focus on the words, but Ian kept snagging my gaze. He hadn't moved from his chair once, and he was still laser-focused on his phone, his hair flopping forward to shield his face.

Right after Christmas Ian decided to stop cutting his hair, and no matter how much my mom begged and threatened, he hadn't let up. Now it was almost to his shoulders and a constant reminder of how unfair the gene pool was. My brothers all had my mom's thick eyelashes and wavy dark hair. My grandmother's fine blond hair had leapfrogged a generation, bypassing my dark-haired dad to land on me.

We all had the blue eyes, though, and even from here Ian's were looking bluer than usual, accented by the heavy dark circle around his left eye, courtesy of me. The bruise looked really painful. And final. A punctuation mark on the end of a long, miserable sentence.

Suddenly, a smile split Ian's face, and a mixture of emotions bunched up in my chest. Because here's the thing about Ian's smile: it was always 100 percent genuine. Ian didn't fake anything for anyone—he never had. Get him laughing, you knew you were actually funny. Make him angry, you knew you were actually being an idiot.

I am such an idiot.

Panic bubbled in my chest, and I jumped to my feet, tucking the guidebook under my arm. I needed fresh air. Now.

As soon as my mom got swept into a conversation with the groom's mother, I took off, hugging the side of the dance floor to burst through the doors and into the courtyard.

Outside, I paused to take a few glorious breaths. If I were writing a travel brochure for Ireland, I'd start with what it smells like. It's a combination of just-fallen rain mixed with earth and something else, something secret. Like the extra sprinkle of nutmeg in the top secret French toast recipe my dad and I had spent Fourth of July weekend perfecting.

What if my dad finds out?

Before my mind could dig its fingernails into the thought, I started moving, walking down the stairs past a trickling fountain overflowing with rainwater. Strings of warm, twinkly lights crisscrossed over the courtyard's path, the yellow bulbs making a cheery clinking noise in the spots where they overlapped. Puddles shimmered in the divots in the stone pavement, and the air ruffled in cool, sparkly perfection. How was it possible to feel so horrible in a place that was so beautiful?

I squeezed my fingernails into my palms, a dull ache blooming in my chest. Sometimes I didn't know if I missed Cubby or if I missed the picture I'd put together in my head of the two of us. It was always the same. It would be mid-September, a week or two after everyone's start-of-school jitters wore off. We'd be walking down the hall, him with his arm slung casually around me, lost in one of those conversations where the only thing that matters is the person you're with. Whispers would follow us down the hall. *That's Addie Bennett. Aren't they cute together? I know. I don't know why I never noticed her before either.*

Well, I'd gotten my wish. They'd be whispering all right. But not about what I wanted them to be.

Finally, I made it to an ivy-enclosed alcove on the far side of the garden—an outdoor version of my hiding place in the library—and I attempted to sit cross-legged, cold seeping up through my mom's constrictive skirt. I pulled out my phone, and my heart bounced when I saw a new text message.

WHERE ARE YOU?????????????????

Lina.

Lina and eighteen question marks. I counted them twice to be sure. Aggressive punctuation was never a good sign with Lina. Normally, she texted like a nineteenth-century schoolteacher who'd gotten ahold of a smartphone: proper use of capital letters, restrained emoji use, and always a complete sentence. Multiple question marks was the equivalent of Lina standing up in the middle of a church service and yelling cusswords through a bullhorn. She wasn't just angry; she was raging.

I hit respond, quickly typing out an exceptionally vague text. **Sorry, can't talk now. Wedding stuff ☹**

I was getting good at vague texting. And avoiding phone calls. The frowny face emoji looked up at me judgmentally.

"What?" I snapped. "For your information I have a great reason for not answering her calls."

I wasn't talking to Lina because I *couldn't* talk to Lina. She knew me too well. The second she heard my voice, she'd know something was wrong, and I refused—*refused*—to tell her about Cubby over the phone. If Lina was going to judge me, I wanted to see it in person. There was also the issue of the sheer number of things I had to tell her. She didn't know anything about Cubby, which meant I had to walk her through my entire summer.

I just had to make it to Italy. Once I got there I'd unpack the story and lay it all out, start to finish, nothing excluded.

I knew exactly how it would go. First she'd be shocked, then confused. And then she'd be struck with a brilliant plan for getting me through my junior year while reassuring me that everything was going to be okay.

Or at least that's what I kept telling myself.

The first time Cubby ever spoke to me was four days after we moved to Seattle. I was making waffles. Bribe waffles, to be more specific, and I wasn't having an easy time of it. Archie and Walter had been assigned to unpack the kitchen, and they'd somehow managed to turn it into one large booby trap. I'd taken a baking sheet to the head and dropped an entire carton of eggs when I tripped over a bread maker. But once my first waffle was on the iron, sending delicious spirals of steam into the air, I knew it would be worth it.

I took a deep, satisfied inhale. The waffles needed to be delicious. They were my ticket into the early-morning hangout Ian had expressly banned me from. No one yells Addiegetoutofhere *to someone holding a plate of hot waffles. Not even when they're trying to impress their new friends.*

"You have batter in your hair."

And there they were. The first words Cubby Jones ever said to me. Admittedly, not the most romantic introduction, but I was only twelve. I didn't have a name for the way my attention funneled to Cubby every time he walked into a room. Not yet.

While I swiped at my bangs with a dish towel, Cubby stepped closer, sniffing the waffle air. The second he was within five feet of me, I pinpointed what was different about him. "Your eyes!" I crowed, abandoning my dish towel. Cubby's eyes were two different colors.

His smile slipped off his face. "It's called heterochromia. It's just a genetic thing; it's not weird."

"I didn't say it's weird," I said. "Let me look." I grabbed his arm and yanked him in close. "Blue and gray?" I whispered.

"Purple," Cubby corrected.

I nodded my head. "Yep. I like that one the best. If you were in a sci-fi movie, that eye would be the source of all your powers."

Both of his eyes widened, and then he smiled, a slow, surprised drizzle that started at his mouth and went right up to his mismatched eyes. That was the moment I realized there were two different ways to look at boys. There was the regular way—the way I'd done my whole life—and then there was this way. A way that made kitchens tilt ever so slightly and waffles go forgotten in Mickey Mouse irons.

The sparkler send-off for the newlywed couple was a joke. Not only did my legally tipsy oldest brother attempt—and succeed at—catching one of the rosebushes on fire, but cameraman number two kept missing his shot of the bride and groom. This meant repeating the whole process over and over again until we ran out of sparklers and even the most camera-hungry wedding guests began to bray mutinously.

"Buses arrive tomorrow morning at six thirty sharp," Aunt Mel yelled over her shoulder as Uncle Number Three carried her back into the hotel. The train of her dress dragged behind her, sweeping up bits of confetti and dried sparklers. The send-off had been just for show. They were staying at Ross Manor tonight with everyone else.

"Finally free to go," my mom said quietly, running a tired hand through her hair. Her mascara was smudged, and it made her eyes look blurry.

The rest of us followed behind her, slogging silently up the billiard-green staircase to our floor, then filed one by one into our closet of a room. Despite the fact that there were five of us, including two college football players who were roughly toddler-size versions of King Kong, Aunt Mel had assigned us what had to be the smallest room in the hotel.

Fuzzy floral wallpaper decorated the walls, and my brothers' cots occupied most of the space, so all that was left over was a tiny corridor running along the base of the beds. And of course my brothers had filled that up with their never-ending supply of junk—candy wrappers, tangled-up phone cables, and more sneakers than should really exist in the world. I had a term for it: brother spaghetti.

I managed to claim the bathroom first and locked the door behind me, turning the tub on at full blast. I had no intention of actually taking a bath. I just needed to drown out the sound of everyone crashing around the room. Traveling with my family made my head hurt.

I yanked off the real estate dress, replacing it with an oversize T-shirt and a pair of black pajama shorts, then brushed my teeth as slowly as possible.

"Gotta pee, sis!" Walt shouted, banging on the door. "Gotta pee, gotta pee, gotta pee pee peeeeee."

I yanked the door open to make it stop. "Cute song. You should trademark that."

He shoved past me. "Thought you'd like it."

I picked my way through the room, avoiding half a dozen sneaker land mines before climbing onto the bed and cocooning deep into my blankets. I couldn't wait to sleep. Forget. It had been my main coping skill over the past ten days—ever since Ian had burst into my room to tell me how badly I'd screwed up his life. *His* life. Like he was the one who would have to spend the whole upcoming year avoiding Cubby and everyone who knew Cubby. My stomach twisted as tightly as the sheets.

"So what's the strategy exactly? Wear my T-shirt until I forget it's mine?" Ian's voice pierced through my blankets, and I slowly uncovered my head. Was he talking to me?

My mom was stuffing her suitcase like it was a Thanksgiving turkey, and Archie lay with his face planted on his cot, still wearing his suit. Ian propped himself up on a mountain of pillows, one earbud in, his face pointed in my general direction.

"You gave it to me," I said, aiming my voice for what a sitcom writer would mark as RETORT, SASSY. It was an exceptionally comfortable T-shirt with a black collar and sleeves and SMELLS LIKE THE ONLY NIRVANA SONG YOU KNOW written across the chest in block letters.

"By 'gave it to you,' do you mean you raided my T-shirt drawer and stole the softest one?"

Nailed it. "You can have it back," I said. *Ian is talking to me. Talking. To me.* A flicker of hope sprang into my chest.

"Do you even get the reference?" he asked, punching his top pillow into shape. His hair was in a horrible attempt at a man bun, with bumpy sides and a large chunk hanging out the back. He clearly hadn't watched the *How to Man-Bun Like a Boss* tutorial I'd forwarded him.

"Ian, I sat with you on Fleet Street and listened to the entire *Nevermind* album. How would I not know what it means?" That had been during Ian's Nirvana period. We'd gone on three different Nirvana-themed field trips, including a trip to Kurt Cobain's red-vinyl childhood home. I'd even agreed to dress up as Courtney Love for Halloween even though it required wearing a tiara and no one knew who I was.

"At least you know what it means." Ian flopped grudgingly onto his side. He hesitated, then nudged at his phone, his voice slightly above a whisper. "When are you going to tell Mom?"

I groaned into my sheets. He was bringing it up *again*. Now? When Mom, Archie, and Walt were all within earshot. Not to mention that's what the black eye had been about. One of Ian's teammates had texted him asking about Cubby. And instead of waiting until after the wedding ceremony, when we would be alone, he'd shoved the phone in my face and whisper-demanded that I tell Mom. Our parents finding out was the worst thing that could happen. Why didn't he get that?

"Ian!" I hissed.

He cut his eyes at Mom, then shot me a warning look. I growled in my throat and then slid down under the covers, forcing my breathing to calm. The odds of me *not* exploding on Ian were only as good as the odds of him not bringing up Cubby every chance he got. That is to say, not good.

Time to put a hard stop to this conversation. "Good night, Ian." I slid even farther under the covers, but I could still feel Ian's glare on my back, sharp as needles. A few minutes later I heard him rustle under the covers, the music from his earbuds filling the air between us.

How were we going to survive a full week together?

* * *

The next morning, I awoke to what sounded like the brass section from our school's famously exceptional marching band rumbling with our famously unexceptional drama team. I opened my eyes a slit. My mom was untangling her leg from the alarm clock and lamp cords. "Damn hell spit," she muttered. Or at least that's what it sounded like she muttered. Walter was right. She needed a swearing intervention.

I opened my eyes a half millimeter more. Weak sunlight puddled under the curtains, and Archie and Walter and their extreme bedhead stood next to the door looking all kinds of ambiguous about the state of their consciousness.

"You both have your passports, right?" my mom asked them, finally freeing herself. They stared at her with blank, sleep-coated expressions, and she sighed before swooping in on me in a cloud of moisturizer. "Your cab will be here at nine. The gnomes will knock on the door to wake you up." She pressed her cheek onto my forehead like she used to do when I was little and had a fever. "Promise me you'll work things out with Ian. You two are the best friends you'll ever have."

Way to twist the dagger. "Love you, Mom," I said, scrunching my eyes shut.

She crouched down next to Ian and mumbled something to him, and then the three of them cleared out of the room, banging loudly into the hallway.

It felt like only minutes later when a slamming noise sprang me out of sleep. I sat up quickly, disoriented, but not too disoriented to notice that the entire vibe of the hotel room had changed. Not only did it feel twice as big without Archie, Walter, and my mom, but the curtains were straining against full, brilliant sunlight. The room was silent, highlighting a distinct ruffling sensation hovering in the air. Had someone just been here?

"Ian," I whispered. "Are you awake?"

He didn't budge, which was typical. Ian could sleep through almost anything.

I rolled onto my back and lay still, straining my ears. The hotel's silence was as thick as black pudding. Suddenly, the door to our room pulled quietly shut, followed by an explosion of footsteps down the hall. Someone *had* been in our room. A thief? A European kidnapper? One of the gnomes?

"Ian," I said, tumbling out of my bed. "Someone was just here. Someone was in our room." I reached out to shake his shoulder, but in a highly disorienting moment, my hand sank straight through him.

I yanked off the covers to find a pile of pillows. Had he *pillow ghosted* me? I spun around, checking the rest of the cots. Empty, empty, and empty. "Ian!" I yelled into the silence.

My eyes darted to the door, and what I saw elicited my first real bit of uneasiness. Instead of the two navy-blue suitcases that were supposed to be standing by the door, there was only one. Mine.

I hustled over to the alarm clock, but it stared up at me blankly. Of course. My mom had ripped it out of the wall. I needed to find my phone.

Not under the sheets, not under the complimentary stationery, not in the scattered brochures. Finally, I ran to the windows and flung open the curtains, only to get kicked in the retinas. The countryside was on fire—green and sunlight combining to create an intense glare. Apparently, Ireland did have sunshine, and it was blinding.

I stumbled my way to the door and burst out of the room, my bare feet making staccato echoes down the hall.

Downstairs I did a fly-by inspection of the breakfast room and lounge, but the only form of life was an obese orange cat who'd taken up residence on a velvet armchair. I sprinted out the front door and into the parking lot, and a wave of cold air hit me head-on. Irish sunshine must be for looks only.

The only vehicle in the parking lot was a lonely utility van parked next to a line of rosebushes waving frantic messages at me in the wind. *Where's Ian? Did you miss your cab?*

I needed to pull it together. Even if I had overslept, it's not like Ian would have left for Italy without me. Maybe he was just out for an early-morning walk. With his suitcase?

The distant sound of an engine starting pulled me out of my trance. I took off after it, the shuddering noise getting louder as I headed toward the side parking lot. When I rounded the corner, I skidded to a stop, giving myself a few seconds to process what I was seeing.

The tortured-sounding vehicle was technically a car, but it just barely qualified. It was tiny and boxy—like when a Volkswagen and a hamster love each other *very much*—with a splotchy paint job and a muffler dangling an inch or two off the ground. And striding purposefully toward it, navy-blue economy suitcase in hand, backpack slung over one shoulder, was Ian.

Adrenaline hit me full force. My legs got the message before I did, and suddenly I was charging across the parking lot, my brother in my line of target.

He saw me just before he reached the passenger door, but by then it was too late. I collided with him like I was the Hulk going in for a high five, which was to say, hard. His backpack went flying, and we both hit the ground, tumbling for the second time in twenty-four hours. It hurt in a white-hot, head-pounding kind of way.

"What are you doing?" he hissed, scrambling to his feet.

"What am I doing? What are *you* doing?" I yelled back, jumping up to shake off the fall.

He lunged for his backpack, but I beat him to it, wrapping

the handle around my fingers. "Are you trying to leave without me?" I demanded.

"Just go back up to the room. I left a note on the bathroom mirror." He wasn't meeting my eye.

"A *note*? Is this the cab Mom ordered for us? Why is it in such bad shape?"

Suddenly, the passenger window began cranking down in jerky, uneven motions. The sound of an appreciative slow clap filled the air followed by an Irish voice. "Ah, Ian, you've been beaten by a girl! I wish I'd been recording. Would love to see a replay."

"Rowan!" Ian hustled over to the window, his voice much happier than someone who'd just been tackled in a parking lot should sound. He wore the same massive grin he'd had plastered all over him last night during his text sessions.

I dropped Ian's backpack on the ground and ran over, butting him out of the way so I could get a look inside.

"Well, hello there," the driver said. He was Ian's age, maybe a little older, with tousled hair, large grayish eyes, and horn-rimmed glasses that should have been perched on an old man's face but managed to be at home on his. His T-shirt said HYPNOTIZING CAT and featured a large feline with whirlpool eyes. Definitely not a cabdriver. He smiled, and a dimple appeared charmingly on one side. Until now I'd thought that dimples only came in pairs.

"Who are you?" I demanded.

He stuck his hand out. "I'm Rowan. And you must be Addie." His accent was 100 percent Irish, singsongy with the vowels getting soft and running together like chocolate syrup in ice cream.

I ignored it. His hand and the chocolate syrup voice. But I couldn't ignore the way he was looking at me—like I was something rare and exciting that he'd just discovered in the wild. "How do you know who I am?" I asked.

"I knew Ian has a sister named Addie, and let's be honest, only a guard or a sibling would tackle someone in the middle of a stony car park."

When I didn't match his smile, he dropped his, self-consciously reaching up to push the corners of his glasses up with both hands. "Or at least I'm guessing that's how siblings operate. Also, you look like the mini female version of him."

"Do *not* call me a female version of Ian," I snapped. My first week of high school, at least five of Ian's friends had made it a point to tell me that I looked like my brother with a blond wig, which was not the confidence booster I'd been looking for.

He held up his hand quickly. "Chillax. I didn't mean to annoy ya. I probably wouldn't like it if someone called me a male version of a woman either." The dimple reappeared. "Also, I come in peace. So please don't attack me, too."

Ian quickly nudged me aside. "Sorry about this, Rowan. Minor glitch in the system. Addie, go back up to the room. Your taxi will be here later. And the note will explain everything."

Had he just called me a minor glitch in the system? "What do you mean *my* taxi? It's our taxi. Why are you out here talking to . . . ?" I stopped. I'd been about to say "Hypnotized Cat Guy," but that just sounded rude.

Ian grabbed my arm, pulling me away from the car and lowering his voice so Hypnotized Cat Guy wouldn't hear. "Great news: your wish is granted. I'm not coming with you to Italy. Go upstairs and read the note—it has all the details."

The parking lot revolved once, then twice. He was serious. "You're not coming to Italy? Since when?" I asked dizzily.

He swiped his hair out of his eyes and put a steadying hand on my shoulder. "Since always. I'll meet you in Dublin for the flight home." My mom had only arranged for our flights to and from Italy. The plan was that we would return to Dublin to fly home with the rest of the group. But now it seemed that plan was about to be compromised.

"But . . . why?" I asked desperately.

Rowan's voice pierced the air between us. "I thought Addie was in on this. Why doesn't she know we're going to Stradbally?" I was momentarily distracted. The way he said my name made it sound like it was being played on an Irish fiddle.

"I left her a note," Ian said, his cheeks flushing pink. He shoved his hair out of his face and slid his eyes guiltily at me. "It's easier this way."

"For who?" I shot back.

Rowan leaned toward the passenger window, his eyes concerned behind his glasses. "A *note*? No wonder she just knocked you over. This must look unbelievably sketchy. You meet some random guy and leave for a place she's never heard of?"

I lifted my hands in the air. "Finally, someone's making sense here."

Rowan looked pointedly at me. "Stradbally is a small town near Dublin. But we're headed to a few other sites first. We have to do research for—"

"Stop—stop—stop!" Ian stuttered. "Please don't tell her anything." He shoved past me again and yanked on the car door handle, but it didn't budge.

"Don't tell me what? Ian, don't tell me *what*?" I grabbed at his backpack.

Rowan smiled apologetically at my brother. "Sorry, Ian. According to the previous owner, that door hasn't worked since the late nineties. The lads always just have to climb in through the window."

"Who are the lads?" I asked. As if that were the most important question that needed answering.

Ian hoisted his backpack in and slithered through the

window before reaching for his suitcase. I lunged for it, but he managed to pull it in. "Addie, just go read my note. I'll see you in a few days."

I clamped my hands onto his window frame. They were shaking. "Ian, were you not in the car yesterday? Didn't you hear what Mom said about us not messing up? This is the definition of 'messing up.'"

His shoulders slumped. "Come on, Addie, you said it yourself. You don't want me to come to Italy, and I get it. I even respect it. So you go have your trip, and I'll have mine. The only way we're going to get in trouble with Mom and Dad is if we tell them, and let's be honest, neither of us is going to do that."

"Ian—"

"Just stopping by Electric Picnic," Rowan added in the kind of soothing voice you'd use on a rabid dog. "We'll be done by Monday morning. Nothing to stress about, ninja sister."

"Electric what?" The Hypnotized Cat looked at me pityingly. My voice sounded hysterical. Strangled.

"Electric Picnic. It's the biggest music festival in Ireland. It happens every year. Lots of indie and alternative stuff. But this year is special. Guess who is headlining?" Rowan paused, his smile suggesting that I'd just dangled something warm and cinnamony in front of his nose.

"Not Ian," I answered weakly.

"Yes, Ian," Ian said. "*Definitely* Ian. And you won't even

care because you'll be off in Italy having an incredible time."

"Titletrack will be at Electric Picnic," Rowan said, his tone a clear indicator that we'd both just let him down.

Titletrack. It took me a second, but my mind leapfrogged to a massive poster hanging over Ian's desk. Four guys, four brooding expressions, and an admittedly unique sound that I'd actually started to look forward to on the mornings when Ian drove me to school. "That band you love. From the U.K."

"Now you've got it," Rowan added encouragingly. "Only they're Irish, not British. And Ian's planning to—"

"Okay, Rowan, that's enough. Addie, have a great time in Italy." Ian cranked at his window, but I threw myself on top of it, using all my weight to keep it down.

"Ian, *stop*." Rowan looked disapprovingly at my brother. "You were just going to roll the window up on her?"

Ian shrank under Rowan's stare, and he dropped his gaze to his fidgeting hands like he was trying to decide something. "Addie, I'll explain it all later. Just make sure Mom and Dad don't find out, and everything will be fine. You'll figure out a way." He took a deep breath, delivering the next part in a rush. "You've been lying to everyone all summer anyway, so this will be easy."

The line was rehearsed. He'd been carrying it around in his back pocket in case of emergency. In case I *got in his way.*

"Ian . . ." Tears prickled my eyes, which of course made

me furious. I couldn't lose it now—not in front of this oddly dressed stranger and definitely not when Ian was already settled in the oddly dressed stranger's car. "Ian, there's no way we'll pull this off. You know they're going to find out that you didn't make it to Italy, and then we'll have to quit our teams."

His gaze collapsed to the dashboard. "Come on, Addie. Sports aren't everything."

"Sports aren't everything?" Now my breath was catching in little bursts in my chest. What was he going to say next? Fainting goats aren't hilarious? "Who are you?"

"This is my only chance to see Titletrack in concert. I'm sorry you don't like it, but I'm going." The edges of his voice set hard and crinkly, his eyes a steely blue. The look set off a chain reaction of panic in me. We had officially entered the Defiant Ian stage, better known as the Never Back Down Ever stage. Unless I did something drastic to stop him, he was going to that concert.

Now or never.

I dove through the window and grabbed the keys out of the ignition, then shimmied out before either of them could process what was happening.

"Addie!" Ian yanked his seat belt off and scrambled out the window. I was already on the other side of the car, the keys imprinting in my palm. "Are you seriously doing this?"

"Wow. You people are really entertaining. Like sitcom-level entertaining." Rowan reclined his seat noisily.

I squared toward my brother. "Ian, you can't do this. You know I have to play soccer if I'm going to get into a good school. Don't ruin this for me."

"Your college plans are not my problem." His voice fell halfway through. He was trying to play the tough guy, but the real Ian was under there, the one who knew how hard I tried—and continued to fail—at school. Sometimes I got the impression that he felt guilty about how easily things came to him, when nothing ever seemed to come easily to me.

We stared each other down, waiting for the other to make the first move. Ian stepped toward me, and I bolted in the opposite direction, using the car as a buffer.

Ian groaned. "Sorry, Ro. Let me just get this out of the way and we can head out. Minor bump in the road."

"Don't you mean glitch in the system?" I asked, purposely making my voice snide. "And 'Ro'? You already have a nickname for this guy?"

Ian shoved his hair back, edging toward me. "I've known him for more than a year."

"How?"

"We met online." Ian lunged at me, but his foot slipped on the gravel, giving me plenty of time to make it around to the other side of the car. He rose slowly, holding his hands up in surrender. "All right, all right. You win."

"Ian, give me some credit. I've fought with you for sixteen

years. You think I don't know that the fake out is your go-to move?"

He just raised his hands higher. "Look, even if Mom and Dad do find out, that just means we're even. I have to deal with the fallout of you messing around with Cubby, and you have to deal with the fallout of me staying in Ireland. Now give me the keys."

"I told you to stop talking about Cubby," I said. "And you being embarrassed in front of your friends is not a *fallout*."

Rowan's voice floated out the window. "Is Cubby your oldest brother?"

"No," Ian said shortly, his eyes on me. "That's Walt."

"Oh, right. Walt." Rowan cracked his door and got out, clutching a jumbo-size box of cold cereal that read SUGAR PUFFS. "Look, guys. As entertaining as this is, we all know you can't keep this up forever. So why don't we head inside and grab a real breakfast?" He shook his Sugar Puffs winningly at Ian. "Or something stronger if you need it. A pint? We could talk it through."

I shook my head. "We aren't old enough for a *pint*. And there's nothing to talk about—"

In a flash of dark hair, Ian slid across the front of the car and clutched my wrist. We settled into a death grip, Ian fighting to wrench the keys from my hands while I curled up like a pill bug, channeling all my energy into keeping my fists closed. Another classic Addie/Ian fight move. In junior high we'd once maintained this position for eleven and a half minutes, and that was over an Oreo. Walter had timed us. "Ian . . . let . . . *go*."

Rowan leaned back against the car, popping a handful of cereal into his mouth. "You two are the best argument I've ever seen for single-child families." He crunched for a moment, then swallowed. "Okay, here's a wild idea. Addie, what if you relinquish the keys to my custody and then join us on our first stop?"

"Not a good idea," Ian said, leveraging his shoulder against mine.

"What do you mean join you?" My elbow plunged directly under Ian's rib cage.

"Addie," Ian groaned. "That hurt."

"That one's my signature move," I said proudly.

"Hear me out." Rowan raised his Sugar Puffs into the air. "The first site is not too far from here. Less than an hour. Addie, you can come with us and learn a little more about what Ian's doing. Then you two can come up with a solid plan to avoid detection by your parents, and then Addie can be on her way. No death matches involved."

First site. Did that mean there was more than one? Curiosity bit into me, but I wasn't about to start asking questions. Not about a trip Ian was *not* taking. And especially not when every bit of my energy was currently being channeled into maintaining possession of Rowan's keys. "We can't risk missing our flight," I said, putting a heavy emphasis on the "we." "Not seeing Lina is not an option."

"Who's Lina?"

"My best friend."

"Oh, duh. The one who moved to Italy."

"What else did Ian tell you about me?" I asked, doubling down on the keys.

"Don't flatter yourself," Ian said. "Believe it or not, we don't spend all our time talking about you."

I spun away and tried to run for the hotel, but Ian executed a half tackle, and the keys flew out of my hands, jangling across the gravel. I scrambled for them, but Ian got there first.

He ran for the car. "Let's go!" he shouted, tossing the keys to Rowan, but Rowan didn't follow. Instead, he carefully placed the keys in his pocket, surveying me seriously. "Just come with us on our first stop. The airport's a straight shot from the Burren. We'll make it in plenty of time."

Burren. Where had I heard that word before? *You know where, buttercup*, a little voice said. Guidebook Lady. Of course.

"Are you talking about the place of stone?" I asked.

He brightened, shoving his glasses up enthusiastically. "You've heard of it?"

"I read about it last night." *Ireland for the Heartbroken* had a whole section on the Burren, right after the Cliffs of Moher entry. What were the odds that Ian's first stop on his not-happening road trip was also in my heartbreak guide? My stance shifted. "You really think we'd make it on time?"

"Absolutely." Rowan flashed me a friendly smile.

Ian made a strangled noise, then positioned himself between us. "Look, Rowan, I appreciate what you're trying to do here, but this is a bad idea." And just in case Rowan didn't get the point, he kept going. "A *really* bad idea. We need to stick to the original plan."

"It is not a *really* bad idea," I protested.

"But we would be following the original plan, just with a minor detour to the airport. It wouldn't put us behind at all." Rowan's voice was slow with uncertainty, his eyebrows bent. He didn't have to say it for us to hear it: *Why are you being such a jerk about this?*

Ian's shoulders sagged, and his right hand disappeared nervously into his hair. "But . . . there's a lot of stuff in your car. Where would she sit?"

"Easy. She's a little yoke. We'll make room." *A little yoke?* Rowan lifted his chin up to me. "You don't mind a tight squeeze for an hour or so, do you?"

I leaned over to look through the back window. Ian wasn't exaggerating. Not only did the car have the tiniest back seat in existence, but it was packed full the way Archie's and

Walter's cars were whenever they left to start a new semester at college. A jumble of clothes, books, and toiletries. For once, being tiny was going to pay off. "I can make it work."

Ian shifted back and forth between his feet, absent-mindedly strumming the zipper on his jacket. He was torn. No matter what he said, he didn't feel okay about abandoning me at the hotel. The big brother was too strong in him. I was going to have to use it to my advantage.

"Look, it makes sense." Rowan held out the cereal box to Ian, but he waved it off. "What you guys need is some time to get used to this idea. Going to the Burren will give us that time."

"This is a bad idea," Ian repeated.

"You already said that." Two scenarios played through my head. Best case, I used the extra time to talk some sense into Ian. Worst case, I saw another guidebook site, and maybe got one step closer to healing my broken heart—that is, if Guidebook Lady knew what she was talking about—before continuing on to Italy alone. My mental Magic 8 Ball tumbled out an answer: *All signs point to yes.*

I took an authoritative step toward Rowan. "I need you to give me the keys."

"Do *not* give them to her," Ian ordered.

One of Rowan's eyebrows lifted, a smile pulling at the corner of his mouth.

"I have to go get my suitcase. And I need insurance that you aren't just going to leave while I'm gone."

"Rowan . . . ," Ian warned.

Rowan nodded thoughtfully and threw them to me in one smooth motion, his grin still playing on his face. His smiles felt like a payday. "Sorry, Ian. She's right: I wouldn't leave us alone in the parking lot either. And I'm a sucker for a well-thought-out argument."

Victory.

Ian shook his hair into his face and crossed his arms tightly. "Addison Jane Bennett, if you are not back down here in five minutes, I will come looking for you."

Rowan's dimple dented his cheek. "Better hurry, Addison Jane."

"Addison Jane Bennett. B-minus in geometry? I thought you were straight As all the way."

I stumbled back into the doorway, hand to my chest. It was early one morning in July, and either I was hallucinating or Cubby Jones was standing in my kitchen looking at my report card.

I blinked hard, but when I looked again, he was still there. Only now he'd deployed the signature grin, one hand still on the fridge. A lot had changed since the morning I'd made him waffles. Cubby's smile didn't go all the way up to his eyes anymore, and something about it looked calculated, like he'd figured out its power and was using it to his advantage. Like now.

"What are you doing here?" I managed to choke out.

He grinned again, then pulled himself up onto the counter in an easy, athletic motion. "Don't try to change the subject. B-minus? What does your honor student brother think of that?"

"I bombed the final," I said, attempting and failing at nonchalant. "And you know report cards are confidential, right? Meant only for the person they're addressed to." I attempted to snatch the paper from his grip, but he held on to it tighter, pulling me toward him before he let go. And suddenly I was twelve years old again, in this very kitchen, looking into his eyes for the first time and noticing that Cubby was different. The memory must have hit him, too, because this time the old Cubby was back, his smile climbing to his eyes.

"So"—he cleared his throat, looking me up and down—"are you going out for a run?"

I quickly crossed my arms over my chest, remembering what I was wearing. A ratty T-shirt and an ancient pair of volleyball shorts that were so short, I only wore them to bed or for quick trips to the kitchen for early-morning Pop-Tarts. Or in this case, quick trips to the kitchen that resulted in running into my longtime crush.

Sometimes I hated my life.

"No run. I'm just, um . . ." I bit my lip nervously, desperate

to get out of there but also desperate to stay. "What are you doing here, Cubby?"

"No one calls me Cubby anymore, Addison," he said, tilting his head slightly.

"Well, no one calls me Addison. And the question stands." I edged toward the hallway, the tile cold under my bare feet. Cubby's stare ignited too many feelings in my stomach—and they tangled into a knot. Why did I have to look so gross? Upstairs, the bathroom door slammed shut.

"I'm picking up your brother. Coach called for an extra practice this morning, and Ian said you had the car today."

"We have joint custody," I said. "This weekend it's mine."

Cubby nodded knowingly. "But you made sure to explain to the car that it isn't his fault, right? And that you both love him very much?"

A laugh burst out of me just as Ian appeared in the doorway. His hair was wet from the shower, and the strings from the two sweatshirts he wore tangled together. He was the only person I knew who ever wore two hoodies at once. How he managed to put them on was an unsolved mystery that I had been attempting to put to rest for several years now.

Cubby lifted his chin. "Hey, Bennett."

Ian nodded at him sleepily, then squinted his eyes at me. "Addie, why are you up so early?"

"I was on the phone with Lina." The time difference meant

I sometimes had to get up really early if I wanted to talk to her.

He looked at my pajamas and wrinkled his face. I didn't have to be a mind reader to know what he was thinking.

"Bye, Addison." Cubby smiled disarmingly, then jumped off the counter, giving me a long look as he followed Ian out.

"Bye, Cubby," I called back, my heart hummingbird-fast. The second he was out of sight I fell against the counter. Why did I always have to act like a lovestruck third grader? I might as well walk around with a T-shirt that reads I ♥ CUBBY JONES.

Suddenly, Cubby's face appeared around the corner. "Hey, Addie, you want to hang out sometime?"

I shot back up to standing. "Um . . . yes?" You'd think that living with so many brothers would mean I'd know how to talk to guys, but I didn't. It just meant I knew how to defend myself. And the way Cubby was looking at me—really looking at me—I had no defense for. It set my capillaries on fire.

Back in the hotel room I set a world record by getting dressed, packing my suitcase, and locating my phone, all in less than six minutes. Once my sneakers were laced, I stuck my head into the bathroom to check for Ian's alleged note. Sure enough, there was a folded-up square of paper wedged into the corner of the mirror, my name spelled out in Ian's miniscule handwriting.

"Ian, come on," I groaned. Chances were I wouldn't even have seen it there.

I jammed the note in my pocket, then wheeled my suitcase to the doorway, pausing when I caught sight of the guidebook peeking out from under my cot. I hurried over and scooped it up. I didn't like the idea of stealing from the gnomes' library, but something about the guidebook's crinkled pages made me feel better. Less alone. And besides, what if Guidebook Lady was telling the truth? What if she *was* an expert on heartbreak? I needed all the help I could get. Maybe I'd figure out how to mail the guidebook back to the gnomes from Italy.

Outside, the car was right where I'd left it and Rowan stood rummaging through the trunk. Now that I wasn't engaged in actively fighting off my brother, I could actually take Rowan in. He was taller than I'd expected and really skinny—like half the size of Archie or Walter. But even so, he definitely had what my mom called "presence." Like he could walk into any lunchroom anywhere and ten girls would look up from their ham sandwiches and whisper, *Who's that?* in identical breathy voices.

Good thing my breathy voice had been scared into permanent hibernation.

"Welcome back." Rowan took my suitcase, tossing it into the trunk.

I pointed to the bumper stickers plastering the back of the car. "Did you pick all of those, or were they a preexisting condition?"

"Definitely preexisting. I've only owned the car for three weeks."

IMAGINE WHIRLED PEAS

THIS CAR IS POWERED BY PURE IRISH LUCK

TEAM OXFORD COMMA

CUPCAKES ARE MUFFINS
THAT DIDN'T GIVE UP ON THEIR DREAMS

"The muffin one is pretty funny," I said, hugging the guidebook to my side.

"I think so too. It may be the whole reason I bought this car. There wasn't a whole lot to love otherwise."

I shook my head. "Not true. This car is equipped with a rare sagging tailpipe. I'm sure people go crazy over those at car shows."

"Wait. Is that a joke, or is the tailpipe actually sagging?" He looked anxiously at the roof of his car, his gaze a solid six feet above where the tailpipe actually resided. Yikes. I think it was safe to say Rowan was *not* a car person.

"Uh . . . that pipe thing?" I said, pointing under the back bumper. "It lets exhaust out of your car. If it starts dragging on the ground, it'll make a loud, horrible noise."

"Oh . . ." He exhaled, a blush spreading across his cheeks. "Actually, I think it was making that noise. On the way here. Especially when the road got bumpy. But Clover makes a lot of horrible noises, so I thought it was just business as usual." He patted the car affectionately.

"Clover?"

Rowan pointed to the most prominent bumper sticker, a large, faded shamrock. "Her namesake."

"How Irish."

"Nothing like a good stereotype," he countered, his mouth twisting into another smile. I wished he'd stop with the smiling. It kept conjuring up memories of another notable smile.

"Time to go." Ian stuck his head out the window, drumming his hands against the side. I don't think he meant for it to, but his excited expression landed squarely on me. "Addie, I cleared you a spot. It will probably work best if you climb in from this side."

I rushed over, eager to keep up the goodwill, but when I looked inside, the glow that Ian's smile had created instantly faded away. He had somehow managed to stack Rowan's items into a teetering pile that almost touched the ceiling. The only actual space was behind Ian's seat, and it was just the right size for three malnourished squirrels and a hedgehog. If they all sucked in.

"Grand, Ian," Rowan said from behind me. "You worked a wonder back here."

He was either a liar or a serious optimist. "Um, yeah . . . a really great job, Ian," I echoed, bracing my hands on either side of the window. I needed to keep things positive. "So how am I getting in there exactly?"

"Tunnel in," Ian said. "You can just climb over me."

"Great." I threw my leg in through the window, managing to keep the guidebook pressed to my side as I climbed onto the middle console.

"What are you holding?" Ian asked, reaching up for the book.

I quickly tossed it into the back seat. "It's a guidebook about Ireland."

"Oh, right. The one you read about the Burren in," Rowan said.

"Right." I hovered, unsure of my next step. Circumventing the pile was not going to be a straightforward process.

"Maybe put your foot on the . . . ," Rowan started, but I was already midfling, Rowan's possessions snagging at every bit of exposed skin on my body. I landed in a heap.

"There was probably a less violent way to do that," Ian said.

Rowan raised his eyebrows. "There was definitely a less violent way to do that. But none quite so entertaining."

Crunchy, sun-faded velvet lined the back seat, which smelled vaguely of cheese. And Ian's seat was so close to mine that my knees barely fit in the space. I jammed my legs in as best as I could, wincing at the tight squeeze, then poked at the pile. "Rowan, what is all this stuff?"

"Long story." He started up the car, pointing to Ian's black eye. "So, are you going to tell me what happened, or will it just be the big mystery of the trip?"

"Ask her." Ian hiked his thumb back at me. "She's the one responsible."

Rowan turned and looked at me appraisingly. "Wow. You always so aggressive?"

"Always," Ian answered for me. Was it just my imagination or was that a thin layer of pride spread atop all that exasperation? Either way, I didn't protest. Rowan thinking I was dangerous might work to my advantage.

"Ready?" Rowan asked. Before we could reply, he hit the gas, accelerating so hard that the pile shimmied, spitting out a handful of records and one dress shoe. A group of birds scattered as we peeled brazenly out of the parking lot and onto the sunlit road, sprays of rose petals shooting out behind us.

Or at least that's what I imagined our exit looked like. There was too much stuff blocking my view for me to know for sure.

* * *

I assumed that once we were on the open road, a few things would be cleared up. For example, what a tourist site in western Ireland had to do with my brother's favorite band. But instead of explaining, Ian produced a massive, scribbled-on map of Ireland that he'd apparently been carrying around in his backpack, and Rowan passed around his box of cold cereal, and the two of them commenced to yell at each other.

Not angry yelling, *happy* yelling, part necessity due to the loud music—because as Rowan explained, the volume knob was missing—and part excitement. It was as if the two of them had been holding back an arsenal of things to say, and now that they were face-to-face, they had to get it all out or risk annihilation. And Rowan was as big of a music nerd as Ian was, maybe even more so. Ten minutes in, they'd covered:

- An eighties musician named Bruce something who was famous for composing guitar symphonies that involved bringing thirty-plus guitarists onstage at once
- Whether or not minimalism is a sign of a truly great musician
- Something called "punk violence," which Rowan claimed (and Ian enthusiastically agreed) was the natural balance to the synth-pop genre that emerged through early MTV
- Why the term "indie" meant nothing anymore now that massive indie labels were churning out artists assembly-line style

I was torn between listening to Ian in his element and trying not to have a panic attack every time I looked at the road. Rowan was the kind of driver every parent dreads. His speed hovered just below breakneck, and he had some kind of psychic method for determining which curves in the road didn't require remaining in his own lane.

But I was the only one worrying. Ian's excited voice climbed higher and higher until it was resting on the roof of the car, and he alternated between his favorite fidget modes: knee bouncing, finger drumming, and hair twisting. Wasn't he supposed to be explaining things to me?

My phone chimed, and I fumbled quickly for it, tuning out their conversation as I pulled up a behemoth text:

> (1) Thank you for subscribing to LINA'S CAT FACTS–the fun way to quit ignoring your best friend and learn something feline in the process! Did you know that when a family cat died in ancient Egypt, family members mourned by shaving off their eyebrows? And bonus fact: Did you know you are in danger of having YOUR eyebrows shaved off? BY ME? (Mostly due to the fact that you are arriving in Italy today and I haven't heard from you in A WEEK AND A HALF?) In order to receive double the number of Daily Cat Facts–please continue to ignore me. Thanks again for your subscription, and have a PURRRfect day!

"Oh, no," I whispered to myself. Immediately, Lina's texts began dropping in like fuzzy hair balls. Egyptian family members were just the beginning.

(2) Cats who fall five stories have a 90 percent survival rate. Friends who ignore their friends for longer than 7 days have a 3 percent chance of remaining friends (and then only if they have a really good reason). Thanks again for your subscription, and have a PURRRfect day!

(3) A group of kittens is called a kindle. A group of adult cats is called a clowder. People who stop talking to their best friends for absolutely no good reason are jerks. This is not a CAT FACT. It is just a fact. Thanks again for your subscription, and have a PURRRfect day!

(4) Back in the 1960s, the CIA turned a cat into a tiny spy by implanting a microphone and camera into her ear and spine. Unfortunately, Spy Cat's mission was cut short when she immediately ran out into traffic and was flattened by an oncoming taxi. This reminded me of the time you decided to visit me in Italy and then the week before completely stopped talking to me. ARE YOU EVEN COMING ANYMORE?? Thanks again for your subscription, and have a PURRRfect day!

Guilt twisted painfully in my gut. I had to respond to that one.

So so so so so sorry. And of course I'm still coming to Italy. Explain everything once I'm there.

"Is that Mom?" Ian's voice bypassed Rowan's pile of stuff to hit me in the face. He held a lock of wet and stringy hair near his mouth.

"That is disgusting," I said, pointing to his hair. "And no. It's Lina."

He chomped down on the lock. "What's she saying?"

"How excited she is to see both of us. You know, because *both* of us will be there?" I wiggled my eyebrows at him. Sometimes humor worked really well on Ian.

"Keep dreaming," he said. Guess it wasn't going to work today.

"Addie, you want any cereal?" Rowan shoved his box of Sugar Puffs through the space between the seats.

"No. Thank you." I leaned back, rubbing my thigh. Being crammed into such a tiny space had set my left leg on fire with pins and needles. "So when are you guys going to fill me in?"

"Fill you in on what?" Ian dropped his hair out of his mouth, and it bounced perkily off his shoulder.

"On your master plan." I gestured to the map. "You can start with what the Burren has to do with Titletrack."

Ian's knee shook. "Nice try, sis. We have one hour until we drop you off at the airport, and the deal is you stay quiet until then. So you just sit tight back there, okay?"

I hated when Ian used that condescending tone with me. It only came out when he was trying to leverage his role as big brother. Fifteen months was not a lot of extra experience, but according to him all of creation had happened during that time period. "What deal? No deal was made."

He flipped around, giving me a bouncy smile that caught me off guard. Even with me here, he was happier than I'd seen him all summer. "Your getting in this car was proof that you agreed to our terms and conditions. It was a contractual agreement."

"And let me guess. You're in charge of the terms?" I asked.

"Exactly." He patted my arm patronizingly. "Now you're getting it."

I shoved his hand away. "You know what? Never mind. This is actually really great. Instead of thinking about an Irish road trip that you're not taking, I can spend my time looking at the view and thinking about what a great time we're going to have in Florence."

"Keep dreaming, sis."

Rowan met my eyes in the rearview mirror, the corners of his mouth turning up in an amused smile. I hoped he'd lobby for me—after all, he was the one who'd suggested we use this little side trip as a way to get things out in the open—but instead, he and Ian dove right back into their conversation. The pull of the music was too strong.

I crouched forward to scout for clues on Ian's map. A string of *X*s looped in a crescent along the bottom of Ireland, each site surrounded by a mini flurry of tiny Ian handwriting. Most of the writing was concentrated around six numbered spots:

1. Poulnabrone
2. Slea Head
3. Torc Manor
4. An Bohair Pub
5. Rock of Cashel

And the grand finale, written in large letters:

ELECTRIC PICNIC

Great. I knew an Ian project when I saw one. Any time he found something he was really interested in, he dug in, and no amount of coaxing could peel him away from it. Once he committed, he went all in. That's what made him such a great athlete.

I shimmied his note out of my back pocket.

Addie,

Change of plans. Not going with you to Italy. Tell Lina and her dad that I had to go home early for practice. Tell Mom and Dad that I'm with you. Will meet up with you for the flight home. Will explain later.

—Ian

Was he serious? I heaved myself forward again, thrusting the paper under Ian's nose. "This was your note? Your big explanation? This doesn't even look like your handwriting! I would have thought you were kidnapped!"

Ian startled, like he'd forgotten I was back there. He probably had. He snatched the note from me. "I was going for brevity."

"Nailed it," I said.

"Let me see it." Rowan took the note and read it aloud, his musical voice making it sound even more cryptic. "Wow, that is bad."

Ian grabbed the paper, stuffing it into his backpack. "I wanted it to be like in war movies where people only have the information they need. That way, when they get captured by the enemy, they can't have the information tortured out of them."

"Tortured out of them?" I said incredulously.

He hunched his shoulders sheepishly. "You know what I mean. I just thought it would be better for you if you didn't have all the facts."

"I still don't have all the facts." I yanked at my right leg, managing to free it from the crevice. If Ian wouldn't tell me what was going on, maybe Rowan would. I fixed my eyes on the back of his neck. His hair was slightly longer at the nape.

"So who are you exactly?" I asked, using my friendliest Catarina-approved voice. She was big on curiosity as a means of persuasion. Start by acting interested.

I don't know if it was my question or sparkly tone, but his eyes flicked toward me warily. "Rowan. We met back at the hotel? You told me my bumper was sagging?"

"That sounds dirty," Ian said.

"It was your tailpipe," I wailed, dropping the act. "Never mind. That part doesn't matter. What I want to know is why you"—I pointed at him—"clearly Irish, and my brother"—I pointed at Ian—"clearly American, are acting like best friends. And don't just say 'online' again. People who only know each other online don't complete each other's sentences."

"Isn't this a violation of the terms and conditions?" Rowan asked, calling upon what Ian had said earlier. Ian gave him a smirk equivalent to a fist bump.

"True, it is a clear violation . . . ," I started, but I paused to think. What I needed was a cohesive argument. It had worked before in persuading Rowan to give me the keys. "Rowan, the thing is that I'm much more likely to be supportive of Ian's plans if I know what is going on."

"Riiiiight," Ian said, dragging out the word.

"I am," I insisted. "I didn't come with you on your first stop just so I could sit back here listening to you guys dissect the music industry." Saying "first stop" felt like a dangerous concession. It suggested the possibility of the road trip.

Rowan took both hands off the wheel to adjust his glasses. "She's right. This is why she's came with us in the first place—to give her some time to get used to the idea."

Or talk you out of the idea, I added silently.

"Fine. Fall for her evil tactics. But don't come crying to me when she makes your life a living hell." Ian fell into a heap against his window. I'd always thought he'd missed his calling by not signing up for drama club.

Rowan lifted his chin curiously in the rearview mirror.

I shrugged. "By all means, continue. I'll let you know when my evil tactics kick in."

His dimple winked at me. "Right. Well, Ian and I talk a lot. Like most days. And we've known each other since last summer. Well, I guess 'known' isn't quite the right word, is it?" No comment from Ian. Rowan continued nervously. "At first I was just familiar with his work. I read his first series of articles, and we started e-mailing from there. And then—"

"You read his first series of what?" I interrupted.

Ian made a barely audible groan, and Rowan's eyebrows knit in confusion. "I'm sorry, but I was under the impression that you two had met? Addie, meet Ian Bennett, esteemed teen music journalist. Ian, meet Addie, parking lot tackler extraordinaire."

Music journalist? I jammed my knees into the back of Ian's seat. "This is a joke, right?"

Rowan cleared his throat. "Um, sorry, but is *this* a joke?"

"Addie, I write articles, okay?" Ian propped his feet up on the dashboard and yanked irritably at his shoelaces. "I used to have a blog, but now I get paid to write articles for online publications."

"Ha ha," I said. "And you also love My Little Pony, right?"

"What are those guys called?" Rowan asked. "Bronies?"

Ian shot me a dirty-as-mud look, and I flinched. He was serious—and hurt. I could see it in the way he jutted his chin out. "Wait. You really do have a blog? Like online?"

"Yes, it's online. Where else would it be?" He scowled.

"But . . ." I hesitated, waiting for the pieces to fall into place, like they usually did. They didn't. "You have a *blog* blog? Like the kind you add entries to?"

"Yeah . . . like a website run by an individual? They're usually pretty informal," Rowan said helpfully, his voice kind. "It's pretty easy to sign up for one."

I blinked a couple of times. Anyone else would have

made fun of me. He was too nice for his own good. "Thanks, Rowan, but it's not the idea of a blog that's tripping me up. I'm just having a hard time believing that Ian has one." The thought of Ian coming home from practice to pour his feelings out in an online diary was so far in the realm of not possible that it technically didn't exist.

"Why can't you believe it?" Ian demanded, his mouth pressed into a tight line. He sounded exactly the way I had when talking to Archie last night. *Why, you think it's impossible that a popular football player would like someone like me?* "Because jocks aren't allowed to do anything but play sports? Thanks for stereotyping me."

"Ugh. Ian, no one's stereotyping you." Lately, Ian had had a huge chip on his shoulder about being seen as The Jock—impossible when he worked so hard to look alternative. And why did he mind the role anyway? It raised him to the level of high school god. "I just don't get how you'd even have time to write. During the school year you're either doing homework or playing sports."

"I make time," Ian said. "And what do you think I've been doing all summer?"

Finally, something clicked into place. Except for when he was at practice, Ian had spent most of the summer stationed at his computer. "Mom said you were working on college admissions essays."

He let out one of those harsh noises that sometimes passes as a laugh. "I have definitely not been working on college admissions essays. Unless you count creating a portfolio for journalism schools as a college application. If so, then yes."

"Journalism school? Does Washington State even have a journalism program?"

Ian slammed his hands on the dashboard, making Rowan and me jump. "I'm not going to Washington State."

"Whoa. Ian, you okay there?" Rowan asked. Ian lifted his chin slightly, as if he was rearing for a fight.

"What do you mean you're not going to Washington State? They scouted you earlier this summer. They're going to offer you a full-ride scholarship," I reminded him. And if this scholarship didn't work out, then another one would. Great grades plus incredible player equals money.

"I don't care about the football scholarship," Ian said, lowering his voice to a simmer.

"Why, because you won the lottery?"

"So fill me in here," Rowan broke in, his voice confused. "You two are obviously brother and sister, but were you separated at birth? Mom took one, Dad took the other? Or did one of you only recently learn English so that's why you've never communicated before?"

The tips of Ian's ears suddenly turned red. "It's pretty hard to communicate with someone who spent their whole summer lying to you."

I grabbed the back of his seat, my ears as red as his. They were our ultimate anger indicators. "Don't try to make this about Cubby. And besides, you're one to talk. You apparently have a whole secret life."

"It's not a 'whole secret life,'" he snapped, imitating my tone. "It was just this summer. And I would have told you if you weren't so busy sneaking around with Cubby."

"You have to stop bringing him up," I yelled.

Rowan tapped Clover's brakes firmly, lurching both of us forward. If we hadn't been the only ones on the road, we would have been rear-ended for sure. "Look, guys," Rowan began, "I get that you're dealing with some issues here, but I've been around enough arguing to last a lifetime. So, Ian, how about you bring Addie up to speed on what is apparently your dual life? I'm pretty curious myself how you've managed to keep this a secret from your family."

"It isn't that hard to keep it a secret. Unless it's about football, no one cares what I do." Ian dropped his shoulders, tension framing his eyes. "Fine. Addie, what do you want to know?"

Where to begin? "What's your blog's name?"

"*My Lexicon*," Ian said.

"How do you spell that?" I pulled out my phone and typed

it in as Rowan spelled. Not only did the blog exist, but it looked way more professional than a seventeen-year-old's blog should, with a sleek monochromatic theme and MY LEXICON spelled out in all caps across the top.

"It's a reference to a Bob Dylan quote," Rowan explained before I could ask. "'The songs are my lexicon. I believe the songs.'"

Ian crossed his arms angrily. "My blog is how I got my gig with IndieBlurb. I do a weekly column with them."

"It's called Indie Ian's Week in Five," Rowan said.

"Indie Ian? That's, like, your handle?" I kept waiting for one of them to crack a smile, but neither of them did. "Fine. What are the five?"

"They're music categories." Ian listed them off on his fingers. "Worth the hype, overhyped, covered, classic, and obscure. Every week I choose a song to fit into each." He exhaled loudly. "Why are you having such a hard time believing this? I've always liked writing. And music. I tried to be on the school newspaper last year, but Coach wouldn't let me do it. He said he didn't want me to lose my focus."

Coach had said that? A flurry of sibling protectiveness roared in my head.

Rowan jumped in. "Ian has a huge following on Twitter. Every time he publishes something, a hashtag goes around—#IndieIanSpeaks. That's how I found him."

"It isn't a huge following," Ian said modestly, but pride ringed the edges of his voice.

"You have ten thousand followers; how is that not huge?" Rowan said.

Ten thousand? Not bad.

Ian shook his hair into his eyes. "No, it's never been ten thousand. Every time I get close, I post something in the 'overhyped' category that offends people, and there's a mass exodus. My tombstone's going to say, 'Always fifty followers short of ten thousand.'" Rowan snorted.

I pulled out my phone to verify the Twitter account. The profile photo on @IndieIan11 was an up-close shot of Ian's eyes, his long hair framing the right side of the square. 9.9K followers. A massive party I hadn't been invited to. Hadn't even been told about.

I gripped the phone hard, a herd of feelings galloping across my chest. At least now I knew why Ian had been so distant all summer. He'd been living a secret online life. "Ian, why didn't you tell me about all this?" I asked.

He shook his head. "Why would I? It's not like you listen to anything I say anyway."

Cop-out answer. "Ian, for the last time, this isn't about Cubby. If Rowan found you a year ago, that means you were music"—I hesitated—"music journaling way before Cubby and I started hanging out."

"'Music journaling.' I like it." Rowan might as well have been wearing a referee jersey. He was desperate to stop our fight.

Ian turned back impatiently. "So tell me again, are you planning to tell Mom about Cubby during or after your trip to Florence?"

"Ian, we've been through this a dozen times. I am not telling her." My words vibrated loudly through the car. How had he even jumped to that? "And it's not my trip to Florence. It's *our* trip."

Even I didn't sound convinced.

The first time I ever lied to Ian, it was about Cubby. It was surprisingly easy.

It was during our last field trip together, and right away I realized something was different about this excursion from the others. Usually, our trips were to my brother's newest and most recent discoveries, but not this time.

"I've been coming here since I got my license," he said, as I aimed the flashlight at the troll's one visible eye, glistening as hard and shiny as a bead. Cars roared above us on the overpass.

Ian climbed up the statue's gnarled hand, settling into the curve between its head and neck. I let my light wander over the statue. The concrete troll was over twenty feet tall, and one of its plump hands clutched a life-size car in its monstrous grip. "Why have I never been here before?"

Ian stretched out over the arm. "I like to come here after practice. To think."

"To think about what? How you're going to dominate at the next game?" I teased.

He made a noise in the back of his throat, quickly changing the subject. "Did you notice how blobby the troll is? It's because people spray-paint him, and the only way to remove the paint is to cover him up with more cement."

"Nice segue," I said. Lately, Ian had been dodging every conversation that had anything to do with football. But tonight I wasn't going to pry. It was nice just to be with him. I felt like I hadn't seen much of him lately.

I tucked the flashlight into my sweatshirt pocket and scrambled up to join him. For a while, we listened to the rhythmic rumbling of cars rushing overhead. Their predictable noises were comforting. I could see why Ian liked it here.

"Where were you last night?" he suddenly asked, and my heart raced faster than the cars on the highway.

I avoided looking him in the eye. "I went to bed early."

He shook his head. "I came into your room to see if you wanted to watch SNL. *You were gone on Tuesday night too. How are you getting out? The window? Kind of ballsy to climb out past Mom and Dad's room."*

Very ballsy. Particularly for a person who was five foot one on a good day trying to descend a tree whose branches were spaced out at least five feet apart.

"I was probably in the kitchen," I said, surprised by how easily the lie slipped through my mouth. I'd never lied to Ian before, never even really considered it. But then, I guess I'd never had a reason before. A small smile invaded my face. I couldn't help it.

He raised his eyebrows. "So now that I know how you're sneaking out, the question is who are you sneaking out with?"

I pressed my lips together, sealing in my secret. Sometimes it felt like everything I owned had once belonged to one of my brothers, and as much as I loved them, I loved the idea of having something all to myself even more.

After a few seconds Ian let out a long and exaggerated sigh. "Fine. Be that way." He slid off the troll, his sneakers thudding heavily onto the ground. "But you know I'll find out eventually."

Taking me to the troll was Ian's attempt at drawing out my secret: I'll tell you one of mine, you tell me one of yours.

Unfortunately, I wasn't going to be the one to tell him.

Rowan's car raced down the twisted road as I watched Ireland suddenly morph into something remote and ferocious. Roofless stone structures lined the narrow roads, moss blanketing them softly in green. Everything looked abandoned, which for some reason made my internal clock tick even louder. I had less than an hour to convince Ian to abandon his plan.

Luckily, I had a secret weapon. Two weeks ago, my mom and I had driven over an hour north to visit her aunt, and I'd gotten stuck listening to a new Catarina Hayford recording called "Modes of Persuasion." Back then I hadn't thought I would ever need it. But now I needed to draw on the experts. Step one: act curious. "So what exactly does the Burren have to do with Titletrack?"

The bruise under Ian's eye looked at me accusingly. "Listen, Catarina. We're working on a strictly need-to-know basis here. Also, no one invited you, so quit asking questions."

"I was not being Catarina," I snapped. I guess he'd listened to that one too.

"Yes, you were. Rule number one," he said in a surprisingly good impression of Catarina's throaty voice, "act curious."

"I'd ask who Catarina is, but you'd probably both rip my head off," Rowan said.

"You're safe on this one," Ian assured him. "She's a real estate guru who spends all of her free time getting spray tans. She turned our mom into a Seattle real estate mogul."

"I didn't know your mom was in real estate." Rowan slid his eyes curiously at Ian. For someone who was so close to my brother, he knew surprisingly little about him. He hadn't even known Walt's name.

"Rule number two: Never meet the client halfway. Meet them all the way." Ian flicked his hair behind his shoulder and pursed his lips convincingly. "Rule number three: Be realistic and optimistic. The future belongs to the hopeful."

I flicked him on the shoulder. "Ian, stop."

He snorted and dropped the pose, ducking down to look out the windshield. "Rowan, is this Corofin?"

"No. That was the first town. This is Killinaboy. Also, I'm overruling your terms and conditions." Rowan's gaze fell on me, light as a butterfly. "Your sister needs to know what we're doing."

"What? Why?" he asked.

"Because if she knows why you're taking off without her, maybe she'll retaliate less."

"Rowan, believe me. She won't retaliate less," Ian said.

"She can hear you," I reminded them, my gaze snagged on yet another attempt by Rowan to adjust his glasses. The way he pushed them up was the perfect combination of endearing and nerdy. If he didn't seem so clueless about it, I'd think he was doing it on purpose. "And, Ian, I'm starting to like your friend here. Unlike you, he actually considers other people's feelings."

I meant for it to be funny, but I heard my mistake the second it was out of my mouth. Ian took loyalty very seriously—just hinting that he was letting someone down was enough to make him snap.

He twisted around. "Right. Because I never care about your feelings. Because I never, ever stand up for you or help you with school or clean up your mistakes."

My cheeks scalded. Had he just lumped helping me with school in with Cubby? "Did you really just say that?" I demanded.

Rowan verbally threw himself in between us. "Okay, guys. Let's talk about Titletrack. When they first started out, they couldn't get anyone to sign them, so they started posting songs online and performing in pubs around Ireland. Eventually, they talked a radio station into playing one of their songs, and it was requested so many times that it ended up on the top ten charts. After that, labels couldn't ignore them."

There was a long, awkward pause, but the oddly timed description worked. We weren't fighting anymore. Ian sank down into his seat, his chin resting on his chest.

Rowan kept going, probably in hopes of squelching another eruption. "And Titletrack's final concert is in three days. They made the announcement earlier this year and swore they aren't going to do that stupid thing bands do where they retire and then do a bunch of reunion tours."

"I hate that," Ian said, rechanneling his anger.

It was Titletrack's final concert? This was more hopeless than I thought. "So what does the Burren have to do with anything?" I asked again, carefully.

Rowan valiantly picked up the torch again. "So Ian's idea—which was brilliant, I might add—is to visit some of those early places that were important to the band and write a piece that culminates at the picnic. Kind of like following their footprints all the way to Electric Picnic." He paused. "Ian, that's what you should title it!"

"Hmmm," Ian said noncommittally.

"Anyway, the Burren is where they filmed their first music video for a song called 'Classic,' which is, in my humble opinion, the greatest song in the world."

"It is," Ian confirmed. He leaned forward, and his hair fell into a waterfall around his face. "I played it for you on the way to school a couple of times. It's the one that talks about slippery simplicity."

I did remember the song. I'd even requested it a few times, mostly because I liked the way the singer rolled "slippery simplicity" through his mouth like a piece of butterscotch candy.

"Right," Rowan said. "We're going to document the whole trip, Ian posting pictures to his blog and social media. Then, when it's all done, he's going to submit the final article somewhere big."

"*Maybe* I'm going to submit it somewhere big," Ian said quickly.

"What do you mean, 'maybe'?" Rowan's voice sounded

incredulous. "If you don't, I'll do it for you. Your writing is definitely good enough, and I have a whole list of Irish music magazines that would go crazy over it."

"So this is like serious fanboying meets research trip," I said. Each new fact pushed me a little closer toward hopeless.

"Exactly." Rowan punched the air enthusiastically. "And your aunt's wedding? Best coincidence to ever befall planet Earth."

Ian smiled at Rowan, his anger forgotten. Zero to sixty, sixty to zero. It could go both ways. After a lifetime of fights, I should be used to it, but it still caught me off guard sometimes. Especially now, when I'd thought we were headed for another grand mal fight, like the one at the cliffs. "I couldn't believe it," Ian said. "I mean, what are the odds of me being in Ireland during their final concert?"

For Ian? High. Life liked to make things work for him.

I crumpled into the back seat, resignation settling over me in a fine layer. Ireland was enchanting, Rowan was Ian's best friend soul mate, and Ian's favorite band was doing a once-in-a-lifetime show. I'd lost before I'd even begun.

I curled up tightly, hooking my arms around my knees. "I need you guys to be really fast at the Burren. And, Ian, did you cancel your ticket to Italy?"

Ian started to look back but caught himself halfway. "No, but I checked with the airline. They'll just give my seat away when I don't show up." He had enough compassion to keep the victory out of his voice.

Italy and Lina reached out, warm and inviting. Sunshine, gelato, art, scooters, spaghetti, my best friend. I closed my eyes and clung hard to the image. Leaving Ian in Ireland wasn't what I'd had in mind, but maybe it would be good for us. The next hour couldn't go fast enough.

"Fine," I said, falling back dejectedly against my seat. "You win. You always win."

The Burren

Ah, the Burren. *An Bhoireann.* The place of stone. Arguably the most desolate, bleak, miserable excuse of a landscape that has ever graced God's (mostly) green earth. An early admirer said, "There isn't a tree to hang a man, water to drown a man, nor soil to bury a man."

You're going to love it.

But before this love affair begins, let's start with a little Irish geography. Three hundred forty million years ago, the Emerald Isle looked a tad bit different than it does today. Not only were there no pubs or Irish preteens scouring Penneys department stores, but it was covered by water—a great big tropical ocean, in fact, that was absolutely teeming with life. Animals, fish, plants, you name it, all paddling around snapping at one another in certain barbaric bliss. But as every Disney movie has taught us, at some point those creatures had to die (usually horrifically and in front of their children), and as their bones gathered at the bottom of the ocean, an ancient primordial recipe was put into action, one that can be roughly summed up in the following equation:

bones + compression + millions of years =
limestone

And that's exactly what was formed. Limestone. Ten square miles of it, in fact. And once it was done with its stint as the ocean's floor, that limestone came rising to the surface, forming the bleak, unique landscape your plucky little feet are standing on today. Which brings me to another equation, not entirely related but helpful all the same:

courage + time = healed heart

Spelled out that way, it all seems rather doable, doesn't it, chickadee? I mean, the fact that you've somehow managed to get yourself to the Emerald Isle lets me know we're all good on the courage bit. And as for the time bit? Well, that will come. Minute by minute, hour by hour, time will stretch and build and compress until one day you'll find yourself standing on the surface of something newly risen and think, *Huh. I did it.*

You'll do it, buttercup. You really will.

HEARTACHE HOMEWORK: See those wildflowers popping up from amongst the stone, pet? Don't worry. I'm not going to make an overworked point about beauty in pain. But I do want you to pick a few of those, one for each of your people. And by "your people," I mean the ones you can count on to stand by you as you wade through this. Put yourself in a circle of them and draw on their power. Be sure to pick one for me.

—Excerpt from *Ireland for the Heartbroken: An Unconventional Guide to the Emerald Isle, third edition*

"WHAT AM I LOOKING AT EXACTLY?" I ASKED AS ROWAN eased into a sticky parking lot. The Burren was less landscape and more hostile takeover. At first it was subtle, a few flat rocks cropping up in the fields like gray lily pads, but slowly the proportions of stone to grass increased until gray choked out all the cheery green. By the time Rowan slowed to pull over, we were engulfed in cold, depressing rock. A sign read POULNABRONE.

Guidebook Lady had said the Burren was depressing, but this was over-the-top.

Ian pointed to a small, drab structure in the distance. He was already poised for takeoff, seat belt undone, notebook in hand. "The Poulnabrone is a tomb. It's over two thousand years old."

I squinted my eyes, turning the tomb into a gray blur. "A tomb? No one said anything about a tomb."

Rowan slid the car into park, and Ian launched himself out the window feetfirst, his notebook tucked securely under his arm. "See you there!" he called over his shoulder. His sneakers made wet squelching sounds as he sprinted toward the tomb.

Rowan whistled admiringly, keeping his eyes on my brother. He'd been quiet ever since I'd conceded defeat to the

Titletrack plan. Ian had talked more, but he looked slightly uncomfortable, like he was wearing a shirt with a scratchy tag. Detecting Ian guilt was a subtle art; his natural energy made it difficult.

"He looks like one of those Jesus lizards. You know, the ones that move so fast, they can run on water?" Rowan said.

I heaved myself into the passenger seat. "Promise me you won't tell him that. The last thing we need is for Ian to get a Jesus lizard complex."

His dimple reappeared. "Promise."

The parking lot was one large, sludgy puddle that seeped into my sneakers the second I hit the ground. A thin shroud of clouds covered the sun, erasing even the illusion of warmth, and I wrapped my bare arms around myself. Why had no one bothered to tell me that Ireland was the climatic equivalent of a walk-in freezer? Once I arrived in Italy, I planned to spend my first few hours there baking in the sun like a loaf of ciabatta bread. And talking to Lina.

Lina will know soon. A violent shiver worked its way down my spine.

"You cold?" Rowan asked, looking at me over the top of the car.

"What makes you think that?" I asked jokingly. My teeth were seconds from chattering.

"Maybe the fact that you're shivering like a puppy in one

of those animal cruelty commercials? You have those commercials in the States, right? *For just sixty-three cents a day, you, too, can stop a blond girl from shivering. . . .* They used to be on the television all the time."

"Yep, we have those too." Archie had a soft spot for animals, and when we were young, we used to wait for the commercials to come on so we could call him into the room and watch him tear up. Siblings can be a special kind of cruel. When my dad found out, he'd lectured us on the fact that we were being cruel about an animal cruelty commercial, and we'd all donated a month's worth of our allowance to an animal rescue organization.

I plucked at my shorts. "When I packed, I was thinking about Italy, so all I brought were summer clothes. I didn't realize that Ireland spends all its time in Arctic winter."

"And you're here on a good day. Give me a minute." He ducked back into Clover, and I pulled my phone out of my back pocket. 9:03. I wanted to be at the airport by ten o'clock.

"Hey, Rowan, how long will it take us to get to the airport?" I asked.

"About forty-five minutes."

"Then we'd better keep this trip short. I don't want to cut our time close."

He reemerged, his hair slightly mussed. "Addie, what is this?"

For a second I thought he was talking about the navy-blue sweater he had wrapped around one arm, but then I realized he was holding something in his other hand too. The guidebook.

"Rowan, that's mine!" I staggered toward him, a tidal wave of embarrassment washing over me.

He studied the cover. "Yeah, I know it's yours. Is this the guidebook you were talking about? Why does it say it's about heartbreak?"

"I need you to give that back." I jumped up, and he let me snatch it from him. I pressed it to my side. "Why were you looking through my stuff anyway?"

"I was just trying to find you a sweater, and your book was under the seat. I thought it was one of mine." He took a step closer. "But now you've got me curious."

His eyes were puppy-dog soft, and I felt myself cave. And besides, explaining the guidebook didn't mean I had to spill everything about my heartbreak. "I found this in the library of the hotel. It takes you to important sites in Ireland and then assigns you tasks to do while you're there. It's supposed to help you get over having your heart broken."

"Do you think it would actually work?" The urgency in Rowan's voice made my eyes snap up. He stared hungrily at the guidebook.

"Uh . . . I'm not really sure," I said. "The writer is a little eccentric, but it seems like she knows her stuff. Who knows? Maybe it does work."

"So you're using the guidebook to help you get over Cubby?" he persisted.

Now he wanted to talk about Cubby too? I straightened up to shut him down, but he must have seen it coming because he quickly backpedaled. "Sorry. That was too personal. It's just that I've, uh"—he shoved his glasses up, fidgeting with the rims—"I've actually been through a bit of heartbreak myself." He met my eyes, and this time his gaze pleaded with me. "So if you've discovered some kind of magic guide for getting through it, please don't hold out on me."

The vulnerability in his eyes made my heart well up, and before I could talk myself out of it, I thrust the guidebook into his hands, the words spilling out of me: "Maybe you should try it out. There's a homework assignment for the Burren, and I could help you if you want." I always did this. Any time someone was in pain, I wanted to fix it immediately. "If you want, I'll leave the book in the car for you. Maybe you could stop by the sites on the way to your music festival."

He turned it over in his hands, slowly raising his eyes to mine. "Wow. That's really nice of you." He bit his lower lip. "Also, I'm really sorry about my part in keeping Ian from Italy. If I had known . . ."

I waved him off. "I'll survive. And I really do need some quality time with Lina, so maybe it will be better if Ian isn't there anyway."

He nodded, then lifted the book eagerly, hope crossing his face. "If you don't mind, I think I'm going to give the homework thing a shot."

"Of course not. I don't mind at all," I said eagerly, my insides glowing the way they always did when I helped someone.

"Then I'll see you out there. And here, for you." He tossed me the navy sweater, and I quickly pulled it on. It smelled lightly of cigarette smoke and fell all the way to my knees, but it felt fantastic—like getting a hug the second before you realized you needed one. Now for the Heartache Homework. I turned and looked at the gray, bleak landscape.

Wildflowers. Right.

* * *

Lucky for me and my homework assignment, up-close Burren was very different from in-the-car Burren. For one thing, it had a lot more dimension. Yes, flat gray stones covered 90 percent of the ground, but grass and moss exploded up in the cracks between them, bright wildflowers popping up every chance they got.

I walked as far from the tomb as I dared, then collected a handful of flowers. Once I was positive that Ian's back was turned, I placed them one by one in a circle, naming them as I went. "Mom, Dad, Walter, Archie, Ian, Lina, and Guidebook Lady," I said aloud. Too bad only one of them even knew about my heartache.

Okay, Guidebook Lady. Now what? I pulled my arms into Rowan's sweater and turned in a slow circle. How was surrounding myself with floral representations of "my people" supposed to make me feel better?

"How's it going?" I looked up to see Rowan making his way over to me, his grasshopper-long legs carrying him from rock to rock.

"That was fast," I said. "Did you read the Burren entry?"

"Yes. I'm a fast reader." He stopped, remaining respectfully outside the circle. "Is it working?"

"I don't know," I said truthfully. "I mostly just feel stupid."

"Can I come in?" I nodded, and he stepped in, holding out a sunshine-yellow flower. "Here. I wanted to be one of your flowers." He grimaced lightly. "Sorry. That sounded really sappy."

"I thought it was nice," I said, running my thumb over the silky-smooth petals. No guy had ever given me flowers before. Not even Cubby.

I placed Rowan's flower next to Ian's, then—because it felt like I should be doing something—I turned in a slow, self-conscious circle, focusing my attention on each flower, one by one.

When I was back to Rowan's yellow flower, he looked at me expectantly. "So? Anything?"

"Hmm." I touched my heart lightly. It didn't hurt any less, but it actually did feel lighter, like someone had slipped their hands underneath mine to help me with the weight. "I actually do feel kind of different. You should try it."

"Do I have to turn in a circle?" An embarrassed flush bloomed on his cheeks. "Or say their names or something?"

"I think you can do whatever you want. You want some time alone?"

"Yes," he said resolutely. "I think I'd be better without an audience on this one."

I stepped out of the circle and headed over to join Ian at the site. The tomb was about ten feet tall with several flat slabs of rock standing parallel to one another to form the walls, another resting on top to create a roof. Ian's pencil scratched furiously across his notebook. What was there to even write about?

"So . . . this is cool," I said, breaking the silence. "You said this is where Titletrack filmed their first music video?"

He didn't look up from his notes. "Right where we're standing. The quality was so bad. In some parts you can barely hear Jared singing, and the cameraman had a sneezing attack at minute two, but they still got a million views. The song's that good."

He dropped his notebook to his side and we stood quietly, the wind at our backs. The Burren felt solemn as a church, and just as heavy. Guidebook Lady's words broadcasted through my mind. *Courage + time = healed heart. Spelled out that way, it all seems rather doable, doesn't it, chickadee?*

That's where Guidebook Lady was wrong, because it didn't seem doable. Not at all. Especially not when Ian and I could barely talk to each other without spiraling into an argument. I glanced back at Rowan. He was still in the circle, his back to us.

"So you're really not going to tell Mom about Cubby," Ian said, reading my mind like normal. I hated the frustration in his voice—his disappointment always felt heavier than anyone else's.

I shook my head. I knew Ian might be right. Not telling Mom and then having her find out from someone else was a huge risk. But I hadn't managed to even tell Lina—how could I possibly expect myself to come clean to my mother?

Ian's voice rang in my mind. *You know what Cubby's been doing, right?* I stepped away from him, unable to say a word.

Maybe some time apart would be good for us.

* * *

9:21. I spent a few minutes wandering the Burren, and when I finally got to the car and checked the time, my anxiety spiked to a record high. Had we really been here for twenty minutes?

"Guys!" I yelled, waving my arms at both Ian and Rowan. They were standing side by side at the tomb. How had that thing kept their attention for so long? "Guys!"

Ian glanced over, and I tapped an imaginary watch on my wrist. "We need to go. Now."

He languidly pulled his phone out of his pocket before he and Rowan began jogging toward me. I hurried around the back of the car, something unexpected catching my eye.

"Oh, no." The tailpipe now sagged lazily to the ground, the tip completely submerged in a puddle of water. I ducked down to assess the damage.

"Sorry. We lost track of time," Rowan said, his breath heavy as he splashed toward me. "Good thing I'm a fast driver." He caught sight of my crouched form. "Oh, no, did the pipe come loose?"

"I think we lost a bolt. We have to fix it before we leave."

Rowan crossed his arms nervously. "Any chance we could fix it later? I don't want to risk getting you to the airport late."

I fought it, but the practical side of me won out. If the tailpipe were to disconnect as we were driving, that would be it. No workable car. No airport. No Italy and no Lina. I had to find at least a short-term solution.

I jumped to my feet. "As long as we can get it off the road, we'll be fine. What do you have that we could tie it up with?"

Rowan tapped his chin, looking at the bumper stickers as if they might be able to help him out. "Dental floss? I might have a bungee cord somewhere."

I shook my head. "It has to be metal, or it will melt through and we'll have to stop and do it again."

"How about these?" Rowan pulled a pair of headphones out of his back pocket, the cords tangled into a nest. "Aren't the wires inside made out of copper?"

Ian's mouth dropped open. "Absolutely not. Those are Shure headphones. They're, like, two hundred dollars."

"You're offering me your two-hundred-dollar headphones?" I asked, shocked. I knew Rowan was nice, but this was over-the-top.

He tossed them to me. "They were a guilt present," he said, bitterness ringing through his voice. "Divorce kid perks." His shoulders sagged slightly, and Ian gave him a surprised look, but it was pretty clear Rowan didn't want any follow-up questions.

It was way too generous of an offer, but I had to take him up on it anyway. I had too much at stake. I gave him a nod of thanks, then dropped down to the ground. "Ian, hold the tailpipe up for me." He obeyed and I crawled halfway under the bumper, water seeping into my shorts as I felt my way around.

I was used to being the family mechanic. The summer after Walter turned sixteen, my brothers and I had a tire blowout on a freeway near our house. I'd dug out the owner's manual, and by the time my dad had showed up, I was covered in grease, and the spare tire was on. Unlike school, cars had just always made sense to me—there was something comforting about the fact that the answer was always just a popped hood or wrench twist away.

The underside of Rowan's car was coated in mud, and it took me way longer than it should have to attach the tailpipe. Nerves were not my friend. What felt like an hour later, I jumped to my feet, anxiety rippling through my center. "Got it. Let's get out of here."

"Maybe you should change before you get back in Rowan's car," Ian said, looking at my clothes. "You look like a mud ball."

"We don't have time," Rowan said, heading for his door. "Hop in, mud ball."

* * *

I was bouncing around the back seat, trying to ignore the fact that the numbers on Clover's dashboard clock were moving at warp speed, when Rowan suddenly let loose with a word that sounded mispronounced. "Feck!"

Feck? I looked up. "What's wrong?"

Rowan pointed out the windshield. "That's what's wrong."

I spiked forward anxiously, and what I saw tied my stomach into a neat bow. About a quarter mile up was a tractor. But not just any tractor—this one was massive, spilling out over both lanes of the road like a giant, lumbering lobster. It definitely wasn't in a hurry. Rowan eased up on the gas and coasted up to it.

"We have to get around it," I said. Were tractors allowed to just take over the road?

Addie, don't panic. Don't panic. We were already late. How was this happening?

"How?" Rowan raked his hand through his hair. "It's too big to even pull over to let us pass. It takes up the whole road."

"There's no way it can stay on the road for long," Ian said calmly, but his knee burst into full bounce. "Rowan, they can't stay on the road for long, right?"

"Well . . . ," Rowan said. He grimaced. "Maybe I should turn around. There's got to be another route to the freeway."

The suggestion made me nervous. Another route sounded messy. And risky. A rumble behind us made us all whip around.

"Feck!" This time it was Ian who yelled it. The tractor's twin was coming up the road behind us. Just as big, just as slow.

"What is this, a tractor parade?" I demanded. Tractor number two was pumpkin orange, and the driver returned our scowls with a cheery wave.

"Great. Tractor buddies," Rowan said.

"I'm going to talk to them." Ian rolled his window down, and before Rowan and I realized what he meant, he'd scrambled out of the still-moving car, stumbling when he hit the ground. "Ian! Get back in here," I yelled. But he ran full speed to the first tractor, mud flipping up behind him.

"Wow. Bennetts don't mess around, do they?" Rowan said.

"Especially not that one," I said.

The driver caught sight of Ian and slowed. He jumped up onto the step, moving his arms animatedly as he talked to the driver.

I was about to climb out after him when Ian jumped off the steps and ran back to us. "He can't get off the road for another ten minutes, but he said there's a shortcut to the freeway. He's going to point when we get close."

"Yes." Rowan sighed with relief.

"Ten minutes?" I said, looking nervously at the clock. It was already 9:39. The procession started up again, sending a splatter of mud onto our windshield.

* * *

The second we hit the freeway, Rowan slammed on the accelerator. "Rowan, drive!" I yelled.

"I'm going as fast as I can," Rowan said shakily. "Addie, I think we can still make it. You aren't checking a bag, right? And maybe there will be a delay."

I wanted to believe him, but the adrenaline coursing through my body wouldn't let me. Flights were never delayed when you wanted them to be. It was only when you had an important connection in an airport that was the size of an island nation that you got delayed. And according to my phone's GPS, we were still a solid twenty miles from the airport. Time was gaining on us. 10:16.

Clover hit a pothole, and the pile of Rowan's belongings slid into my side. I fought it back, my heart a jackhammer. I felt like one of the bottle rockets my brothers and I used to set off on the Fourth of July. Another few seconds and I was going to shoot out of the car's flimsy soft top.

"It's okay, Addie. We're going to make it," Ian said, his fingers wrapped tightly around the grab handle. He'd said it four times now. 10:18. It hadn't really been a full two minutes, had it?

"This can't be happening." The words burst out of my mouth, as frantic as I felt.

This time, no one even attempted to comfort me. We were all in the same state of panicked despair. It had taken us a solid ten minutes to even get to the detour road, and what the tractor driver had failed to mention to Ian was that our "shortcut" was actually a narrow, bumpy dirt road that slowed us to a pace just above tractor speed.

"Airport!" Rowan yelled.

I exhaled in relief. A large green sign read AIRPORT/AERFORT, the Gaelic word accompanied by a picture of a jet. We weren't there, but we were close. So long as I made it to the aiport an hour before my 11:30 flight, I should be fine. Rowan hit the gas like a NASCAR driver, unfortunately timing it with a sudden pothole. We hit the road hard, and suddenly a loud screeching noise erupted from under the car.

"No!" I screamed.

"What? What was that?" Ian's fidgeting was so bad, he could have been dancing a tango.

I turned to look out the back window, but I couldn't see anything. It sounded like the tailpipe was dipping up and down off the road, screeching every time it hit asphalt. The two-hundred-dollar headphones were not going to hold for long.

"Please hold, please hold, please hold," I prayed aloud.

BAM. A clanging noise filled the car, and I shot to the rear window to see sparks flying out the back. The car behind us slammed on its horn and swerved into the next lane.

"No!" I yelled again.

"What? Addie, what?" Rowan said. "Did it fall?"

I crumpled into my seat, tears filming over my eyes. "We have to pull over."

Rowan and Ian both visibly deflated, and Rowan pulled to the side. I jumped out. The shoulder was narrow, and cars passed by much too close for comfort as I ran to the back and crouched down. The tailpipe was barely connected, Rowan's headphones dangling helplessly. How was this happening?

"10:21." Ian's hands fell to his sides, his voice shaky. The misery in his voice said it all. 10:21. There was no way we'd make it on time.

I'd missed my flight. I fell back onto my butt in the mud. A large, shuddery sob worked its way to my throat and stuck.

Ian crouched down next to me and rhythmically patted my back. "Addie, it's okay. We'll get you another flight. I'll pay for it myself if I have to."

"I feel so bad," Rowan said, crouching down on my other side. "I should have accounted for tractors. I can help pay too."

"I can't believe this," I said weakly, tears flooding me. A plane passed overhead, its engines a dull painful roar. Insult to injury. And I knew the real reason I was upset. All this time I'd been counting down to the exact moment that I could unburden myself by talking to Lina, and now that was delayed. My secret pressed hard on the walls of my chest, burning hot. I couldn't wait one more second.

I jumped to my feet, leaving the guys behind as I fumbled for my phone. What was I going to say? *Hi, Lina. Do you have a second? Because not only did I just miss my flight, but I have something important to tell you.* Telling Lina about Cubby from the side of a freeway in Ireland was not what I'd had in mind, but it was going to have to do.

Where would I even start?

If I absolutely had to pinpoint the day things started with Cubby, I guess I'd start with the night he jumped into my car.

I was waiting for Ian after football practice, like I usually did. Rain spattered merrily onto the windshield, and I hugged my knees tightly up against the steering wheel. I refused to turn on the heat on principle alone. It was July. Why couldn't Seattle act like it?

"Ian, come on," I muttered, looking at the school doors. My friend and soccer teammate, Olive, had invited me to her house for one of her famous B-movie showings. She had a way of making the worst movies spectacularly entertaining, and Ian was absolutely going to make me late. Suddenly, a TIGERS *sweatshirt appeared in the passenger window, and the door yanked open.*

"Finally. What took you so long?" I complained, reaching for my seat belt as he slid into the front seat. "Next time I'm going to leave you."

"You'd really leave me?" I startled at the voice. It was Cubby. Freshly showered, with rosy cheeks and droplets of water clinging to the ends of his hair. He smiled, his bright eyes meeting mine. "You're staring at me like I'm a ghost. Why?"

"Because . . ." My words tried to catch up with my brain. Because I think about you all the time and now you're in my car.

"Um, I guess practice is over?" I finally managed. Brilliant.

He grabbed the seat adjuster, reclining a few inches. "So glad it's over. Practice was brutal." His head dropped, and if I weren't so shocked to have him in my car, I probably would have noticed how spent he looked. Ian had mentioned something about the football coach being exceptionally hard on Cubby this year. I guess it was getting to him. "And Ian might be a while. Coach cornered him for strategizing." He paused, his gaze heavy and invigorating all at once. "Do you still want to hang out? We could go somewhere."

A hot spiral formed in my stomach. Is this really happening? Do things you daydream about actually happen?

"Where?" I asked, careful to keep my voice even.

He looked out the passenger window and traced his finger over the fogging glass. "Anywhere."

It took all my effort not to slam my foot on the accelerator. When it came to Cubby, that was my real problem. I never stopped to think, not even once.

"I missed my flight. My parents can't know and Ian and I got in a fight and there were tractors and Ian's going to a festival and Lina I missed my flight." Instead of the calm explanation

I'd planned on, everything came out in one big tumbling blob, my words piling on top of each other.

"Addie, slow down," Lina said sternly. "I need you to slow down."

"What's going on?" It was Ren, Lina's boyfriend, in the background. He was always in the background these days. Did they ever spend time apart? I wished it didn't bug me so much.

"Just a minute." She shushed him. "I'm trying to figure that out. Addie, what is going on with you?"

"I told you. I—I just missed my flight." Tears poured from my closed eyelids, and my voice sounded as shaky as Rowan's car.

She blew into the phone, sending hot static into my ear. "Yeah, I got that part. But I mean what is going on with you? You've been avoiding my calls for the past week and a half, and now you're standing on the side of the road having a breakdown. This isn't just about the flight. Or the wedding. Why have you been avoiding me?"

Cubby dropped down like a marionette, swinging in the space between us. Of course I hadn't fooled Lina. She'd always had this sixth sense about when I needed her. Half the time I didn't even need to call; she just showed up.

And evasion wasn't going to work. Not when she'd cornered me like this. I took a deep breath. "Lina, there's something I need to tell you. About this summer. I was going to tell you as soon as I got to Florence, but—"

"Is this about Cubby Jones?" she asked impatiently.

"I— What?" I cringed, my shoulders shooting up. Had word really spread to Italy? "Who told you?"

Now Lina's voice was all business. "No one told me anything. You've been hiding something since July. Every time we talked, you were just barely holding back. And then you kept casually dropping his name, like, 'Oh, remember when we were in pottery class and Cubby's pot exploded in the kiln?' Not that great of a story, Addie."

My head fell into my hands. I'd never been very good at lying, doubly so when it was to someone I loved. Walter claimed I was the worst liar in the world. My dad claimed that was a compliment. "Yeah, I guess I was sort of trying to tell you. But not really."

There was a long pause, and I pressed the phone closer to my ear, desperately trying to read her silence. Could silence sound judgmental? I turned to look at Ian. He and Rowan both slouched miserably against the car, Ian's hands deep in his pockets.

"So which airport should I fly into? Shannon or Dublin?"

It took me a moment to realize what Lina was saying.

"Wait. Did you just ask which airport you should fly into?"

"Yes." She exhaled impatiently. "That makes the most sense, right? You just told me that you missed your flight and your parents can't know, so obviously I'm coming to you."

"You'd . . . fly here?" I'd clearly missed the jump somewhere. "But how would you . . . ?" I brushed away the fresh flood of tears staining my cheeks.

Lina made another impatient noise that was distinctly Italian-flavored. "Listen to me. I have tons of frequent flier miles, and Ren does too, and we've both been dying to visit Ireland. I'll just tell Howard that you need me. You stick with Ian, and I'll get to you as fast as I can."

I shut my eyes, letting Lina's plan unfurl. I stay with Ian. Lina comes to me. Maybe our parents don't find out. Maybe I still play soccer. Maybe I figure out a way to make Ian stop looking at me like I'm a burr hitchhiking on his sock. It was the best possible plan for the scenario.

"Are you sure?" I managed. "Flying to Ireland is not a small deal."

"Flying to Ireland is not a huge deal, not when friendship is involved. And, Addie, it's going to be okay. Whatever it is, it's going to be okay."

I wanted to tell her what this moment meant to me, but the words dammed up in my throat. She'd come through with a solution I hadn't even considered. It made me feel bad about ever having doubted her.

"Thank you," I finally managed between tears.

"You're welcome. Sorry you don't get to taste gelato, but at least we'll be together. That's the important part, right?"

"Right." I opened my eyes to a brilliant swath of sunlight. A small pink bubble formed in my chest. Precarious, but hopeful all the same.

* * *

"No. Absolutely not." That was all it took for Ian to snuff the spark in my chest. "This is my trip. Our trip. It's once-in-a-lifetime. We've been planning this for months now." Ian edged toward the car protectively. Rowan had managed to find a wire hanger in the trunk, and I'd used it to refasten the bumper.

"Which is why I'm in this position to begin with," I snapped back. Every time a car went by, I felt like I was about to get sucked onto the road. "If you hadn't messed with the original plan, then none of this would be happening." My voice was high and whiny, but I didn't care. His trip had cost me Italy. "Do you think I wanted to miss my flight?" Though the more I thought about Lina's plan, the more it made sense. Our best chance of surviving this trip unscathed was to stick together.

"Ian, come on. . . . It does make a lot of sense. Don't your chances of not getting caught go way down if you're together?" Rowan asked, echoing my reasoning. I looked at him gratefully, but he was completely zoned in on my brother.

Ian kicked at the ground angrily. "Fine. *Fine.* But listen to me. This is my trip. No fighting. No Addie drama. No stuff about Cubby. Got it?"

"I do not want to talk about Cubby!" I yelled. "You are the one who keeps bringing him up." A large truck whooshed by and blew my hair around my face.

"Whoa." Rowan stepped between us, palms up in stop signs. "We need to establish something right away. I'm completely for this new plan, but I'm not spending the next few days trapped in the middle of whatever's going on between you. If we do this, there has to be a truce. No fighting."

To my surprise, Ian calmed almost immediately, his mouth turned down apologetically. "You're right. Addie, I won't talk about Cubby if you won't."

Really? It was that easy? "Okay," I said warily.

"Okay?" Rowan's eyes darted back and forth between us. "So . . . everyone's good?"

"Good" was a little generous, but I managed a nod and so did Ian. It may have been a forced truce, but it was a truce. It would have to be enough.

* * *

We were fifteen minutes into the new plan, the road spooled out in front of us, everyone still slightly shell-shocked, when one aspect of my life suddenly became startlingly clear: I needed a restroom. Immediately.

I elbowed my way into the front of the car. "Rowan, could you please stop next chance you get? I really need a bathroom."

Ian whirled around, his face tense. "But our next stop isn't until Dingle."

"How far is that?" I asked, looking down at his map. Dingle was a finger-shaped peninsula that reached out into the Atlantic Ocean, a good hundred miles away. Definitely beyond the capacity of my bladder.

"Are you joking?" I ventured.

He set his mouth firmly. He wasn't joking. "We have this trip all mapped out. The tailpipe and tractors have already put us way behind."

"Ian, that's crazy. The last time I had access to a bathroom, I thought I was going to Italy. Either you let me have a bathroom break or I pee on the back seat."

He threw a hand up dismissively. "Great. Pee back there. It will be like the coffee can incident on the way to Disneyland."

"Ian!" I growled. The coffee can incident may be a part of Bennett road trip lore, but that didn't mean I had any interest in hearing about it all the time. Why couldn't my brothers ever let anything go?

"What's the coffee can incident?" Rowan asked, his eyes hinting at a smile.

"What do you think?" I snapped.

"You get the basic elements, right?" Ian said. "Road trip. Coffee can. Girl who—"

"Ian!" I threw my arms around the seat to cover his mouth. "Tell Rowan that story and I swear that I will never speak to you again."

Ian's laugh rumbled through my hands, and he pulled them off, but the mood already felt softer. At least the coffee can story was good for *something*.

"I actually need to put a call in to my mom, so a stop would work great for me. How about we stop in Limerick?" Rowan pointed to a sign. LIMERICK: 20 KM.

"Perfect," I said gratefully. I could handle twenty kilometers.

* * *

Turned out that twenty kilometers of grass-sprouting Irish road was very different from twenty kilometers of, say, any possible other road, and by the time Rowan pulled off the road into a gas station, I had to pee so badly, I was practically immobilized.

"Outoutoutout!" I yelled.

Ian turned, his hand on the headrest. "You have five minutes. And this is the absolute last stop before Dingle."

"Just move!" I pleaded.

Ian jumped gracefully out of the car and beelined for the convenience store. I did my best to follow, but halfway out I lost one of my shoes, and when I tried to reach for it, I lost my balance and belly flopped onto the ground, which was not ideal for the bladder situation.

I rolled to my side. Rowan's sweater was studded with gravel, and my elbow screamed in pain.

"Addie, are you okay?" Rowan sprinted around the car to help me up. "Where's your shoe?"

"No time," I managed. My bare foot throbbed as I sprinted for the store, but my bladder was now giving me the twenty-second countdown. This was no time for protective footwear.

Inside, I wasted a good five seconds stumbling through the aisles of unfamiliar junk food before realizing there was no restroom inside. Finally, I hurried up to the register. An older woman with braids wrapped around her head had her hip to the counter. "I told her, marry him or don't. But don't come crying to me—"

"Hi, love," the clerk said, latching his gaze onto me eagerly. *Save me*, his eyes pleaded. "What can I do for you?"

"Wheresthebathroom?" I didn't have time to space out the words; the situation was too desperate.

He understood the urgency, barking out directions in admirable alacrity. "Toilet's outside, around back. Just that way."

I sprinted past Ian filling up a basket with neon-colored caffeine bombs. My stomach was literally sloshing. Finally, I made it to the back, but when I yanked on the handle of the women's restroom, it didn't budge. "Hello?" I called, banging my fists on the door.

"Occupied," replied a cheery Irish voice.

"Could you hurry up, please?" I jiggled the knob desperately. I was going to pee my pants. I was absolutely going to pee my pants.

Suddenly, the men's room door shifted, and I hurled myself at it just as a bearded man stepped out. "Oh. Men's room, love," he said nervously.

"I'm American," I said, like that explained things. *I'm American, so I don't have to follow gender conventions.* He seemed to accept it as a valid explanation—either that or he thought I was crazy—and he darted out of my way. I quickly locked the door and turned around. Even in the awful lighting, the floor was *disgusting.* Damp and covered in wet toilet paper slime. I instinctively clamped my hand over my nose and mouth.

"Addie, you can do this," I instructed myself motivationally.

I had to. My only other option was to wait it out in the back of a clown car until Dingle.

By the time I'd hopped my way through the bathroom and then back out again, Rowan was at the car, his phone pressed to his ear. I quickly darted back into the store and picked up the largest box of Sugar Puffs I could find and carried it to the counter. The clerk's situation hadn't changed much.

"—so I told her, if she wants to live in a trash heap, that's fine. She just can't expect us to—"

"Can I point you to the milk?" The clerk lunged to take my cereal, almost losing his Santa Claus–looking spectacles in the process. How long had he been trapped there?

I shook my head. "Thanks, but I'm on a road trip. We wouldn't have anyplace to store it."

Interest sparked in his eyes. "I took a road trip or two myself back when I was your age. Where are you headed?" The braided-haired woman made a little huffing noise, shifting her bags from one hand to the other so I'd be sure to know what an inconvenience I was being.

"Right now we're going to Dingle, but after that we're going to a music festival."

"Electric Picnic?" he asked.

"You've heard of it?" Rowan and Ian had said Electric Picnic was a big deal, but I had no way of knowing if they meant big deal in their alternative music world or big deal in the real world. Real world it was.

"Absolutely. I'll pray for your parents." He winked. "I've

never been myself, but my daughter went last year. I get the feeling I heard only a very censored version of what she did there. But, of course, you know the stories."

His eyes crinkled at the edges. "People getting married in unicorn costumes, outdoor hot tubs made from old claw-foot bathtubs, rave parties in the forest, a sunken double-decker bus . . . petting zoos made entirely of three-legged animals. That sort of thing. Everyone's in costume and acting badly."

Was he joking? He didn't look like he was joking. Plus, who could come up with a list like that on the spot? I stared at him in horror.

"You hadn't heard the stories," he said, his eyes crinkling even more.

This brought the need for secrecy to a whole new level of desperation. My parents would flip. It was one thing to sneak off to see a bunch of no-name sites in Ireland, but it was quite another to sneak away to a wild party. Getting caught would probably require them to come up with an entirely new category of punishments.

"Well, I didn't mean to scare you." He laughed at my expression. "Keep your head and you'll be fine. Is there a particular music act you're going to see?"

I nodded, regaining my footing. *Keep your head.* So long as Cubby Jones wasn't involved, I could handle that.

"My brother's going to see his favorite band. They're called Titletrack."

"Titletrack! Their final show," the woman interjected, clutching her hand to her chest. "You lucky, lucky girl, you!"

I turned to her, aghast. *She* was a fan? "I love that first song of theirs—Aaron, what's it called, the one with the music video in the Burren?"

"'Classic,'" the clerk said. "We're definitely fans around here."

"We're actually on a Titletrack road trip. I just left the Burren."

"A Titletrack road trip!" She looked like she was about to faint. She yanked on one braid. "What a *wonderful* idea. Aaron! Isn't that a wonderful idea?"

"Wonderful," he replied dutifully.

"Yes, my brother is a huge fan. He's right . . ." I turned to point at Ian, but the store was empty. "Uh-oh, I'd better go. Thanks so much for the advice."

"Stay hydrated," the man called after me as I rushed through the door.

"Take hand sanitizer!" the woman yelled. "And be careful out on the peninsula. Big storm coming today. One of the worst of the summer."

"Thanks," I called over my shoulder.

The second I stepped outside, Rowan's voice punched

me in the ears. "Mum, I told you, I'm not ready to talk about this. You said I had until the end of the summer, and that means two more weeks. And if you want to talk about Dad, call him. . . . Mum, *stop*." He hung up, then whirled around, his expression leaping with dismay.

My first instinct was to bolt, but instead I stood there stupidly, clutching my cereal box, resting my bare foot on my shoed one. I probably looked like I'd been eavesdropping. I mean, I had been eavesdropping. It just hadn't been on purpose. And now I was curious. What was Rowan not ready to talk about?

"Hey, Addie," Rowan said weakly. "Been there long?"

Please say no was written in a thought bubble over his head. I shook my head as I handed him the cereal. "Not long."

His face drooped sadly. *Fix this*, my inner voice demanded. My inner voice had a lot to say about other people's feelings. I looked around, trying to think of a way to lighten the mood. "So . . . remember when I belly flopped out of your car?"

His face instantly brightened. "On average, how many times a day would you say you dive into parking lots?"

I looked up at the gray sky, pretending to think. "Three. Today's a slow day."

His smile increased, then he looked down, kicking a rock toward me. "You know, Addie, you aren't at all what I expected."

"Hmmm," I said, folding my arms. He had a slight smile, so I was pretty sure he'd meant it kindly, but I wasn't positive.

"'Hmmm,' what?" he asked.

I shrugged my shoulders. "That was one of those compliments that could easily be an insult. Like 'Did you do something different with your hair? It looks so nice.' Meaning it looked like crap before." Rowan's mouth twitched into a smile. I was talking too much. I steered us back on course. "If you don't mind me asking, what *did* you expect?"

His dimple deepened. "Someone more average. I can see why Ian talks about you so much."

Surprise flooded me. "He told you about me? But I thought you guys didn't talk about a lot of personal stuff."

"Just the important things," Rowan said. "He told me you two are very close. Which is why I'm a little confused that you guys are, uh . . ." He flourished his hand.

"Fighting all the time?" I filled in.

"It was a little surprising," he admitted. He folded his arms, dropping his gaze down again. "Anyway, I'm glad you came out here, because I have something to show you." He reached through the window into the back seat and pulled out the guidebook. "While you were in there, I checked the sites against Ian's map, and a lot of them are pretty close to each other. A few of them even double up with Titletrack sites. And guess what? One of them is on the Dingle Peninsula, which is where we're headed next!"

He handed me the guidebook, flipping open to an entry

marked DINGLE PENINSULA. I clutched the pages tightly.

"What about Ian?" I said, glancing back toward the store. "I don't know if you've noticed, but every time my love life comes up, someone starts yelling."

"Really? I hadn't noticed." He grinned a cute, lopsided smile that transplanted onto my face. "I'll handle Ian. Look, I technically could do the guidebook on my own. It's just that it feels a little . . ." He twisted his mouth. "Pathetic. But if we do it together . . . Maybe it's dumb."

"It's not dumb," I said quickly. My flower ceremony at the Burren hadn't exactly been the life-changing experience I'd hoped for, but I did like the thought of having some dedicated time to cope with Cubby. Plus, Rowan was really putting himself out there—there was no way I was going to leave him hanging.

I pitched my tone to sound more enthusiastic. "I mean, why not? Worst case, we see some interesting places. Best case, I leave Ireland with an unbroken heart." *Yeah, right.* I didn't believe it for a second.

His face split into a huge smile. "Thanks, Addie. You work on finding your shoe. I'll work on finding Ian. I'm sure I can talk him into this."

He took off across the parking lot at a happy sprint, and I turned to watch him. Was it possible that I'd managed to find the only person in the world who was more heartbroken than I was?

The Dingle Peninsula

If Ireland were a cake, and you the nervous recipient of something coming out of my oven, I would serve you a thick slice of Dingle. Tart, sugary, chewy Dingle.

It's a combination of absolutely irresistible ingredients—crushed velvet hills, roads disappearing into milky mist, jelly bean–hued buildings crammed together on winding roads—all blended and whipped together into a ladyfinger-shaped peninsula that you're going to want to dunk into a cold glass of milk.

Now, I know what you're wondering, dove: *What does this idyllic bit of perfection possibly have to do with the pathetic state of my heart?* I'm so glad you asked. And, my, aren't you catching on nicely?

It's about the circle, love. The process. At some point (maybe it's already happened?), you're going to wrestle your heartache into a sturdy brown box and then lug it all the way to the post office, where you'll drop it off with a huge sigh. *Glad that's over*, you'll think. *Such a relief.* You'll skip back home, your heart as airy as cotton candy, only to realize—with horror—that that heavy brown box is sitting on your front door. It was delivered back to you. Return to sender. Shipping incomplete. *But I just did this*, you'll think. *I already dealt with it.*

I know you did. But you're going to have to do it again. Contrary to popular belief, getting over someone is not a one-time deal.

It might be helpful to look at the process of heartache like you would a peninsula. One with a long, looping road carrying you past a myriad of delights and wonders. Grief requires you to circle around the issue at hand, sometimes passing by it many, many times until it is no longer the destination but just part of the landscape. The trick is: do not give in to despair. You are making progress, even if some days it just feels like you're going in circles.

HEARTACHE HOMEWORK: Find Inch Beach, then walk out into the water as far as you dare. You'll get cold. Then colder. Then numb. And when you can't stand the cold for one more second, I want you to stand the cold for one more second. Are you surviving this moment of discomfort? Have there been other moments of pain or discomfort that you thought you couldn't survive and yet you did? Interesting, pet. Interesting.

—Excerpt from *Ireland for the Heartbroken: An Unconventional Guide to the Emerald Isle, third edition*

THE STORM HIT JUST AS WE ENTERED THE PENINSULA. And by "hit," I mean came at us as if we were trespassers that had to be forcibly shoved back to the mainland. There was no buildup, either: one second it wasn't raining, and the next raindrops pummeled the roof so loudly, they may as well have been on the inside my skull. Rain slid down our windows in heavy sheets, and Rowan kept over-correcting against the wind. "It's really bucketing down," he said nervously.

"Hey, Rowan. I think we need to pull over," I said, gesturing to Ian. Ian balled up against the window, the green tint of his face highlighting his black eye. I'd seen Ian throw up more times than I could count, and he was exhibiting four out of five of the warning signs. Puke was imminent.

"I'm not sick. I just . . . ," Ian started, but he couldn't even make it through the sentence before gritting his teeth.

"Pull over the next chance you get," I instructed Rowan, grabbing the empty cereal box and shoving it into Ian's hands.

Ian was the poster child for motion sickness, but he was also the poster child for stubbornness. He never wanted to admit that things made him sick, which meant he was constantly doing things that made him sick. None of us had sat next to him on a roller coaster in years.

"Just a little Irish holiday weather. I'm sure we'll be through it in no time." Rowan attempted nonchalance, but the wind blew at us again and he gasped, jerking the wheel as Ian doubled over.

"Ian, you okay? You never told me you had motion sickness."

"I don't," Ian answered. "I must have eaten something bad at the wedding."

Sometimes I thought my brothers were incapable of admitting to weakness. "Rowan, he's lying. This is an ongoing condition. A windy road during a storm is the worst possible scenario."

I turned away from Ian's scowl and pressed up to my blurry window, focusing on the view. Even without the storm's theatrics, the Dingle Peninsula was Ireland 2.0—the drama factor turned on and cranked as high as it would go. We were still on a narrow two-lane road, but everything had been pumped up to Dr. Seuss level. On our left, neon green mountain peaks disappeared into pudding-thick clouds, and to our right, a thick nest of rain rested on top of the ocean.

Ian's phone chimed. "Oh, no. Text from Mom."

"What does it say?"

He attempted to swivel his queasy face toward me, but the motion made him shudder. "She wants us to check in when we land. I'll text her back in a few hours."

Suddenly, a gush of wind blasted Clover, bumping us off the road and into the shoulder. And this time, Rowan's choice of language was a bit more potent than "feck."

"Rowan, you got this?" I asked. He cranked frantically at the steering wheel, trying to regain equilibrium, but the hardest gale yet caught us on the opposite side. For a nanosecond, Clover favored her left two wheels. Ian lurched for the cereal box, dry heaving.

I gagged. I could see Ian puke a million times and never get used to it. I patted him clumsily, keeping my face averted. "It's okay, Ian. It's okay."

"Now I'm pulling over." Rowan pulled over to the foot-wide shoulder, then threw the car into park, collapsing over the steering wheel. Ian rolled his window down, sending in a spray of rain as he stuck his head outside.

"Well, that was traumatizing," I said, taking a few deep breaths of my own.

Suddenly, the car began vibrating. "What—" Ian started, his eyes wide, but just then a massive tour bus sliced around the corner.

"Hang on," Rowan warned. I pulled Ian inside, and we all braced for death as we watched the bus narrowly miss our front bumper. A large swell of water slammed into the car. We all screamed, haunted-house style.

"We are all going to die!" I wailed, once we'd all stopped

screaming. Water trickled in through Ian's window, and he quickly rolled it up.

"Death by tour bus." Rowan sighed.

Suddenly, a terrible non-storm-related thought popped into my head, and I grabbed the back of Ian's seat. "Ian, there's no way we're going to run into the wedding tour, right? Didn't Aunt Mel say they're touring western Ireland?"

Ian made a little *X* with his fingers, which I guess was supposed to mean "no." "I hacked into Mom's e-mail and printed out a copy of their itinerary. We aren't going to be anywhere near them."

"Hacked?" I said. "By that do you mean you used her password?" Our mom either didn't know or care that you're supposed to change your passwords often. Archie had figured it out one December, and we'd been using it to track our Christmas presents ever since. "Can you imagine if we ran into them?"

Ian shook his head. "It's impossible. I scheduled our trip to make sure there was no possible way for us to run into them. Also, I don't know if that's our biggest concern right now," he said, pointing to the sky. His face was shamrock green.

Suddenly, a shot of ice-cold water trickled down my back, and I catapulted forward. "Cold!" I screamed, water pouring down from my window. The inside of my window. "Rowan! The car is leaking."

He arched back just as the stream transformed from a trickle to a gush. "No! Max said the new top was fine."

"What top? Who's Max?" I asked, like details would solve the fact that it was raining in the back seat.

"The guy who helped me repair—"

"It's my window too!" Ian yelped, his pitch identical to mine. He grabbed his handle, frantically trying to roll up his already-rolled-up window.

"Ian, that's not going to help," I said.

Rowan turned the key and jetted onto the road, and Clover responded by giving up on any attempt at being waterproof. Water flooded in through every possible crevice. We sped over a small bridge, water flowing in at full speed as we pulled into a tiny two-pump gas station.

Ian frantically rolled down his window and stuck his head out, gasping like a beached flounder. I was soaked. Water pooled in the seat of my shorts, and my hair hung in stringy clumps.

"Did that really just happen?" Rowan fell back against his seat.

"Addie, how do we fix it?" Ian asked.

Mechanic Addie to the rescue. I reached up to wiggle the roof, and beads of water tumbled in. "Do we care about pretty?" I asked.

Rowan tapped his hand on the dashboard. "Does it look like we care about pretty?"

"Valid," I said. "We need tape. Really strong, thick tape."

Rowan nodded vigorously. "Tape. Got it. I'll just pop in the shop and ask." He grabbed a beanie from the cup holder and pulled it on as he sprinted for the gas station.

"We almost just drowned in a Volkswagen," Ian said, drumming his fingers on the dashboard. "Can you imagine the obituary? Killer car traps trio—"

"Ian." I reached over to still his restless fingers. I had a theory that Ian had spent a previous life as a hummingbird. Or an athletic coffee bean. "What's up with Rowan's mom?"

He glanced back, his eyebrows bent. "What are you talking about?"

"Back at the gas station I overheard him yelling at her. He said something about making a decision before the end of the summer."

"Really?" Ian tucked a strand of hair into his mouth and chewed thoughtfully. "I don't know very much about his family. I didn't even know his parents were divorced until he brought it up back at the Burren."

"Are you serious?" This was so my brother. All of my brothers. I wanted to know everything about my friends—right down to the name of their first pet and what toppings they liked on their pizza. Lina claimed to remember our first sleepover as more of a police interrogation. My brothers, on the other hand, seemed to need only a few similarities to form a bond. *You like football and tacos? Me too.*

Ian followed a bead of rain down the windshield with his finger. "Rowan and I don't talk a lot about stuff like that."

I rolled my eyes. "Because you're too busy talking about Titletrack?"

"No." He blew his breath out loudly. "I mean, of course we talk about music, but most of the time we talk about deeper stuff, like about things we care about and what's bugging us. Stuff like that."

I couldn't help but grin. "So you're saying that you and Rowan talk about your feelings?" Once Archie had asked me what Lina and I could possibly have to talk about on our multi-hour phone conversations and I'd finally told him, "How we're feeling." Now every time she called, they made fun of me. *How's Lina? How are her feelings?*

"Yeah, I guess so," Ian admitted. He flashed me a look that I recognized immediately. Eyes open and vulnerable—it was what I saw before he revealed something about himself. "Have you ever wished you could have someone see you without all the other layers? Like, not how good you are at sports or school or being popular, or whatever, they just see you?"

I wanted to grab him by the shoulders and yell, *Are you kidding me?* Of course I'd felt that way. That was the defining feeling of my life.

Ian had felt that way? This was news to me. "Like I could

just be Addie instead of being Archie's/Walter's/Ian's little sister?"

"Exactly," Ian said.

Suddenly, I realized something—Ian was talking to me like he used to, like Cubby wasn't hanging out in the bruise under his eye. I chose my next words carefully, not wanting to break the spell. "But the label thing is just part of being human, right? We like to categorize people, so everyone gets labels slapped on them whether they're right or not." I'd never thought about it that way before, but it was true. We even labeled ourselves: Bad at math. Flirt. Clueless.

"They're never right," Ian said, a hint of venom in his voice. "Labels aren't big enough for people. And once you try to categorize someone, you stop looking for who they actually are. That's why I like talking to Rowan so much. We're friends but completely out of context. I never thought someone I met online could be such a close friend, but I really needed a friend, and he was there."

I waited for him to crack a smile on the *I needed a friend* part, but he just dropped his gaze to his lap, his knee bobbing. If Ian felt friendless, then the rest of us were doomed. We could barely go anywhere without someone yelling his name and wanting to talk about the football season—kids, adult, everyone.

"I didn't know you were feeling that way," I said carefully. "You could have told me."

His hair whipped back and forth. "You were busy—with Lina and soccer and . . ." Cubby. He didn't have to say it. We both averted our gazes. "So Rowan told me about the guidebook."

"And?" I said, careful to keep my voice neutral.

"And I care about him and I care about you, so if you guys think it will help you, then fine, I'm up for it." He twisted around, his eyes fastening earnestly on mine. "But you know that following some guidebook around isn't actually dealing with what happened, right? It isn't going to make it go away."

My anger flared up, hot and bubbly. "And telling Mom is? Getting our parents involved will just make things get bigger."

"It's already getting bigger," Ian said, mounting his big-brother soapbox. "Addie, at some point you're going to have to deal with it. Don't you want it to be on your own terms? Admit it. You're in over your head."

I wasn't just in over my head; I was gasping at the bottom of the pool. But there was no way I was going to admit that. "I told you back at the Cliffs of Moher, I am done talking about this," I snapped.

"Well, I'm not. Not until you do the right thing," he insisted.

The right thing. The right thing had been to listen to Ian and trust my gut, and ditch Cubby the second things had started to feel off. But I hadn't done that, had I? It was too late now. "Ian, stop!" I shouted.

"Fine," he breathed, falling back against his seat moodily. Why did he have to ruin the moment? For a second there, things had felt almost normal between us.

* * *

I didn't have to see the sign to know we were in Dingle, because Guidebook Lady's description was spot-on. It was *Alice in Wonderland* meets Ireland—a mash-up of charm and color spiked with whimsy. Stores with names like Mad Hatters and the Little Cheese Shop lined the road in every color on the neon spectrum: tangerine, cotton-candy pink, turquoise, and lime. Rowan snaked carefully through the flooded cobblestoned streets, talking a blue streak the entire time.

"Dingle is a huge draw for Irish teenagers. Every summer they come here for Irish camp. You learn Irish language, dances, that kind of thing. The peninsula was pretty cut off from the rest of the world for a while, so a lot of people here still speak Gaelic."

The talking had started as soon as Rowan came out of the gas station with the tape and picked up on the tension between Ian and me. He was obviously someone who tried to bury conflict underneath a lot of words—even if we'd wanted to get a word in edgewise, we couldn't have.

"That's cool," Ian finally said, hedging his way into a rare silence. Our argument had sapped the energy out of both of us. Ian was crunched up into a little ball, buried in his phone, and I was slumped against my window, my anger dissolving into sadness.

"So . . . you're sure you guys are okay?" Rowan asked the quiet car.

"Rowan, we're fine." My voice came out more forcefully than I meant it to, and a shadow covered his face. Ian shot me an annoyed look. Poor Rowan. He hadn't asked for this. I straightened up, swallowing my tone. "Sorry about that, Rowan. Thanks for filling us in on the history. So what's this next Titletrack stop about?" I snuck a glance at Ian's map. "Slea Head?"

"Ah, this one's kind of brilliant," Rowan said, doing the double-handed-glasses move. "When Titletrack first started, they signed with a tiny record label called Slea Head Records. It doesn't exist anymore, but the place it was named after does. It also happens to be one of my favorite places in Ireland."

"Because of Irish camp, right?" I said, to prove that I had been listening to his monologue.

"Right." He beamed.

The road led us through town and onto a windy road that thinned until we were sandwiched between a hill and a cliff. Thick, fluffy fog billowed on the road, and the ocean all but disappeared into the distance. We kept traveling farther and farther out onto the peninsula, and just when I thought we'd drive straight into the ocean, Rowan bumped off the road, stopping at the base of a steep hill where a goat trail snaked its way up to the top.

"Here?" I said.

"Here," Ian confirmed, his knee starting in on one of its specialty spastic dances.

"Too. Much. Wind," Rowan grunted, struggling against the door. Finally, he managed to pry it open, dousing us all with a salty spray of rain.

"Please tell me we're not going out there," I said, but Ian was already scrambling over the console, following Rowan out into the mist, and I followed quickly behind. It's not like the situation inside the car was much drier.

Outside was wet and freezing, and the view was even more intense. The water shimmered a deep turquoise, and a thick afghan of clouds rested on gently sloping hills. All the colors looked oversaturated, especially the green. Before Ireland, I thought I knew what green was. But I hadn't. Not really.

"This way," Rowan said, pointing to the unbelievably slippery-looking goat trail. It rose up a steep hill, disappearing into the mist. Ian bounded forward without a second of hesitation, Rowan close on his heels.

I may as well have been climbing up a sheet of glass. My

usually lucky Converse sneakers were completely useless in this situation, and I ended up on all fours, digging my fingers into the mud and pretending not to notice slugs nestled in the grass.

Up top, Rowan was waiting to haul me up the last few feet, and I stumbled, finally upright, onto the grassy clearing. Nearby, smooth black rock plunged into the water at a forty-five-degree angle, the ocean wild and frothy in front of us.

"People surf here!" Rowan yelled to us over the wind. I looked down in disbelief, watching the water throw itself against the cliff. He shrugged. "Extreme people."

"Good thing Aunt Mel didn't see Slea Head; she would have moved her wedding here," I said to Ian, but he was bent over his notebook again, scribbling furiously through the rain.

I stepped toward the edge, the wind blasting me like a challenge. "Careful," Rowan said.

I extended my arms out wide, feeling the way the wind fought and supported me at the same time. Rowan grinned, then mimicked my stance, the two of us standing like *T*s, spray hitting us full force.

He touched the tips of my fingers with his. Rain speckled his glasses. "I feel like we should yell."

"Yell what?" I asked.

"Anything." He took a deep breath, then let out a loud "Harooooo!"

"Harooooo!" I echoed. My voice sailed out over the water,

overlapping with Rowan's. The sound made me feel alive. And brave. I wanted to feel this way all the time.

"What are you guys doing?" Ian dropped his notebook and stepped next to me, the wind whipping his hair into a frenzy.

"Yelling," I said.

Rowan pointed his chin to the curtain of fog. "Know what's out there?"

"The Loch Ness Monster?" Ian guessed.

"America," Rowan said. "This is the westernmost point of Ireland. It's the closest you can get to the States while still being in Ireland."

I squinted out into the horizon. America. No wonder I felt so good here. There was an entire ocean between me and my problems.

Ian bumped his shoulder into mine—intentional or not, I didn't know—and for a second the three of us stood there, the wind pushing as hard as it could and us pushing back. Together. For one second, I imagined what it would be like if this were real life. Me and Ian against the pressure of everything back home.

I wanted this to be real life, not a detour.

The summer had been full of detours, usually of the nocturnal kind.

It was just after eleven p.m. when I snuck out the back door, creeping through the yard and running down the sidewalk to

Cubby's car. His face shone blue, lit up by his phone in the dark, and his radio played softly. I slid into the passenger seat, quickly pulling the door shut behind me.

"What would your brother think of you sneaking out with me?" Cubby's voice was its usual laid-back drawl, but a thin line of nervousness etched the surface.

"Ian? Good question. Are you going to tell him?" I asked, pointing my finger at his chest.

"Nope," he said, grinning.

Ian didn't know I was out. He also didn't know about the postpractice drive Cubby and I had gone on, or how during the drive Cubby's hand had just casually made its way over to my knee, as if that was where it had always belonged. And I didn't push his hand away either. I wanted it there.

There were a lot of reasons I wasn't going to tell Ian, but the main one was this: Over the past few years my brother's voice had taken on a specific quality whenever he talked about Cubby. Like he'd just taken a bite of bitter chocolate. And tonight was not about Ian's approval or disapproval. It was about me.

Me and Cubby.

"You're sure you want to stay here?" Ian asked skeptically. We sat parked in front of a peeling, burnt-orange building that looked more like a prison than a hostel. Chains tethered the wrought-iron furniture to the porch, and bars lined the windows. "Are they trying to keep people out or in?"

"I think it looks nice," I said. "Very . . . homey. Authentic." Rowan and I exchanged a look. It had taken some convincing to get Ian to agree to stay in Dingle overnight. He'd wanted to keep going, but our guidebook stop was at a place called Inch Beach, and this was not exactly beach weather. There was also the minor issue of hypothermia, which was starting to feel like more and more of a possibility.

There was still one problem, though: Dingle was in high tourist season. And that meant no vacancy—except for the Rainbow's End Hostel, whose way-too-cheerful, Flash-heavy website claimed to ALWAYS HAVE AVAILABILITY!!!! Now, having seen the hostel and all of its charm, I understood why.

"Somewhere over the rainbow," Rowan deadpanned. "How Irish is that?" He took the key out of the ignition.

"Come on," I added. "Anything has to be better than driving in that storm."

"And you get to work on your article," Rowan joined in. "I'm sure you have plenty of material after visiting the Burren and Slea Head."

"True," Ian admitted. "It would be nice to keep up on my writing. That way it isn't a huge job at the end. Plus, I need to post to my blog."

"Perfect! Let's go," I said. Half a day in Clover, and already every bit of me ached. I couldn't get out of the back seat fast enough.

For someplace named Rainbow's End, the interior was surprisingly lacking in color. All except for brown. Brown floors, brown carpet, brown linoleum, and a brass light fixture missing two out of five bulbs. Even the smell was brown: a mixture of burnt toast and the lingering of a pot roast.

I made my way up to a rickety wooden desk. Papers cluttered its surface, and a cup of coffee sat on top of a grubby three-ring binder.

"Hello?" I called out. Brown swallowed up my voice.

"It doesn't look like anyone is here. Maybe we should try somewhere else," Ian offered.

"There is nowhere else. Believe me, we tried." I bypassed the desk and headed down a dark hallway. Light trickled from underneath a door. "Hello?" I called, pushing it open slightly. "Anyone here?"

A guy with a mass of curly white-blond hair sat playing a video game, his dirty feet propped up on the table in front of him. A large pair of headphones encased his ears.

"Excuse me?" I reached out to tap his shoulder, but just before I made contact, he whirled around, crashing noisily to the floor.

"Are you okay?" I scrambled to help him up.

"Okay? Not terribly." He yanked the headphones off. He

was in his late teens or early twenties, furiously tan, and built small and muscular like a rock climber. His accent was decidedly not Irish. Was it Australian? British? He smiled wide, and his white teeth contrasted sharply against his tanned face. "How are you going?"

How are you going? What was the correct answer to that? Good? To Electric Picnic?

He didn't wait for me to figure it out. "So sorry about the mattresses. I know they're utter crap. But I guess that's why we have such an affordable rate. And be honest, you didn't come all the way to the Emerald Isle to sleep anyway, right? You're here to explore."

I raised my eyebrows, completely lost. "I think you're mistaking me for someone else." Someone he'd spoken to before.

His eyes widened. "Oh, no. You aren't with the German group, are you? Forget what I said about the mattresses. Sleeping at the Rainbow's End is like sleeping on a cloud." He sang the last part.

"Nice save," I said. "Do you have space for three people?"

He clapped me on the shoulder. "Didn't you see the sign? We always have availability. I already told you about the mattresses, but let me sell you on the good parts of our humble Rainbow's End. We have a killer nightlife here. Party out front after dark every night, heaps of people, amber fluid, everything you could ask for." He winked, erasing my ability to tell if he was joking or not. "I'm Bradley, by the way. Welcome to the Rainbow's End, the most westernly youth hostel in Europe."

"I'm Addie." I shook his hand. "You didn't by chance write the content on the website, did you?"

He bobbed his head enthusiastically. "That I did, Addie. That I did. Built the whole thing in forty-eight hours. That thing is pretty bodgy, but it does a lot of my work for me, which means I get to spend my afternoons surfing."

"Do you surf at Slea Head?" I asked.

"What kind of crazy do you think I am?" He folded his arms and gave me an appraising look. "Why do you look like you floated here? You weren't out walking in the storm, were you?"

"Driving. Our car isn't waterproof."

"Ah," he said, like he knew all about it. "I'm not supposed to let anyone in until after evening, but this looks like an emergency. You could use a hot shower."

"Yes, I could," I replied gratefully.

He grabbed a grimy white binder from the table and began flipping through pages full of names and phone numbers. The hostel's record book, I assumed. "Where are you from?"

"Seattle. Well, that's where my brother and I are from. The other guy we're with is from Dublin." A loud creak erupted behind me, and Rowan and Ian poked their heads in. Bradley immediately launched himself at them. "You must be brother. And other guy. I'm Bradley." He shook their hands enthusiastically. "But why aren't you two as wet as this one? I thought your car wasn't waterproof."

Rowan grimaced. "The back leaks the most."

"And the back is where I sit," I filled in.

"Way to be gentlemanly," Bradley said brusquely, his gaze drifting back and forth between them.

Ian yanked at his sweatshirt strings, his cheeks slightly pink. "She wasn't supposed to come; we weren't prepared."

"Yeah, yeah, save it." Bradley waved them off. "Now come sign the book while little sister takes a shower." He turned to me. "Bathroom is past the bunk room. Towels are in the closet next to it." I was out of the room before he even finished his sentence.

* * *

Despite the bathroom's questionable cleanliness, the shower felt life-changing. I changed into a fresh set of clothes and wandered back into the lobby, tugging a comb through my hair. Bradley sat paging through a dog-eared copy of *Encyclopedia of Surfing*. When he saw me, he slow clapped. "Huge improvement. Huge. You look one hundred percent less like a boiled rat."

"Thank you," I said, biting back a smile. "I wasn't aware

that I ever looked like a boiled rat, but that's an incredible compliment. Do you know where the guys are?"

He nodded his head to the dining room. "Bouncy one's in there, trying to track down the Internet signal. Good luck to him. Sad guy is in the bunk room."

Sad guy?

"Sad guy is here," Rowan interrupted, walking into the room.

Ouch. "Oh, sorry, bloke. I meant, um . . ." Bradley backpedaled.

Rowan ignored him. "Addie, you ready to go to Inch Beach? It looks like it's clearing up out there."

"Already?" I turned to look out the window. A patch of blue beamed brightly among the gray clouds. "That was fast."

Bradley dropped his book. "Weather turns pretty quickly around here." He straightened up, dropping back into a sales pitch. "And might I interest you two in renting bicycles for the small fee of three euro apiece? I can also toss in the best free tour guide Dingle has to offer." He extended his arms out wide. "Me."

Stretching my legs on a bicycle sounded like perfection. "That's a great idea! Rowan?"

He hesitated, keeping his eyes firmly away from mine. "Bikes would be great. I have no interest in getting back in that wet car. But . . . I've spent some time on the peninsula, so I think I can manage the tour guide role." He didn't want an audience for the Heartache Homework. Rowan was really taking this seriously.

"Ahhh," Bradley sang, looking between us.

"We're just doing this guidebook thing," I said quickly. My cheeks boiled even though I had nothing to hide.

"Guidebook thing, is that what the kids are calling it?" Bradley winked. "No worries. I know when I'm not wanted. Bikes are around back in the shed. You can have them on the house. Just don't tell my uncle Ray. And you'll come to the party tonight, right? People start gathering on the porch at about nine o'clock."

Party? I'd forgotten about the party. "Maybe," Rowan answered for us.

"We'll be there," I said. Bradley winked, then took off down the hall.

Rowan exhaled slowly. "That guy is too much."

"I like him." I studied the fresh T-shirt Rowan had changed into. This one featured a cat holding a piece of pizza in one hand and a taco in the other. A purple-and-black galaxy played out in the background.

"I think I like this one even more than the hypnotized cat," I said, pointing at it.

"Thanks." He lifted the familiar coffee-stained book into the air. "Ready for an adventure?"

"You mean am I ready to walk back out into the cold?" I flourished my hand toward the door. "Why not?"

* * *

Poststorm Dingle had a completely different temperament. The heavy clouds had thinned into a soft haze, and water lapped restfully against the edges of the cliffs. We rode past a marina filled with colorful bobbing boats and signs about a local hero, a dolphin named Fungie, who, according to Rowan, had been visiting tourists for decades.

"We're here," Rowan called back to me. We coasted off the main road, our bikes picking up speed as we curved down to a small inlet.

"Wow," I said.

"I know, right?" Rowan said.

The sand at Inch Beach sparkled a deep gray, the sun kissing it with a touch of glitter. The tide was low, and silver ruffles of water unfurled lazily onto the shore. Out on the water, sunlight fragmented into kaleidoscope shapes. Stress melted from my shoulders, and my lungs opened up. I took the first deep breaths I had in days.

Next to the sand was a small, sea-glass-green building with SAMMY'S STORE stenciled on the side. Large swirly script read:

Dear Inch must I leave you
I have promises to keep
Perhaps miles to go
To my last sleep

It reminded me of a paper I'd written for English last year about the similarities between Robert Frost's "Stopping by Woods on a Snowy Evening" and Emily Dickinson's "A Bird, came down the Walk." I loved Emily Dickinson. She didn't get things like capitalization and punctuation right, but it didn't matter because you could still hear exactly what she was saying.

As we made our way toward the beach, two messy-haired kids emerged from the store holding ice-cream cones and chasing each other in a feisty game of tag. Their mom played along, lifting the young girl up in the air once she caught up with her.

"She reminds me of my mom." I nodded toward the woman. The girl now sat comfortably on the mom's shoulders, the little boy speeding around them in a circle.

Rowan pulled his beanie over his ears. "How so?"

"The way she's running around with them. She played with us. Lots. Even when it meant she didn't get other stuff done." My mom had never been a picture-perfect type of mom—the kind with a clean kitchen floor or a PTA résumé. But she was excellent at building blanket forts, and when she read to us, she did all the voices. Plus, she was just always there. Her going back to work had rocked me more than I'd thought it would.

"She sounds really great," Rowan said, shoving his hands into his pockets. "Once, I was talking to Ian, and your mom came in to talk to him about school. I could tell she really cared."

"She does." *So why aren't you telling her about Cubby?* a little voice inside my head asked. I brushed it away.

"So what's your family like?" I asked carefully. I'd have to be deaf to miss the longing in his voice.

"Ha," he said unhappily. "It's just the three of us—my mum, my dad, and me—and we're a mess, that's what we are. Sometimes I wish there were more of us, to spread the misery around."

In my experience, that wasn't how misery worked. Or happiness, for that matter. Both tended to expand until everyone had an armful.

I dug my big toe into the sand. "I'll bet there are lots of perks to being an only child." The words felt false as they slid off my tongue. Not that being an only child couldn't be great—I was sure it had its pluses and minuses just like every family situation—but I didn't even know who I'd be without my brothers. Especially Ian.

"I guess so," he said very unconvincingly. He straightened up, squaring his shoulders to the horizon. "You ready to do this?"

The wind heard its cue, skipping off the water and blasting us with cold air. I had officially given up on being anything but frozen on this trip. "What Guidebook Lady wants, Guidebook Lady gets."

We headed toward the water, our toes sinking in the cold sand. When a cold wave slipped over our ankles, we both looked at each other in shock. "Cold" didn't even begin to describe it. It needed a more dramatic word, something like "arctic" or "glacial." Maybe "arcticglacial."

"We've got this," Rowan said, extending his hand to me. Before I could overthink it, I grabbed tight, his hand warm and comfortable in mine as we plunged into the water.

"So, back to the guidebook. What's your thing?" Rowan asked. "What's something you survived that you thought you couldn't?"

"Losing Lina's mom to cancer." I was surprised by how easily the words bypassed my filter. I didn't usually talk about that experience with anyone but Lina. I'd tried a few times, but I found out pretty quickly that most people don't actually want to know about the hard things you've been through. They just want to look like they care and then move on to the next subject as quickly as possible. Rowan felt different.

He looked up, his gray eyes stricken. "I didn't know her mom died. How long was she sick?"

"Only a few months. It was so disorienting. One minute she was running us around town looking for the best fish taco, and the next . . ." I trailed off. The water tingled against my shins. Whenever I thought about those months after Hadley's diagnosis, I remembered the sounds. The beeping hospital machines. The whooshing of the ventilator. How quiet Lina's apartment was in the afternoons when I brought her her homework. I was supposed to be the go-between, delivering homework both ways, but the teachers all knew the score, so they never cared that I rarely brought any back.

The water inched above my knees. "I don't know if Ian told you, but Lina moved in with us right after the funeral. She was really shut-down. She even stopped eating, which is a huge deal, because she loves food more than anyone I know. I ended up getting really obsessed with cooking shows because the only way I could get her to eat was by making things I knew she couldn't possibly turn down."

"You can cook?" Rowan said hungrily. "What did you make for her?"

A tall wave slammed into our knees, sending a spray of salt water into my face. I wiped my eyes on the neckline of my shirt. It was taking every ounce of my willpower not to turn and run out of the water. "Triple chocolate cupcakes. Bacon-wrapped asparagus. Wild blueberry pancakes with whipped cream. Gourmet mac 'n' cheese . . . That one was probably my best. It had four kinds of cheese plus bacon and truffle oil."

Rowan moaned. "I haven't eaten anything but Sugar Puffs since I left Dublin yesterday."

"I thought you loved Sugar Puffs."

"I do love Sugar Puffs," he said adamantly. "But I love bacon and truffle oil more." He looked down at the water, then squeezed my hand. "How's this? We far enough?"

For a second I didn't know what he was talking about, but then I realized water was up past my midthigh, waves kissing the hem of my shorts. "Can you feel your legs?" I asked.

He grimaced. "What legs?"

"This is worse than being in the back seat of Clover." We dropped hands, and I skimmed my fingers across the water's icy surface. Rowan's turn. "What about you? What's the hardest thing you've survived?"

"This year." No hesitation. And no eye contact. Which for most people meant door closed.

But me being me, I had to at least try the knob. "This year, because of your breakup?"

He exhaled, then wiggled his shoulder like he was trying to shake off his mood. "Is this too depressing? I know you're going through your own heartache; I don't want to burden you with mine."

"You aren't burdening me," I said, telling the truth. I liked that he felt like he could talk to me. We were a support team of two. "And what was your girlfriend's name, anyway? Or . . . sorry, girlfriend? Boyfriend?" I shouldn't assume.

"It was actually a goldfish," he said seriously. "We dated for a whole year, but every few hours she forgot who I was and we had to start over."

"Oh," I said, adopting his serious tone. "That sounds challenging. Did the goldfish have a name?"

He hesitated for a second and his smile faded. "It's my parents," he finally said. "They're getting divorced."

"Oh." I didn't know what to say. His answer was not what I was expecting, but it shouldn't have surprised me so much. Heartache came in all sorts of flavors. "I'm really sorry," I said.

"Me too." He gave me a rueful smile. "If they could get past their issues, I think they'd actually be pretty great together, but . . ." He trailed off, shivering violently. I suddenly became acutely aware of the cold. He gave me a lopsided smile, his eyes not quite meeting mine. "I think I'm about to succumb to hypothermia."

"That means we have to stand here for one more second," I said. *Are you surviving this moment of discomfort? Have there been other moments of pain or discomfort that you thought you couldn't survive and yet you did?*

"Now!" I said, turning back to shore. We ran. My legs were so frozen, I could barely feel them churning the water to white, but Rowan's warm hand found its way back to mine, and suddenly I felt that same lightening sensation I had back at the Burren.

It was possible that Guidebook Lady was onto something.

* * *

Bradley was not exaggerating about the nightlife at the Rainbow's End. Music blared from a miniature speaker, and every light blazed. More people than I'd seen on the entire peninsula were crowded onto the porch and steps. Someone had built a fire in a garbage can, and flames licked the edges of the metal.

"The Rainbow's End's infamous nightlife," Rowan said, skidding to a stop. The way back had taken us twice as long since we had to pedal uphill, and my shaky legs meant sore muscles tomorrow. "Any sign of Ian?"

"No, but there's our host." Bradley sat holding court in an anemic-looking lawn chair. He'd paired a too-small button-up shirt with a tee featuring Jesus on a surfboard. Bradley caught sight of me and waved, gesturing dramatically to the seat next to him.

The seat of honor. Part of me wanted to coast on the calm feeling I'd carried back from Inch Beach by going straight to bed, but Bradley kept waving his hands excitedly at me.

"I'll take the bikes back," Rowan said, grabbing my bike handlebars. "Better get over there. We don't want to keep the king waiting."

As I made my way over to Bradley, Ian suddenly appeared at my side, latching on to my arm. He wore double hoodies, and his hair looked more tangled than usual. "Where have you been?" he asked urgently.

I shook him off. "Inch Beach. Didn't Rowan tell you?"

"I didn't think it would be all day."

"All day? We were only gone for a few hours." Suddenly, I realized that Ian was rocking back and forth from his heels to the balls of his feet, which was Ian speak for *I have something to spill.*

My heart fell. Not another text. Please not another text from back home. "Ian, what is it? What's going on?"

He set his mouth in a grim line. "Mom called."

"And?" Huge rush of relief. That was manageable. Mom was manageable. "What did she say?"

"She wanted to talk to Howard."

Yikes. I hadn't even thought about that. "Oh, right. We should probably come up with a plan of what to say next time she calls."

He rocked onto his heels again, spitting the rest out. "I got nervous and I had Bradley pretend to be Howard."

"What?" I yelped so loudly that a cluster of long-haired girls looked up from the fire. "You asked Bradley to pretend he was Howard? Please tell me you're joking."

He grabbed for his hair, twisting the same snarled piece. "It actually wasn't too bad. His American accent was sort of . . . questionable, but I think she bought it."

"No," I whispered. This was a disaster. Less than a day in, and Ian was already jeopardizing us. We were never going to pull this off. "Ian, what were you thinking? You should have waited to talk to me."

He threw his arms up defensively. "She kept calling and calling. You know how she is about the persistence thing—I think Catarina warped her brain. I had to improvise. And besides, you said you were stopping at a site, not leaving for the whole night."

The accusation in his voice was too familiar—*You know what Cubby's been doing, right?* "This isn't my fault, Ian," I snapped. "It was your decision to stay in Ireland, not mine." I shoved past him, heading for the porch steps.

"Addie!" Bradley called. "Did you hear I talked to your mom?"

"Sorry, Bradley, now's not a good time." I stomped into the building and made a beeline for the bunk room, collapsing onto my bed. I was exhausted. And starving.

But instead of leaving the room to forage for food, I dug my phone out of my pocket and searched for Indie Ian. I wanted to see for myself what this trip—and the possible end of our sports careers—had been about. Two articles came up automatically: "Is the Garage Band Dead?" and "I Went to the Mall. Here's What Happened."

"Here it goes," I said aloud.

Two sentences in and I fell headfirst into the world of garage bands. The article blew me away. Ian's voice rang through loud and strong, but with an extra gloss, like it had been coated with furniture polish and set out in the sun to shine. It was well written and intellectual but approachable, too, packed full of personality and enough enthusiasm to make me actually care.

I quickly pulled up the second article, "I Went to the Mall. Here's What Happened." This one was about him wandering around the mall near our house reviewing the music played in individual stores. When had he done that? The only time I'd ever seen him at the mall was when our mom dragged us at the beginning of the school year.

I dropped my phone to the bed, my chest heavy. There was a whole part to Ian that I'd never known existed. One that he hadn't told me about. That he'd chosen not to tell me about.

You did the same thing, my brain nudged silently.

I hadn't told Ian about Cubby; he'd found out all on his own. And then he'd confronted me immediately.

"Addie, not him. Anyone but him." Ian's voice startled me so much, I almost fell back out the window. It was two a.m., just a few days after our field trip to the troll, and he was sitting at my desk in the dark, his headphones pushed down around his neck.

I recovered just in time, stumbling into the room and turning to pull the window most of the way shut. Cubby's car was already gone. "What do you mean? Not who?" I said, pulling my shoes off and tossing them onto the floor. I'd taken to wearing running sneakers at night—it made the climb easier.

"I just saw you get out of his car." Ian stood, sending my desk chair spinning. "Addie, not him," he repeated, his face pleading.

A slow fury built in my center, surprising me with its intensity. Why did he think he got a say in who I dated? "Ian, I get that Cubby's your teammate, but you don't get to tell me whether or not I hang out with him."

He pulled his headphones off his neck, balling them into his fist. "Addie, I'm with him a lot. I hear how he talks about girls. You don't want to hang out with him. Believe me."

But I didn't want to believe him. And so I didn't.

I can usually count on sleep to polish out the hard edges of whatever I'm worrying about—like a broken bottle tumbling through waves to become sea glass. But I spent the night as jagged as they come.

The mattresses were, as promised, utter crap, and a little after one a.m. the entire party, including Ian and Rowan, descended on the bunk beds in a stampede. Finally, morning came, and I woke to light filtering softly through the barred windows. I rolled to my side. An orchestra of different snores and breathing patterns wafted through the room. Most of the beds still contained lumps of people. Everyone's, that was, except Ian's.

I jumped to sitting. Ian's and Rowan's beds were empty,

the sheets and pillows removed. Even their bags were gone.

"Are you kidding me?" I yelped into the silence.

They'd left me. Again. Even Rowan. I hurled myself out of bed, stumbling over a child-size backpack propped up against my bed before crashing loudly into a bedpost.

"Hallo?" a startled voice said from the top bunks.

"Sorry." I raced barefoot out into the hall and into the dining room, colliding face-first with Ian, who, of course, was holding a steaming hot mug of something.

"Addie!" he yelled, the drink sloshing everywhere. "Why are you running?"

The relief was so intense that I nearly folded in half. I rested my hands on my knees, waiting for my heart to slow. "I thought you left me."

"Left you? What would possibly make you think that?" He opened his eyes wide and then snorted, laughing at his own joke.

Laughing. He was laughing. Had he forgotten about last night's fight? He grabbed a handful of napkins from the kitchen table and swiped at the spill on his shoes.

"Yes, really funny. So, so funny." I jabbed him in the shoulder. His black eye looked a little better today. The outer edges were already fading to a dull green.

"What's so funny?" Rowan asked, joining us in the hallway.

"The fact that I now have PTSD over being left behind,"

I said. Rowan's hair was nicely rumpled. Today's cat shirt featured a bespectacled cat with the words HAIRY PAWTER.

"That's not new," Ian said. "You did that every time one of us graduated to the next level of school. I thought you were going to have a breakdown when I graduated from elementary school to junior high."

"Ian, shut up," I demanded, but I relaxed a little. His tone was still teasing. "Why are you in such a good mood, anyway?"

He held up his phone. "I'm only two followers away from ten thousand. Everyone loved the photos of Slea Head and the Burren."

"Ian, that's great," I said, meaning it. I wanted to tell him how much I'd liked his articles, but covered in coffee at the Rainbow's End didn't feel like quite the right time. I wanted it to be special.

He nodded happily. "Hopefully, the next stop will put us over the edge. Get dressed—we're leaving in five."

"How about six?" I asked. Rowan caught my eye and grinned.

"Five," Ian said. "Don't push me, sis."

Killarney National Park

Are you enjoying the wooded delights of Ireland, love? Have you noticed the trees standing in tight communal bunches, branches locked together in an embrace of mutual affection and appreciation? Does it remind you of me and you? The way we just *get* each other?

Me too, pet. Me too.

Muse with me for a moment—have you ever stopped to think about how much work a tree represents? How many steps it's gone through to get to where it is today? Take one of those mammoth trees outside your window, for example. Their ancestors had to migrate to our bonny island. Birds and animals carried seeds like hazel and oak across land bridges that once connected Ireland to Britain and Europe. Other seeds—the light ones, like birch and willow—arrived on a puff of air. And that was just the beginning. Once they were here, those tiny seeds had a lot of work to do. All the growing, stretching, reaching.

Makes me think about all the work you're doing.

What work? Heartache, love. The aching of the heart. And unlike so many other tasks, it's one only you can do. No delegating or shortcuts allowed. We humans love to try to circumvent pain. We want a shortcut, a trapdoor, something that will slurp us up and spit us out on the other side, no sticky messiness necessary.

But the sticky messiness is required. The process is built into the name. If you want to get through heartache, you're going to have to let your heart, you know, ache. And no matter how many distractions you pile on—cartons of ice cream, shopping binges, marathon naps—you can't outsmart heartache. It has nowhere to be, nothing to do. It will just stand there, buffing its nails, waiting until you're ready.

It's a persistent little devil.

So let's get to work, sugarplum. Let's quit drowning our pain in music and credit card bills and cyberstalking. Let's confront it. Let's own it. You've got a job to do, and the sooner you get to work, the sooner you can get back to frolicking through a forest like the sparkly little forest nymph I know you to be.

HEARTACHE HOMEWORK: Ready to do the work, love? I thought so. Find a tree that speaks to you and nestle up at its base. And then, when you're good and comfortable, name the thing that hurts the most about this heartache of yours. Don't flinch. Don't look away. Just face it. Why the tree, you ask? Because trees are exceptionally good listeners, of course.

—Excerpt from *Ireland for the Heartbroken: An Unconventional Guide to the Emerald Isle, third edition*

"WELL, THIS SUCKS," ROWAN SAID FROM THE OTHER SIDE of the tree.

"Agreed," I answered. We'd decided to use the same mossy-trunked tree, him on one side, me on the other. And so far, the Heartache Homework was making my heart feel . . . achy. Which I guess was the point. Looking right at heartache was like looking at the sun. It burned.

I shivered, rubbing at my goose bumps. My clothes were soaked again. A night in the Rainbow's End carport hadn't done the magic we'd hoped for. Clover's back seat had morphed subtly from soggy to mushy, and even though Bradley had donated a few towels to what he called Operation Keep Addie from Looking Like a Boiled Rat, my shorts were soaked through before we even hit the main road.

I was also dealing with some extra stress. Lina had found a flight that would get her and Ren into Dublin by tomorrow evening, and Ren had even managed to secure three tickets to Electric Picnic so we could all go to the concert together. Seeing the e-mail sent insecurity ricocheting through me. What if I didn't like Ren? Or worse, what if he didn't like me? Could a boyfriend and best friend coexist if they didn't like each other? And if not, who got the ax?

I wrapped my arms around myself and looked up through the trees, trying to refocus my mind. The forest was absolutely drenched in moss. Every surface and every branch dripped and glistened with it, softening everything to a green glow.

"We'd better do this before Ian gets back," I said. We'd convinced him to take a walk, but I doubted he'd be gone long. He was antsy to get to the next Titletrack site.

"Okay, you first. What's the worst part of your heartache?" Rowan asked.

Mine was a hard call. Was it public humiliation? Letting my brother down? An unexpected answer rose to the surface. "I didn't listen to myself. There were so many red flags, but I ignored them. I let myself down." I exhaled slowly, sadness coating me from head to toe. "What about you? What's the worst part?"

Rowan shifted, crunching some twigs. "Knowing I don't have any control over the situation."

"I might steal that one."

Rowan hesitated again. "You can tell me to shut up, but what happened exactly? Did you break up with him, or did—"

"It was him." I pressed my head against the bark, my heart sending out another pulse of ache.

Rowan absorbed my silence for a moment, then stood and crunched his way around the tree, sitting next me. "Hey,

Addie, you know I'm here for you, right? Like if you need to talk?"

I met his eyes. They were big and liquid, ready to absorb whatever ugliness I had for them. And suddenly the whole ugly story rose up until it was pushing against the back of my teeth. I did need someone to talk to about it all, but I'd been telling myself the story for ten days now, and it had become pretty clear what part I played in it: loser girl who throws herself at a guy because she's desperate to keep his attention. Not exactly flattering. Or friend-attracting.

"Thanks, Rowan, but I think I'm done here," I said, climbing quickly to my feet. At the car, Ian narrowed his eyes at us. "Why do you guys look so mopey?"

He was right. The time in Killarney National Park had really brought my mood down. I'd always heard you were supposed to distract yourself from heartbreak—not zero in on it. Why was Guidebook Lady so insistent on digging into heartache?

"We don't look mopey," Rowan said. "We're sad. They're two different things."

"Well, this isn't going to help," Ian said, tossing me his phone. "Text from Mom. That woman is relentless."

"Great," I groaned. I pulled up the text.

How's Italy? How are things with Addie?

"Well, at least she actually seems to think we're in Italy," I said.

He shook his head, unconvinced. "Or she's testing us."

I wrote back, Hey Mom, this is Addie. Things are going great!! Italy is so beautiful and WARM. You were right, we just needed some time together!!!! Really feeling some great sibling vibes!!

I regretted the text the second I hit send. It sounded like it had been written by a deranged cheerleader. A deranged cheerleader who was obsessed with the fact that her body temperature hadn't been normal in days. If Bradley's cameo hadn't tipped her off, this would. She wrote back immediately: Had no idea Howard was Australian. How interesting!

Ridiculous. Either she was laying a trap, or spending so much time with Aunt Mel was warping her brain. She knew Howard was American—it was a requirement for running the American cemetery.

I was so absorbed in trying to decipher my mom's text that it took me several minutes to realize that Ian and Rowan were now arguing.

"Ian, I'm being serious. I can't get caught." Rowan's hands were as tense as his voice, and his eyes darted nervously to the rearview mirror. I turned to look behind me, but the road was empty except for a long, fuzzy strip of grass growing through the middle of it. Roads had no chance here—Ireland liked to swallow them whole. "I just don't think we should risk it."

Ian's mouth settled into a hard line. "Rowan, it took us three weeks to track down where the Red Room is. And you just want to throw that all away?" He jabbed his finger accusingly. "I thought you were a fan."

"Whoa," I said, perking up. Those were fighting words. But they didn't seem to ruffle Rowan.

He shook his head soundly. "Stop acting the maggot. Not wanting to see it and not wanting to get caught are two different things."

This sounded interesting. I abandoned Ian's phone and scrambled forward to read the next site on the map. "What's Torc Manor?"

Rowan inclined his head slightly toward Ian. "Should I tell her, or do you want to?"

"Be my guest," Ian said, dropping his head back down to his map. Back at the Rainbow's End, he had peeled the tape off his window, and now he had his right hand out, fingers spread in the wind.

"I'm waiting," I prompted.

Rowan sighed heavily, then met my expectant eyes. "Torc Manor is a summer house that used to belong to the drummer's uncle. They recorded an entire album in the sitting room there."

"It's called the Red Room," Ian added, taking over. Whenever he was excited about a story, he had to get involved in the telling. "They went in thinking the album would be more upbeat and kind of poppy, but the room was full of heavy drapes and carpet, and all the fabric absorbed some of the sound and completely changed the way the songs came out. After that, they started producing songs that had that same moody vibe. They even re-created the same atmosphere in real recording studios with pillows and things. The room changed their whole musical direction."

This was exactly the kind of musical fact that Ian loved to geek out over. Thanks to Ian, I knew tons of odd music trivia—things like Paul McCartney hearing the melody for "Yesterday" in a dream, and Bill Wyman being asked to join the Rolling Stones solely because he had access to an amplifier. No wonder Ian's knee had graduated from bouncing to marching. Seeing something as iconic to him as the Red Room was his dream come true. "Okay . . ." I studied Rowan's grim face, allowing the "dot-dot-dot" to settle. Then I jabbed him in the shoulder. "So what's the problem here? Why are you so nervous?"

Rowan exhaled, giving his glasses a shove. "I just don't want to get caught trespassing. School's about to start, and if I get in any kind of trouble with the law, I'll get expelled."

"'Trespassing' is such a harsh word," Ian said, a grin swallowing his face whole. "I prefer 'unlawful entry.'"

Trespassing? I transferred my jabbing finger from Rowan to Ian. "No way. Priority number one is keeping Mom and Dad from knowing about our side trip. Which means we are not doing anything that could potentially involve police."

"No one is going to call the police." Ian tugged on his hair. "Why are you guys being so dramatic? All we're going to do is drive in there, snap a few photos, and get out. The owners will never even know we were there."

"Until photos of their house show up online and then they remember that you heckled them with e-mails for a full month." Rowan dragged his eyes away from the road and tapped his chin in mock-thoughtfulness. "What did that last e-mail from them say? Oh, yes. I believe their exact words were, 'Come near our property and we will not hesitate to notify the authorities.'"

"But they didn't say which authorities," Ian said, his smile still plastered on his face. "Maybe they meant the town water authorities. Or the leading authority on climate change."

Oh, Ian.

This plan—whatever it entailed exactly—was so my brother. One part danger, two parts music trivia, three parts rebel. Add a handful of jalapeños and some marshmallows and we had ourselves the perfect Ian recipe. Nothing I said was going to matter. May as well conserve energy—I might need it for running. I tried to send Rowan an abandon-all-hope shrug, but his eyes locked onto the road.

"'Look for a mossy, broken-down fence a few kilometers past the bent speed limit sign,'" Ian read from his phone. He stuck his head out into the wind, and his hair puffed into a large dandelion. "Addie, did you see that sign back there? Did it look kind of bent to you?"

"It was a Guinness advertisement," I said.

"But, Ian, what about the fan who got arrested?" Rowan hadn't known Ian long enough to understand what he was up against. "The break-in wasn't that long ago. You know the owners are going to be on high alert. They're probably sleeping with shotguns under their pillows."

"A fan got arrested?" I flicked the back of Ian's head. Was the fan part of his brain completely overriding the common-sense part?

Ian's smile only grew. "That was a whole year ago, and that girl was a mega stalker. You don't just walk into a stranger's house. Not when they're home."

"Because you only walk into a stranger's house when they're not home?" I clarified.

"Oh, she did more than walk in." Rowan pulled his glasses off and wiped at his eyes in a move that made him look like an old, tired businessman—but because it was Rowan, a cute, old, tired businessman. "She made a ham-and-banana sandwich in the kitchen and then ate it while rolling around on the carpet. The owners were sleeping upstairs, and she woke them up."

"Ew," I wailed. "Ham and banana? Is that a Titletrack thing or an Irish thing?"

"Definitely not Irish," Rowan said, a wry smile crossing his face. "Haven't you heard? All we eat are potatoes and beef stew."

Ian clasped his hands prayerlike in front of him and pushed his lower lip out in a pout. "Come on, guys. I promise not to make a gross sandwich and roll around on the carpet. No one will see us; no one will know."

I shook my head disgustedly. "Ian, the lower-lip-pout thing stopped working about ten years ago."

He pooched it out even more. "The lower lip pout is successful at least seventy-three percent of the time. How do you think I passed Español last year? Señora Murdock can never resist it."

I shook my head impatiently. "Quit trying to change the subject. Rowan's telling you that he doesn't want to go to Torc Manor, which means we are not going to Torc Manor."

"That was the bent speed limit sign!" Ian shrieked, hurling his body partially out the window. "We're almost there. Rowan, we have to, have to, have to go."

"Fine." Rowan's gaze swiveled back and forth from my brother to the road. "But listen to me. I cannot get caught. *Cannot* get caught. My parents are already in a constant state of stress. I can't stir the pot by getting in trouble."

"That's it!" Ian yelled.

Rowan hit the brakes, and Ian all but threw himself out

the window, extending his face toward the tall, ivy-covered fence. An oversize NO TRESPASSING sign cozied up to an even larger BEWARE OF DOGS sign.

I pointed to the image on the sign. "What a cute snarling shadow dog."

Ian waved me off. "That sign's a fake. Half the time people put those up when all they really have are goldfish."

"Rowan has a goldfish," I said.

His mouth twitched. "Had a goldfish. *Had*, Addie."

"Look, as long as we stick to the plan, we'll be fine. We already know that the room is ground level and faces the backyard. It will probably take me ten seconds to find. Rowan, all you have to do is drive in and wait. I'll do the rest."

This was train-mode Ian. I couldn't stop him. Rowan couldn't stop him. A slab avalanche couldn't stop him. Our best bet was to do exactly what he wanted—get in there, get a photo, and run.

"Fine." Rowan sighed, rolling his eyes to the ceiling.

Ian bounced giddily, pulling his notebook out. "Thanks, Rowan. I really owe you."

Rowan put the car into reverse. "Yeah, you really do."

"What about me?" I asked, yanking my legs out of the crevice behind the passenger's seat. Over the course of the day, I had reached a new and alarming mental space where I now accepted my legs being asleep as normal.

Ian petted me on the head. "Thanks, Addie. I really owe you, too, I guess?"

I shoved his hand away. "No, I mean what do you want me to do while you take photos of the inside of someone's house? Go with you?"

"No. It will be better if you stay right where you are. Guard Rowan's stuff." He tried to pet my head again, but I ducked out of the way.

I was about to insist on going with him, but when I straightened up, Ian had already moved into his pregame routine, a ritual I'd seen just shy of a million times. First he tied and retied his shoes—once, twice, three times—then he cracked his neck back and forth, finishing with a firm shoulder shake.

Watching him soothed me. If anyone could outrun an angry shadow dog, it was Ian. If he weren't the quarterback of the football team, he'd be the running back. He was the fastest sprinter on the team.

There was also the semicomforting fact that Ian was unequivocally lucky. If, for instance, the owners saw us and decided to shoot our car with flamethrowers, Clover would choose that exact moment to hit a pothole, and Ian would be launched from the car at just the right second, tumbling into soft grass and surviving the ordeal completely unscathed. It was Rowan and me who would end up crispy.

* * *

"Where is he? It's been donkey's years," Rowan hummed under his breath. Our eyes met over the clock on the dashboard. I wasn't sure about donkey's years, but it had been a lot longer than the two minutes Ian had promised before he'd disappeared out the window. Now we were both impersonating him, jiggling anxiously.

Torc Manor was trying very hard to be charming, and the ingredients were all there: a steeply pitched roof, white-trimmed windows, well-kept flower garden. But the longer we sat there, the more I realized there was something eerie about it too. Thick white sheets shrouded the patio chairs, and the surrounding trees grew in a wild tangle, filling the sky with branches and making the afternoon feel much darker than it actually was.

At least Ian was right about no one being there. There weren't any signs of life—no cars in the driveway, no shoes at the door, and no noise. Even the birds and insects were quiet.

Suddenly, Rowan ducked low. "Did you see that?"

My heart skittered as I followed his gaze to the upstairs window. But the curtains were drawn; no movement anywhere. "See what?"

"I thought I saw something. A flash of white." He cleared his throat. "Sorry I'm being a dope. I'm not that great at stress."

Ian suddenly materialized at the car window, startling

me so much that I flung my arm into Rowan's chest, hitting him with a dull thud.

"Oof," he wheezed.

"Sorry, Rowan," I said. This was not an isolated incident. Startled Addie equaled flailing Addie. Once, during a particularly intense cinematic moment, I'd showered an entire row of moviegoers with popcorn. Now I had my snacks doled out to me at movies.

Ian crossed his arms, reveling in a self-satisfied smile. "Why are you so jumpy? I told you, no one's here."

I looked at the house again. I couldn't shake the feeling that we were being watched. "Can we get out of here? This place creeps me out."

Ian shook his head. "The windows back there are too high. I need you to come with me so I can lift you up."

Instinct told me to hijack the car and get us out of there, but reason told me to go along with Ian's plan and get it over with. Also, I liked the fact that he was asking me for help. It felt pre-Cubby. "Let's just make it quick."

Ian dragged me around back. The back lawn was carefully maintained, with a wall of well-tamed rosebushes. Wind rippled through the trees, making a low shrieking noise. "I think it's that one," he said, pointing to a large window.

"Let's check." He knelt down so I could climb onto his shoulders, then wobbled to a stand. I leaned in, careful not to touch the spotless window. “Impressive,” I said. “You found the Red Room on the first try.”

“I did? What does it look like?” He bobbed around happily, and I had to grab his hair to keep from falling off.

“It looks . . . red.” Heavy red drapes drooped down to the oxblood carpet, tufted sofas and chairs rounding out the remaining hues of red. Even the portrait over the mantel depicted a redhead holding an armful of poppies.

He handed me his phone, but between the glare and my proximity, all I could see in the image was my own reflection. “Can you move to the right? The glare is really bad over here.”

Ian moved, stumbling on a garden hose but catching his balance quickly. This time the image was perfect. I took a stream of photos, capturing as many angles as I could. “These are going to turn out great.”

“Addie, thank you so much. This is really great of you!” The excitement in his voice narrowed the chasm between us.

“I read your articles,” I said, holding tightly to the small bridge between us.

The swaying underneath me immediately stopped, and his shoulders tensed. My opinion still mattered to him. “And?”

“They were incredible,” I said simply. “Really, really incredible. You’re meant to write about music.”

He squeezed my ankle. “Thanks, Addie. That means a lot. I’ve wanted to show you for a long time, but at first it was nice to keep it secret, because it was less pressure. And then this summer . . ." He hesitated.

A long, clunky silence filled the air, and I suddenly felt desperate to keep the camaraderie going. I missed the easy parts of our friendship.

"Ian, maybe you're right. Maybe I should tell Mom." The words ran out of my mouth faster than I could catch them. *Oh, no.* Why had I just said that?

"Really?" Ian's voice bounced off the house, his relief heavy as an anchor. "You have no idea how happy I am to hear you say that. Telling Mom is the right thing. That's what being an adult is, you know? You have to own up to your mistakes."

Mistakes. I felt myself bristle at the word. But I couldn't afford to get angry; I needed to focus on letting him down gently. "Ian, listen . . ." I steadied my fingertips on the glass and took a deep breath. But before I could speak, something caught my eye and I looked up. A woman stood at the glass, a vein bulging in her pale forehead, her face as close as my reflection. Her mouth stretched open in a wordless howl.

"Aaaaaah!" The scream ripped out of me and I hurled my body backward.

"Addie!" Ian tried to catch me, swiveling back and forth. I lost my balance and fell onto my back, hitting my head on something solid. A rock? Black polka dots invaded my vision.

"Addie, are you okay? Why did you scream?" Ian stood over me, his eyes tight with panic.

"Because—" My brain felt too confused to explain.

Suddenly, the porch door slammed, bringing me back to coherence. "Brutus, Marshall, get them!" The sound of scrambling erupted across the patio, followed quickly by barking.

"Addie, we have to run!" Ian yanked me to my feet, dragging me behind him as he charged for the car.

Rowan's phone was pressed to his ear, and his eyes widened when he saw us. "What happened? What—?"

"Just drive!" Ian stuffed me in headfirst, then jumped in behind me, and Rowan dropped his phone, tearing down the drive as two of the largest dogs I had ever seen threw themselves at our back tires.

* * *

Even though the dogs stopped dead at the edge of the property, Rowan spent the next ten minutes driving like a madman, swerving through lanes and overtaking every car he possibly could.

My hands would not stop shaking. Seeing the woman in the window reminded me of a game I'd played in elementary school called Bloody Mary. A group of us would turn off all the lights in the girl's bathroom and then chant *BLOO-DY MAR-Y* into the mirror in hopes that her ghost would appear. Nothing scary ever happened except for the occasional appearance of the crabby old janitor who came in to shoo us out. I'd always wondered what I'd do if a face actually appeared, and now I knew: crumple into a ball and wait for Ian to rescue me.

"Follow my finger," Ian commanded, moving his index finger left to right. "Do you feel dizzy? Nauseated?"

"Ian." I slapped his hand away. He was running through concussion protocol. All the student athletes had been required to attend a meeting on it back in March.

"What about sensitivity to light?" Ian shined his cell phone flashlight directly in my eyes, and I quickly blocked the brightness with my hands.

"Ian! Forget a concussion. You're going to blind me." I pushed him back into the front seat and carefully touched the back of my head. "It hurts, but it's just a bump." I winced, feeling the goose egg already forming. "No concussion."

"Good." Ian nodded, pointing to his black eye. "Call it even?"

I shrugged, and Clover flew over a bump and soared through the air.

"She didn't see me, right?" Rowan kept saying. "We're positive that woman did not see me?" His phone had been ringing ever since he'd dropped it, and he stuck his hands down between the seats, groping around.

"Rowan, how would she have seen you? You were in

the car the whole time," Ian said cheerfully. At least he was happy; he had his photos to keep him going. "Addie, these are incredible."

I knew his sunniness wasn't just about my excellent photo-taking skills—it was about what I'd said right before diving into the flower bed. *Maybe I should tell Mom.* What had possessed me to say that? It was only going to make things worse. I carefully touched the back of my head, wincing again.

"Tackling people in parking lots, surviving head injuries . . ." Rowan sounded amused, his worry about being seen lifting. "Addie, I have a new nickname for you, and I think it fits perfectly." He met my eyes in the mirror, pausing dramatically. "Queen Maeve."

"Who's that?" I asked.

"She's a famous Irish queen. Part myth, part real. And she was a warrior. I'll find a picture." He hit silent on another incoming call and then passed his phone to me. Ian crowded in close to look. A blond, long-haired woman sat slumped over on a throne, like someone was trying—and failing—to entertain her. Her foot rested on a golden shield.

"She seems . . . cool," I said, trying to disguise how flattered I felt. I'd always identified with characters like this. The limp-noodle princesses never felt right—who wanted to sit around in a tower all day?

Rowan took his phone back, nodding. "They buried her

standing up; that way she's always waiting for her enemies. The best part is that her tomb keeps getting bigger because any time someone hikes up the hill where she's buried, they take a rock with them and add it to the pile." He quickly turned his head back to me when he said, "So she's always getting stronger."

I loved the sound of that.

Just as I was about to thank him, Rowan's phone started ringing again, and I quickly handed it back to him. He angrily hit the silence button.

"Who keeps calling?" Ian asked, his nose just a few inches from the photos.

"My mum." The words spat out of his mouth, too vehement for either of us to ignore. It was the same tone he'd had when he was on the phone at the gas station.

Ian's eyes quickly found mine. "Everything okay?" he asked.

Rowan shook his head roughly. "I'm not her friend. I'm her kid. She can't keep coming to me with her problems." His foot pressed heavily on the accelerator, and suddenly we went from flying to jetting, the scenery rushing past.

Ian and I exchanged a worried look. The speedometer was rising. We were still in the okay range, but very high speed could be in our immediate future.

I tapped him lightly on the shoulder. "Uh . . . Rowan.

You're going pretty fast. Do you need a break? I could drive for a while."

"Or I could," Ian offered, his hands twisting nervously. "I can't promise I won't drive us into a wall, but I could try."

"I'm the only one with a license to drive here." Rowan let up slightly, but he was still going way over the speed limit. His hand gripped tightly around his phone.

"Rowan, let me take that for you." I reached forward, gently prying his phone away. "I think you and your phone need some time apart." I tossed it discreetly to Ian, then rested my hand on Rowan's shoulder. "Hey, Rowan, I don't know what's going on exactly, but you aren't alone. We're here for you." It was almost exactly what he'd said to me back in Killarney.

A long moment of silence unspooled, and then Rowan sagged forward, his speed slowly ticking down. Ian looked at me with appreciative eyes.

"Sorry, guys. My parents are putting a lot of pressure on me. It's been a really tough year. I just . . ." His voice wobbled.

Ian's eyes met mine again, and the message was clear. *Help him.*

"Um . . ." I glanced down, my eyes landing on the guidebook. "What if we add an extra guidebook stop? There's a castle between Killarney and Cobh. It's a little bit off our trail, but it sounds really interesting."

"Blarney Castle?" Rowan's voice instantly perked up.

"That's a great idea. I could really use some time to decompress."

"Uh . . . ," Ian broke in. "I obviously want you to have some time to decompress, but I'm worried that another stop will make us late to Cobh. It took me a month of e-mailing to get the owner of the pub there to respond, and then she said she only had a one-hour window. I really don't want to risk it."

Why was he being so clueless? Could he not tell the level of despair Rowan was in?

"He really needs a break," I said, shooting daggers at Ian through my eyes. "We'll be fast. Also, how many Irish people have you been cyberharassing this summer?" Poor people. When he fixated on something, Ian could be relentless.

"Only two," Ian muttered, the tips of his ears glowing red.

"We have plenty of time. And back there you did say that you owe me." Rowan looked at Ian expectantly.

Ian hesitated, a clump of hair disappearing into his mouth before he relented. "Okay. As long as we're fast, it should be fine. I just don't want another tractor situation."

Rowan and I shared a victorious smile in the mirror.

The Blarney Stone

There comes a moment in every heartbroken traveler's life when she finds herself dangling upside down from the top of a castle, lips planted on a saliva-coated rock, and she thinks, *How on earth did I get here?*

Let me assure you, this is a perfectly natural part of the heartbreak process.

The place? Blarney Castle. The saliva-coated rock? The Blarney Stone, a hunk of limestone with a sordid history and the propensity for attracting more than three hundred thousand visitors a year. Rumor has it anyone who locks lips with the magical stone will find themselves endowed with "the gift of gab"—the ability to talk and charm their way out of just about anything.

I'm not entirely sold on the gab bit, but I do know two things the Blarney Stone is excellent for: communal herpes of the mouth and discussions about rejection. Let's delve into rejection, shall we?

Because you're a human and because you're alive, I'm going to assume that you've faced your own Blarney moment. A time when you've put yourself out there—vulnerable, dangling—but instead of the blessed reciprocity your heart yearned for, all you got was a slimy stone that did *not* in fact create any oratorical prowess.

Been there. And I know exactly how that feels. I also know it's tempting to believe that you're the only person who's been left hanging. But you're not. Oh, you're not. In fact, the pain of rejection is so common, it's served as the inspiration for roughly half of history's art (and, I would argue, acts of lunacy). And yet when it happens to *you*, it feels like something brand-new. Like the world has cooked up the worst thing it could think of and then called you in for dinner.

That's love for you. Universal and yet *so damn personal*. Solidarity, sister. Anyone who hasn't gotten hurt is either a liar or a robot, and we all know that liars and robots make for terrible friends. Also, robot uprisings. Can we talk about the fact that we don't talk about them enough?

HEARTACHE HOMEWORK: You know what you're going to have to do, don't you, pet? Climb the castle, plunge into a gaping hole, and kiss the damn stone. Embrace the communal germs. They're there to remind you that you are not alone.

—Excerpt from *Ireland for the Heartbroken: An Unconventional Guide to the Emerald Isle, third edition*

AS USUAL, IRELAND HAD NO INTEREST IN KEEPING TO OUR time frame. Roadwork cluttered the road into Blarney—mostly construction workers yelling jovially to one another as they set up unnecessary-looking traffic cones. The castle wasn't much better. The site was stuffed full of tourists and the variety of ways they'd gotten themselves there.

After twenty long minutes behind a cranky row of tour buses, Ian threw his hands up. "How about I park, and you guys get out and do your thing?"

"Don't you want to see the castle?" I asked, craning my neck to get a glimpse. The castle managed to give off the impression of being both imperious and decrepit, a spindly old lady in a crown.

Ian stuck his head out the window. "Seen it."

Rowan laughed. "All right, Ian. Take the wheel." Rowan and I both jumped out, and Ian slid into the driver's seat.

"Watch out for roundabouts," I said.

"Ha ha, very funny. I'll probably have moved two feet by the time you get back." He lowered his voice, addressing me. "Keep it quick?"

"Of course."

Rowan and I took off together, following signs that explained the Blarney Stone's location at the tip-top of the castle. We crammed our way inside, shoving through giant picture-taking masses to get to the swirling staircases.

I started up first, and I must have climbed fast because when I got to the top, I had to wait several minutes for Rowan to emerge. When he finally popped out of the staircase, he was breathing heavily, a light sheen of sweat on his forehead.

"It wasn't a race, Maeve," he said, throwing his arm around me and collapsing dramatically.

I liked hearing my new nickname again. "I've been conditioning this summer." I couldn't quite extinguish the pride in my voice. I'd missed only two workout days the entire summer. The plan was to be as ready as possible for college scouts.

"Just to be clear, you know you just ran up a hundred flights of stairs to wait in line to kiss a manky stone, right?"

"No . . . *we* just ran up a hundred flights of stairs to kiss a manky stone," I corrected, enjoying the chance to try out some Irish slang. At the front of the line, a Blarney employee carefully lowered a woman backward into a stone cutout, her upper body disappearing into the hole. "Look how much fun that is. You get to hang upside down."

"A bit of a thrill seeker, eh?" Rowan said, his gray eyes shining.

"One hundred percent." My brothers called me a thrill junkie, which was decidedly more negative. But it was the truth. Heights, roller coasters, the bigger the better.

Rowan grimaced. "I'd expect nothing less from you. But sorry, Maeve, what I'm trying to say is that there is no 'we' in this enterprise. My mouth is not going anywhere near the Blarney Stone."

"Why? Is it a height thing?" I stood on my tiptoes to see over the wall. Besides the Cliffs of Moher, the top of Blarney offered the best panoramic view I'd had so far. Down below was an ocean of subtly shifting green, people scattered like colorful confetti. It even gave me the same sensation as the cliffs—I felt free, disconnected from all the heaviness waiting for me down below.

Rowan joined me on tiptoe, even though he could see over the ledge just fine. "Heights aren't the problem, Maeve." He shoved his glasses up. "Look, I'm sorry to be the one to tell you this, but locals really mess with Blarney Stone. They pee on it, spit on it, all kinds of stuff. Trust me, you don't want to kiss it."

I wagged my finger at him, a breeze blasting over the top of the castle. "Do you need me to reread the guidebook entry to you? Those communal germs are the whole reason we're here. And besides, I grew up sharing a bathroom with three brothers. Being afraid of pee is not an option."

Rowan's eyebrows shot up amusedly, just the way I knew they would. I liked surprising him. And besides, it was completely accurate. Once when I was in elementary school, I'd gotten so fed up with the situation that I'd drawn a bunch of arrows plus the words IN HERE on the toilet seat in permanent marker. My mom had laughed for a solid hour.

"Queen Maeve, your bravery knows no limits. If you kiss the pee stone, I kiss the pee stone. You have my undying allegiance." Rowan swept into a low bow.

"Thank you, my lord," I said, bowing back.

* * *

When it was finally our turn, even my daredevil instinct faltered slightly. The cutout the stone was located in was really just a hole, the long drop down to the lawn safeguarded with just three metal bars.

The worker beckoned to me. "Ready for the gift of gab, love?" He wore a cap, and his collar was pulled up against white stubbly whiskers.

"Ready," I said resolutely, ignoring the way my stomach spiraled. Rowan gave me a reassuring smile.

I sat quickly on the ground, shimmying back until my butt was on the edge. The hole felt cavernous behind me, wind gushing up through it.

"All right, then. Lean back, hand on each bar, back, back,

all the way back," the man chanted rhythmically, like he must have done a million times before. I followed his instructions until I was completely upside down, the man's hands firmly on my waist. Blood rushed to my head along with Guidebook Lady's words. *Because you're a human and because you're alive, I'm going to assume that you've faced your own Blarney moment. A time when you've put yourself out there—vulnerable, dangling—but instead of the blessed reciprocity your heart yearned for, all you got was a slimy stone.*

Cubby's face appeared, and a dart of pain traveled from my heart to the rest of my body. But instead of forcing the feelings away, I sat with them. Or dangled with them, I guess. Just like I had in Killarney. Again, none of the pain went away, but they did shift over slightly, revealing something that had been hidden. My feelings—my heartache, embarrassment, pain, all of it—weren't me. They were something I had to go through, but they weren't me any more than a pair of sneakers or a T-shirt was me. I was something else entirely.

"Kiss the stone, love," the man called down patiently, breaking me out of my epiphany.

Right. I planted a quick kiss on the stone. It was, in fact, manky. And oddly empowering. I kissed it again, this time for Rowan.

"Success!" Rowan grabbed my hand to help me once I was upright. "You okay?"

"A little dizzy." I wasn't sure what to do with my new realization. It wasn't like I could just throw off my heartache like a sweaty jersey. But could I look at it in a new way? As something that didn't define me?

I looked up at Rowan. "You don't have to kiss the stone. I did it for you."

He grinned. "And now you have truly earned my undying allegiance." He kept a steadying arm around my shoulders as we made our way back to the staircase.

Back on ground level, I was just about to try to put my revelation into words when a voice shot through the crowd, spearing my attention. It was the kind of voice you couldn't ignore. Bossy. Female. American.

My feet froze to the ground. That couldn't be . . .

"All right, people, listen up. Cameramen are going first. The rest of you? Single file. I need one good shot and then we're moving on to the next site. We're already behind, so I need you to make this speedy."

"No," I whispered.

"What?" I felt rather than saw Rowan turn toward me. I couldn't move. Twenty feet away, just past a long steel bench, my aunt Mel stood in full camera makeup.

"No," I said more forcefully. Aunt Mel shifted to the left, yanking at her perfectly tailored blazer, and a second heaping of panic poured over me. It was Walter. And my mom. Walter must have sensed my gaze, because suddenly he looked up, his eyes locking on mine. A single thought erupted in my brain. *Run.*

There was no time to warn Rowan. My feet pounded the pavement, and I rounded the corner of the castle so quickly, I slipped on mud. I needed a solid hiding place, somewhere I could gather my thoughts. Someplace . . .

Like that. I spotted a small opening in the bottom of the castle and hurtled toward it, ducking under the low doorway and stumbling up two steps to a small room. It was barely the size of a walk-in closet, dark except for a thin shaft of light working its way through a chink in the wall. I sank to my knees, adrenaline rushing through my body. Now what? I had to warn Ian.

"Addie?" My heart seized, but luckily it was just Rowan in the doorway, a serious frown crowding his features. "I know we haven't known each other long, but there's such a thing as common decency. You don't just tear away from your travel partner with no explanation."

Common decency? Travel partner? Rowan reverted to the role of stuffy English professor when he was angry. Before I could assign this particular trait the label of "cute," I grabbed his sleeve and pulled him in, our bodies colliding clumsily as he stumbled up the steps. The ceiling was much too low for him, and he ended up in a half stoop over me.

"My mom's out there. The whole wedding party's out there," I stammered.

His jaw dropped—I'd never seen anyone's jaw actually drop before—and he turned to gape at the doorway. "Which one was she? Did she see you?"

"No, but Walt did. We have to find Ian, and we have to get out of here." I crouched down to the ground, trying to still my trembling legs.

"I'll text him right now." He started for his phone, but just as he pulled it out, a second voice boomed into the cave, sending me toppling and Rowan's phone clattering.

"Addie?"

I sprang to my feet. Walt's eyes were as wide as I'd ever seen them, and he blinked unsteadily into the darkness. "I thought I was going crazy. I saw you, but you're supposed to be in Italy and . . ." His gaze snapped down to Rowan, who was still hunting for his phone, and suddenly Walt's face switched into Big Brother Mode. "Who the hell are you?"

"Walt!" I threw myself at him just as he charged Rowan, managing to pin him back against the wall. This was escalating way too fast.

"Whoawhoawhoa." Rowan stumbled backward, holding his phone up like a shield. "I'm her friend."

"Everyone, listen!" I yelled at the top of my lungs. It was a risk, but it worked.

I stepped back from a now-still Walter. "Walt, this is Rowan. He's Ian's friend. He's safe."

"But . . . but you're not in Italy." Walt's voice shot up to dog whistle levels. If he could hear how he sounded, he'd be mortified. "Mom thinks you're in Italy. *Everyone* thinks you're in Italy."

"And that's how it has to stay. Mom can't know we're in Ireland. You have to keep this a secret." I leaned in to emphasize my point and got hit by a solid wall of fragrance. Walt had a lot of things going for him—he was sweet and uncomplicated, and he could be extremely thoughtful. But he was not good at cologne regulation. Which was unfortunate, because he also really, really loved cologne.

"Addie, what are you thinking?" His piercing voice lifted another octave, raising my anxiety with it. If I didn't derail him, he was going to run out and ruin everything. Time to deflect.

I waved my hands in front of my watering eyes. "Walt, your cologne! I thought Mom said you couldn't pack any."

"I only did two spritzes," he protested. "Two spritzes and a walk-through. That's what you're supposed to do. Why can't any of you get that?"

Rowan suddenly piped up, catching on to my plan. "That's got to be a John Varvatos. What is it? Artisan Acqua?"

The shift was instantaneous. "Artisan Blu," Walter said, his mouth twisting into a grudging smile. "You wear it?"

Varvatos to the rescue. Rowan nodded vigorously as the tension in the cave lowered. "I've noticed that sometimes I have to water mine down a little because it's one of the stronger scents. Might be worth a try." Rowan was a master at argument disruption. My mom would adore him. I just hoped she wasn't about to meet him.

Walt dropped his hands to his sides, his voice now calm. "Addie, why aren't you in Italy?"

Insert plausible/convincing/nonincriminating explanation here. Minor problem: I was not good on my feet. Maybe if I just started talking, something brilliant would come out. "We stayed because of Ian. He's . . ." I hunted through my brain for some sort of lifesaver, but nothing emerged.

"They stayed because Ian's doing research for a college admissions essay." Rowan to the rescue again. "I'm a student mentor from Trinity College. Ian hired me to help him write the perfect paper. Right now we're researching famous historical sites."

Not bad. Too bad Walt was never going to buy it. People were always falling for Walt's laid-back-surfer-guy act, but it was just that—an act. Despite his lack of cologne awareness, Walt was most definitely not clueless. He had straight As and was working toward an accelerated degree in chemical engineering.

"But Ian doesn't need a college admissions essay," Walt

said, unconsciously flexing his left biceps. "He could fail his whole senior year and still get into any sports program in Washington. Why is he wasting time writing a paper?"

I automatically jumped to Ian's defense, my voice coming out in a snarl. "Maybe he likes writing." *This is what Ian meant.* Any time the subject of his future came up, it was automatically wrapped in a helmet and shoulder pads. Suddenly, a new idea popped into my head. One that might actually work. I quickly softened my voice. "Ian's trying to get into Notre Dame or Penn State. They have stricter admissions rules, so the paper matters."

"Penn State?" Walt whistled admiringly. "You're right, he might need something a little extra to get admitted there."

"Exactly!" My voice was way too amped-up.

"So . . . why is this a secret?" Walt asked, doubt edging its way back into his voice. He looked Rowan up and down, and Rowan straightened, lifting his chin slightly, maybe in an attempt to look more professional.

"He really wants to surprise Mom and Dad," I added quickly. "Can you imagine how excited Dad would be if Ian played for Penn State? And it was so hard for Ian to get matched up with a good . . . student adviser. He was really lucky to get Rowan."

Walt still looked a little unsure, but he nodded slowly. "All right, I've got you, sis. Your secret is safe with me."

"Thanks, Walt, I really appreciate it. Now, I think you'd

better get back to the group; we don't want them to notice that you're gone."

He sighed wearily. "Remind me to never travel with Aunt Mel again. The last two days have been a nightmare." He tilted his head at Rowan. "Nice to meet you, man. Take good care of my brother and little sis."

"She's pretty good at taking care of herself, but I will," Rowan said.

Walt gave me a quick, strong-smelling hug, then ducked back out of the room.

"That wasn't so bad, right, Maeve?" Rowan collapsed back against the cave.

I fell back next to him. "Thanks for jumping in with the college admissions story. I think it may have worked."

It may have worked short-term, but it definitely wouldn't work long-term. Secret keeping simply wasn't a part of Walt's chemical makeup. I'd just activated a ticking time bomb.

* * *

We waited as long as my adrenaline would allow—about seven minutes—while Rowan texted Ian and then traded me his hoodie for the navy sweater so I could cinch it around my face. Under the circumstances, it was the best disguise we could muster. We crept carefully out of the cave and then ran full speed, me praying fervently that no one from the group was watching the grounds too closely.

Back at the car, Ian was a solid mess of nerves, so bouncy that he could barely get the window down. We both ducked low, Rowan attempting to tear out of the parking lot. "They weren't supposed to be here until tomorrow," Ian said. "I checked the itinerary."

"Sounds like they aren't following the itinerary."

"I can't believe you saw Walt," he moaned. "Of all people, Walt." My thoughts exactly.

"Maybe it will be okay." I was trying to emulate the yoga instructor who sometimes came to our pregame practices to help us with visualization. Her voice was smooth and melodic and always worked to calm my nerves. "Rowan came up with a great story about you staying in Ireland to work on a college admissions essay. Plus, he promised to not tell Mom."

"Addie, he's Walter."

I abandoned the yoga teacher voice. "I know he's Walter. What do you want me to do about it?"

"Guys, remember the sibling treaty? No fighting?" Rowan hunched over the steering wheel, looking anxiously at the road. We were stopped at a crosswalk, a flood of people blocking our exit.

"I just can't believe this happened." Ian's leg bouncing slowed, and he slumped dejectedly against the side of the car.

Suddenly, my phone chimed and he whipped back around. "It's Mom, isn't it? Walt lasted a whole ten minutes."

"It's not Mom," I said, my relief quickly replaced with confusion. It was from one of my soccer teammates, Olive, and was in her signature all caps.

DID IAN REALLY GET KICKED OFF THE TEAM????
EVERYONE IS TALKING ABOUT IT AND FREAKING OUT!!!!

What?

I looked up, meeting Ian's nervous gaze. "Who is it?" he asked, his voice drum-tight.

"It's . . . Lina," I said, making a split-second decision to lie. Olive prided herself on always knowing what was going on, but this text couldn't be true. And bringing up some stupid rumor would probably just make Ian angrier. "She's just confirming her flight."

The crosswalk finally cleared and Rowan surged forward. "Tomorrow evening, right? And they're going to take the train to the festival?"

I nodded, my head too cloudy to form words. What had kicked off this rumor? And of course people were freaking out. Ian was the star player—the MVP. If he got kicked off, there'd be riots in the street.

I rubbed my thumb over the screen, and an uncomfortable thought popped into my head. One of my parents' favorite phrases: *Where there's smoke, there's fire.*

Something had started this rumor. What was it?

* * *

Once we cleared Blarney, the road became extra twisty, relegating Ian to his balled-up position against the car door. I'd been studying him carefully since Olive's text. Part of me wanted to shove my phone under his nose and ask him what it was all about, but the other part was afraid of opening another door—who knew what kind of ugliness was on the other side?

Rowan's voice pierced the silence. "Addie, do you know what this light on the dashboard means? It just turned on."

I set the guidebook down and scrambled forward to get a look. The temperature gauge was all the way up to the red *H*, and a small orange indicator light glowed next to it. I almost wished I didn't know what it meant.

"It's bad news, isn't it?" Ian said, watching my face.

"The car is overheating." I rose to look at the hood. At least there was no steam. Yet.

"Is that a big deal?" Rowan asked, tapping his thumb nervously on the steering wheel.

"Only if you want to keep your engine." His complete lack of car knowledge was almost endearing. "Almost" because it kept getting us into trouble. "Pull over, but don't kill the ignition."

Ian spun his carsick face away from the window, his voice wobbly. "Addie, we don't have time to pull over. My interview appointment is in an hour."

"Then we definitely don't have time to break down on the side of the road. We need to stop. Now."

"Just do it." Ian sighed, admitting defeat. I was the final word in car maintenance, and he knew it. Even our car-ogling dad had started asking me for advice on his old BMW.

Rowan pulled up alongside a line of trees. I crouched down near the hood, coming face-to-face with a small, steady trickle of liquid. I stuck my hand under, and a drop of green goo landed in my palm. "Great," I muttered, wiping my hand on my shorts. The guys squatted down on either side of me.

Ian clenched his fists nervously. "What is it? What's that green stuff?"

"It's antifreeze. Max probably overfilled the radiator, which causes too much pressure, and then you end up with leaks and your engine can't cool itself."

"I'm going to kill him." Rowan punched his fist into his hand. "And then I'm going to get my money back and kill him again."

"So now what? We tie up the radiator with a hanger? Plug it with bubble gum?" Ian asked, tugging anxiously at the ends of his hair. "Because missing the interview is not an option.

Miriam is a huge deal in the music world. The fact that she agreed to see me was a complete—"

"Ian, I get it," I interrupted, trying to think up a quick solution. I'd once seen a car show host crack an egg into a steaming radiator, allowing the heat to cook the egg and plug up the hole. But we didn't have any eggs, and it would probably gum up the engine anyway. "How far are we from Cobh?"

Rowan shielded his eyes to look up the road. "Maybe twenty kilometers?"

I jumped to my feet. It was never a good idea to drive on an overheating engine, but if we sat around waiting for a tow truck, we would definitely miss Ian's appointment. Was it worth the risk?

I looked down at Ian's still-clenched fists. It was either Clover or Ian. One of them was going to blow. I mentally flipped through the *Auto Repair for Dummies* book I kept on my nightstand. It was the only book that simultaneously stuck to my brain and made me feel calm. Something was clearly wrong with me.

"Ian, go turn on the heat. We're going to idle for a few minutes. Rowan, I need you to pop the hood and find me some water. I'll refill the radiator and we'll watch the gauge the whole time. And, Ian, find us a mechanic shop in Cobh. We need to drive directly there."

His smile filled up the entire road. "Done."

Cobh

Cobh, pronounced COVE. Or as I like to call it, the town of LISTEN TO YOUR UNCLE. NO, REALLY, LISTEN TO HIM.

Yes, there is a story, honey bun. But first, context.

Cobh is a good-bye kind of place. See that dock down by the water? It was the stepping-off point for 2.5 million Irish emigrants. It was also the site of one rather famous good-bye: the *Titanic*. You've heard of it? The Unsinkable Ship made its final stop in Cobh, adding and subtracting a few passengers before slipping off into the icy Atlantic and infamy. I'm going to tell you about one of the lucky passengers.

Francis Browne was a young Jesuit seminarian with an uncle who had a flair for gift giving. His uncle Robert (bishop of the spiky cathedral you see in the center of town) sent him a ticket for a two-day birthday cruise aboard the *Titanic*. The plan was to start in Southampton and end in Cobh, where he'd disembark, enjoy a slice of chocolate cake, and spend some quality time with good old Uncle Rob.

It was a great plan. And a thrilling ride. Along with snapping more than a thousand photographs, Francis did a good deal of schmoozing. One wealthy American family was so taken with him that they offered to pay his full voyage to America in exchange for his company at dinner. Hurray! Ever the dutiful nephew, Francis sent a message to his uncle asking for permission to stay aboard and received this rather terse reply: GET OFF THAT SHIP.

Francis and his iconic photographs got off that ship. Arguably, it was the most important decision he ever made.

All this in preparation for the rather terse and important message I have for you, my jaunty little sailor: GET OFF THAT SHIP.

What ship? You know what ship, love. It's the one you built back before the water got cold and the sailing treacherous. The one you stocked full of optimism and excitement and *look what's up ahead—this is so thrilling!* When hearts get involved, heads like to join in too, creating hypothetical futures full of sparkling water and favorable tides. And when those futures don't work out? Well, those ships don't just drift away on their own. We have to make a conscious effort to pull up anchor and let them go.

So get off the ship, dove, and send it out sea. Otherwise, you run the risk of allowing the thing that once carried you to become the thing that weighs you down. Solid land isn't so bad. Promise.

HEARTACHE HOMEWORK: Find some reasonably sturdy paper and draw your ship, pet. The plans, the dreams, all of it. I don't care how bad you are at drawing. Just get it all down. Now we're going to have ourselves a little send-off party. Use the PAPER BOAT FOLDING 101 instructions at the end of the book to create a tiny vessel. Fold that future of yours into a boat, and then put it in the water. Let the water do the rest.

—Excerpt from *Ireland for the Heartbroken: An Unconventional Guide to the Emerald Isle, third edition*

WE PULLED INTO COBH A HOT, SWEATY MESS. TO DRAW heat from the engine, we'd had to keep the car's heater on full blast, and by the time we made it to the auto shop, we were all dripping in sweat. And I only got hotter when the mechanic—a vaguely tuna-fish-smelling man named Connor—took one look at me and predecided that I couldn't have any idea what I was talking about. "I'll just have a look myself," he said.

"There's a hole in the radiator," I insisted. "I already found it."

His mouth twisted into a patronizing smile. "We'll see."

Before I could blow up, Ian yanked me toward the door. "We'll be in touch."

We hustled down the waterfront streets, carrying our bags past candy-colored row houses with lines of laundry out back. Ships bobbed against the wooden docks like massive rubber ducks, and a spiky stone cathedral stood tall and commanding, its steeple piercing the clouds.

The church was surrounded by visitors, and as we approached, bells suddenly split the air, their song surprisingly cheerful for such a grim-looking structure. "Wow." I skidded to a stop, my neck craning up toward the bell tower.

"Man down," Ian called over the clanging, circling back to

grab my elbow. "Those bells mean we're supposed to be there by now. You can stare at churches later."

"We have to come back for our homework anyway," Rowan said, pointing to the harbor.

"Fine." I sighed, slinging my backpack up higher on my shoulder and breaking into a run.

Au Bohair Pub was hard to miss. The two-story structure had been painted a startling robin's-egg blue and was sandwiched between a lime-colored hat shop and a cranberry-colored bakery. Even this early in the day, it had a festive, game-day feel, music and people spilling out onto the sidewalk in front of it, a collective cloud of cigarette smoke hovering in the air. When we got to the edge of the crowd, Ian ran up to a man standing near the doorway wearing worn denim overalls. "Do you know where I can find Miriam?"

"Miriam Kelly?" He smiled wide, revealing corncob-yellow teeth. "Stage left. She's always stage left. Just make sure you don't bother her during a set. I made that mistake once."

Ian nodded nervously, shoving the handle of his suitcase into my hand. "Addie, could you just . . . ?" He shot through the doorway, disappearing in a crush of people.

"Nope, don't mind at all," I called after him. It wasn't like I already had my suitcase to deal with. The man gave me an amused smile.

"Here, let me help you," Rowan said, absentmindedly

shuffling the guidebook from under my arm and disappearing just as quickly as Ian had.

"Really?" I muttered, grabbing hold of the bags. I bumped clumsily through the entryway, running over toes and sloshing people's drinks as I went. It was only when I'd squeezed into the middle of the room that I took a moment to look around. Wooden tables littered the floor, and the walls were almost completely eclipsed by music posters. A well-stocked bar stood in one corner of the room, customers filling every inch of remaining space.

"Ian!" I called. He and Rowan stood on tiptoe, staring hungrily at the stage. "Stage" was a bit too grand of a word for it. It was actually a small wooden platform, just a foot or two off the ground, that was somehow managing to accommodate a large tangle of musicians, their various instruments belting out a decidedly Irish tune.

I mashed my way over to them. "Could have used a little help."

Neither of them acknowledged me. They were too busy fanboying. Hard.

"That's Titletrack's first stage," Rowan was saying, his glasses practically fogging up with excitement. "This place is lethal. So, so lethal."

"I can't believe we're here," Ian said. "We are standing in the first place Titletrack ever performed."

I wriggled between them to get their attention. "Remember when you left me with all the bags?"

"Is that my baby music journalist?" a raspy voice boomed from behind us.

We all spun around, coming face-to-face with a short, round woman wearing thick spectacles and a shapeless brown dress, her hair pulled back into a tight knot.

"Um . . . are you . . . ?" Ian managed.

"Miriam Kelly." She yanked him in for a hug, patting him enthusiastically on the back. "You made it! I was worried you'd stood me up."

Ian cleared his throat, trying and failing to get over the shock of the most important woman in Irish music looking like the kind of person who baked banana bread and crocheted afghans in her spare time. "Um . . . ," he said again.

Suddenly, she dropped her smile, pointing a finger at him seriously. "So, tell me, Ian, is the garage band really dead?"

"You read his article!" I crowed, recognizing the title from when I'd read it back at the Rainbow's End.

She turned her bright eyes on me. "Of course I have. This young man left me five voice mails and sent an ungodly number of e-mails. I either had to turn him over to the guards or arrange a meeting. You must be the little sister."

"I'm Addie," I said, accepting her firm handshake. "And this is our friend Rowan. He's a huge fan of Titletrack too."

"So, so nice to meet you." Rowan pumped her arm, his face splitting into a smile. "Such an honor."

"An Irishman amongst the Americans. I like it." She turned back to me. "Addie, your brother here is quite the writer. I was very impressed."

"You—you were?" Ian's face lit up like a birthday cake, and he stumbled back a few steps. I'd never seen a compliment hit him so hard, and on the field they rained down on him constantly. "Thank you," he choked out.

Miriam slapped him heartily on the back. "And I love that you're so young. When you get to be my age, you realize that age has nothing to do with what you can accomplish—if you've got it, you've got it. Why wait until you grow up? And then once you're all grown-up, why stop? Or at least that's my motto."

Forget Titletrack. We should start a fan club about *her*.

She kept going. "I want all of you to find a table. I've been on the road all summer, but they let me back in the kitchen today and I made my famous Guinness beef stew. Bruce Springsteen claims it changed his life."

"Bruce Springsteen?" Ian looked like he was about to collapse.

She tapped her chin with one finger. "Or was it Sting? Funny, I sometimes get those two confused. I'll tell the kitchen staff you're here—see you in two jiffs." She bustled away, leaving ripples of shock in her wake.

"Ian, that was savage!" Rowan enthused.

Ian turned to me, his eyes round. "I just talked to Miriam Kelly."

"No, you were just *complimented* by Miriam Kelly," I pointed out, pride bubbling up in my chest. Whenever Ian was this happy, it always spread to me.

* * *

Miriam had ushered Ian to a table near the small stage, so Rowan and I chose another one closer to the door, in an attempt to give Ian some space for the interview.

"So why is Miriam such a big deal?" I asked, keeping one eyeball on Ian. His face had settled on a subtle shade of cranberry, and so far he'd dribbled stew onto his T-shirt and dropped his pen twice. If he was going to be a music journalist, he was going to have to work on the starstruck thing.

Rowan nodded. "She's like an informal talent director. At first she was just booking people to play here at her pub, but after she pushed some of the biggest acts in Ireland, all the record companies started hiring her to scout talent. Fifteen years ago, she heard Titletrack playing at a university contest and invited them here for a summer. It's how they started building up their fan base."

I dug my spoon into my bowl. "She's also an incredible chef." Miriam's Springsteen stew was a mixture of carrots, potatoes, and gravy topped off with two big ice-cream scoops of mashed potatoes. It was so rich and warm that I wanted to crawl straight into the bowl.

"Hey, did you read the guidebook homework yet?" Rowan asked, nudging the book across the table to me. "We have to build a paper boat and put it in the water."

"Are you going to do it or are you going to bail again?" I teased, flipping open to the Cobh section.

"Look, as long as it doesn't involve body fluids, I'm in."

"Fair." I leaned back in my chair happily. I was stuffed, and relaxed for the first time in days. The live music had been replaced with a Queen album that I recognized from when my dad cleaned out the garage, but mostly all I could hear was Ian. He kept dropping his head back and laughing.

When was the last time I'd seen him laugh so hard? Over the past few years, he'd gotten more solemn, which was probably football-related. You'd think that being the star player meant you got special treatment, but if anything it seemed to make the coaches harder on him. And he took his games so seriously. I didn't even have to check the schedule to know when a game was coming up because he always became quiet and moody for a few days beforehand.

Thinking about football reminded me of Olive's message, and I glanced down at my phone, a pit forming in my stomach. DID IAN REALLY GET KICKED OFF THE TEAM???? The text was obviously something I had to deal with. If rumors of Ian were flying around back home, then he deserved to know about them. *But what if it isn't a rumor?* my brain asked quietly. I quickly shushed it. Of course it was a rumor. Ian would have to set the school on fire before they'd do something as crazy as kick him off the team.

Regardless, I needed to tell him about it the next chance I got. The last thing our relationship needed was another secret.

I glanced over at Ian, and he met my gaze, waving us over. At their table, Ian's bowl sat half-full, the lines of his notebook packed full of his cramped writing. His face glowed with excitement. "Guess what? Miriam said we can stay here tonight."

"Are you serious? Where?" Rowan turned like he expected a bed to appear on the bar.

Miriam smiled, pushing her chair back. "Upstairs. We keep a few rooms to rent out, usually for the talent. Jared must have stayed in that main bedroom for an entire month. Which reminds me, he still owes me for that month, the gobshite. I think he can afford it now, don't you? I'm going to give him a call."

"Jared?" Rowan's mouth dropped open. "Lead singer Jared? He stayed here? And you *have his number*?"

"Of course I do." She shrugged lightly, looking at Ian.

"Let me know when your article is finished. If you'd like, I could forward it on to Jared."

"You—" Ian choked on his own words, his face reverting to a deep vermilion. "I—"

He gasped, and I whacked him on the back. "Ian, breathe."

Miriam raised her eyebrows at him. "Ian, you'll be okay. Once you've been in the business as long as I have, you figure out that musicians are just people. Interesting people, but people just the same." She turned to me. "Speaking of interesting people, let's talk about you, Addie."

My face attempted a copycat of Ian's. Miriam's attention felt sparkly, and a little too heavy. "What about me?"

She poked her finger at me. "I hear you are *quite* the mechanic. That's a talent. Maybe not one I can book, but a talent just the same. Ian said this trip wouldn't have worked without you."

Happiness bloomed in my chest. "Ian, you said that?"

He shrugged, a hint of a smile on his face. "Well, it's true, isn't it?"

Rowan piped up. "If it weren't for Addie, we'd still be dragging our tailpipe across Ireland. She even saved us today. Right after Blarney, my car started overheating and she managed to get us to the mechanic shop down the street."

Miriam sighed. "Let me guess, Connor Moloney's place? I hate to say it, but that man is as useless as a chocolate teapot." She crossed her arms. "So, mechanic. What do you have to say for yourself?"

What did I have to say for myself? "Uh, cars are just something I enjoy."

"And that you're *good* at," she insisted.

"I call her Maeve," Rowan said. "Because the first time I saw her, she was tackling Ian in a parking lot. She's like a warrior queen."

Now I was really blushing. "Sorry, *why* are we talking about this?"

"Because we need to!" Miriam pumped her arm. "We need more warrior queens around here. Especially ones that own up to their power." She leaned in, studying my embarrassed expression. "Addie, you know what I do, right? For work?"

I nodded uncomfortably. "Yeah . . . you book talent."

"Wrong." She jabbed a finger at me, her voice rising into an enthusiastic crescendo. "I *empower*. I find people who are out there singing their songs, and I put a microphone in front of them and make sure the world is listening. And you know what? I want to do that for you, Addie."

What was she talking about?

Before I could figure it out, she leapt to her feet and wrapped her arm around mine, dragging me up to the stage.

"Hey, Miriam, I don't sing. Or play anything." Or do stages. Unless it was on a field, I hated being in the spotlight.

I desperately tried to wrench away, but she just yanked me up onto the platform, positioning me in front of a standing microphone. Ian and Rowan watched with wide eyes, but neither of them attempted to rescue me. Traitors.

"Pat! The microphone!" Miriam yelled.

One of the bartenders ducked under the bar, and suddenly the mic stand crackled to life. Miriam shoved it into my face. "Go on, Addie. Tell the nice people what you did."

I looked at her in horror. True, the pub wasn't nearly as crowded as it had been earlier during the live performance, but there were still plenty of people, and every one of them looked up from their tables, amused smiles etched on their faces. They were clearly used to Miriam's antics.

"Go on," she insisted, giving me a nudge. "Tell the nice people your name and how badass you are. Making a declaration can be very powerful."

Do I really have to do this? Right as the thought entered my mind, her arm constricted around me like a boa. There was no way she was letting me off this stage. I cleared my throat. "Um, hello, everyone. My name is Addie Bennett."

"Queen Maeve!" Ian shouted from the audience, his hands cupped around his mouth.

I blushed straight down to my toes. Once this was over, I was going to murder him. "So . . . Miriam wants me to tell you that for the last couple of days I've been on a road trip. Our car keeps breaking down, so I've been fixing it. And . . . that's it." I hastily shoved the microphone back toward Miriam's hands and attempted to dive off the stage, but she grabbed hold of the back of my shirt.

"Wait just a minute, Addie. You know what I like to see? A woman who knows her strength. A woman who owns the fact that she is smart and creative, a woman who can *get things done*. Addie, you are a powerful woman." She grabbed my hand and raised it over our heads, victor-style. "Go on, Addie. Say it."

I cringed. "Say what exactly?"

Rowan and Ian grinned at each other. They were loving every minute of this.

"Say, 'I am the hero of my own story.'"

"I'm the hero of my own story," I said quickly.

"No, no, no. Louder. Open up the diaphragm. Really belt it out."

Was she not seeing the irony in forcing someone to declare how powerful they were? *Just get this over with*, I told myself.

I took a deep breath and yelled right into the microphone, "I am the hero of my own story!"

"Yes! Again!" Miriam shouted.

This time I really let loose. "I AM THE HERO OF MY OWN STORY."

"Good girl." Miriam dropped my arm, her face glowing with perspiration.

It actually did feel good to yell. It would probably feel even better if I believed it.

* * *

"So that was weird," I managed, dragging my and Ian's suitcases over to the staircase. As soon as Miriam had dismissed me from the stage, Ian had jetted off, intent on seeing our rooms.

Rowan grinned. "You stood on a stage and yelled to a bunch of strangers about what a hero you are. What's weird about that?"

I attempted to slug him, but the suitcases made it impossible.

Rowan grabbed one from me, shuffling it over to the stairs. "I'm going to run over to the mechanic shop, make sure Connor can have our car ready by morning. Can you believe Electric Picnic is tomorrow?"

"No." I couldn't believe it. Had the past few days dragged or flown? "I'll stay here. It's probably better if Connor and I don't see each other again."

He flashed me a smile. "Too bad. I was hoping to see Hero Maeve in action."

"Ha ha." I followed Ian up the stairs, the weight of the suitcases sending me bumping back and forth between the walls.

Finally, I made it to the top, dropping everything into a heap.

"I can't believe this." I followed Ian's voice through the doorway. The room's ceiling was slanted, and two twin beds crowded the far wall, the fading light streaming in from a single octagon-shaped window.

Ian was writhing around on the nearest bed. "Which bed do you think Jared slept in? This one?"

"I have no idea," I said, averting my eyes. Ian's dedication to Titletrack bordered on embarrassing. I fled for the next room, taking way longer than was necessary to set up my suitcase next to the bed. Olive's text was burning a hole in my pocket. I had to talk to Ian. Now.

When I walked back in, Ian had switched to the other bed, his arms tucked under his head, a peaceful smile on his face. Was I really going to do this? *I am the hero*, I thought ruefully.

"Thanks for getting us here," Ian said before I could open my mouth. "It really means a lot.

"Oh. Sure," I said, lowering myself onto the other bed. "So, Ian, there's something I need to talk to you about."

"Me too!" He rolled onto his stomach, reaching for his notebook. "I wanted to tell you that you should tell Mom about Cubby as soon as you possibly can. Maybe even before we get home. If you want, I could distract Archie and Walter at the airport while you tell her."

"What?" I felt the bridge between us collapse in one fell

swoop. Now he wasn't just insisting that I tell her, but he was dictating the time and place, too?

He sat up. "I think you should tell Mom about Cubby before—"

"Ian, I heard you," I said, falling against the closet door behind me. "But I'm not ready to tell Mom yet. Not that soon."

He slammed his notebook shut. "But you said I was right about telling Mom. When we were at Torc Manor."

"I said *maybe* you were right. I never said I was going to do it for sure."

Ian jumped to his feet and began pacing furiously. "You have got to be kidding me. Addie! Why not?"

"Because I'm not ready. If I want to tell Mom, I'll tell Mom." And even though I knew it would cause an explosion, I couldn't help but add the last part. "And besides, what happened with Cubby is none of your business."

"None of my *business*?" He stopped in place, his eyes shining angrily. "Addie, I would be thrilled if that were actually the case, but we both know it isn't true. It became my business the second I walked into the locker room."

My throat tightened. The locker room. Any time I tried to conjure up the scene of Ian walking in, of my *brother* being the one to stop Cubby, my brain grabbed a thick set of curtains and slid them shut.

"How was I supposed to know Cubby would do that?" My mouth was dry.

He pointed at me. "Because I warned you about him. I told you he was bad news." It was the same fight we'd been having all summer. It made me feel tired, right down to my bones. "Addie, for once, just listen to me. You can't keep this a secret anymore. You have to tell Mom the first chance you get."

"Stop telling me what to do!" I exploded, my heart hammering in my chest. "And who are you to talk about secrets, *Indie Ian*?"

I spat the name off my tongue, and his eyes hardened. "Don't turn this on me."

"Why not?" I opened my arms out wide, encompassing the room. "Secret Irish friend. Secret writing career. Secret college plans." I needed to pause, reel it in, but I was too angry. I reached into my pocket and then thrust my phone in his face. "And this. What is this about?"

He yanked the phone from my hands, his posture deflating as he read Olive's text. "How does she know?" he said quietly.

His words stopped me in my tracks, sending my brain spiraling. "Wait, are you saying it's true? You got kicked off the team? Why didn't you tell me?"

He tossed the phone onto the bed. "It was because of you, okay? I'm off the team because of *you*."

No.

I backed out of the room, my hands shaking as a mountain formed in my chest, heavy and brand-new.

Now his voice was pleading. "Addie, I got kicked off the football team. Mom and Dad don't know yet, but I can't keep it a secret forever. You have tell Mom. You have to tell her about the photo, and about Cubby passing it—"

"Ian, *stop*!" I yelled, clamping my hands over my ears. My body spun around, and suddenly I was running, the steps rising up to meet me, Ian at my back.

* * *

I made it all the way down to the harbor before I slowed. My chest was heaving, the tears making it hard to breathe, and I fell heavily onto an iron bench, the cold slats pressing into my spine.

Here's the thing that shouldn't have happened this summer, not to me, not to anyone. After weeks of Cubby asking, I'd sent him a topless photo of myself. I hadn't felt completely okay about it because one, all his joking about it had started to feel uncomfortably like pressure, and two, no matter how many times I swatted at Ian's warning, it refused to stop buzzing in my head. *I hear how he talks about girls. You don't want to hang out with him.*

But Cubby and I had been together all summer. Didn't

that mean I knew him better than Ian did? Didn't that mean I could trust him? And besides, maybe this was how you went from secret late-night meet-ups to walking down the halls of your high school together. You took a leap of faith.

So I'd hit send. Even though my hands were shaking. Even though the buzzing in my head got even louder.

And then two days later, Ian had come home from football camp and all but thrown himself through my bedroom door, angry tears pooling in his eyes. *You know what he's been doing, right? He's been showing everyone your photo. Why didn't you listen to me?*

I'd been too stunned to even ask what happened next, but now I knew. After Ian walked in on Cubby passing my photo around to the entire varsity team, he'd fought him. Of course he had. And then he'd gotten kicked off the football team. And the fact that I hadn't meant to involve my brother—hadn't meant to let my life spill over into his—didn't matter, because that came with being family. Whether you wanted them to or not, your actions always affected the entire unit. I took a deep, shuddery breath. I needed to tell Ian why I hadn't listened to him. The real reason. He deserved to know.

A few seconds later I heard his footsteps behind me, just like I knew I would. "Addie . . . ," he started, but I whipped around, forcing the words out before they could retreat.

"Ian, do you know how hard it is to be your little sister?"

He froze, a searching expression moving over his face. "What do you mean? This summer excluded, I've always felt like we had a great friendship."

"We have." I shook my head, groping for the words as he slid onto the bench next to me. "What I mean is, do you know how hard it is to be *Ian Bennett's* sister?"

He shook his head almost imperceptibly. "I don't understand."

"You're the star of our high school. Star of the football team. The star athlete in a house *filled* with star athletes." My voice wavered, and I picked a spot in the ocean to stare at, steadying my gaze. "You're good at school, and sports, and writing . . . and of course you were right about Cubby. You were completely right. And deep down I knew it all along."

Ian dug his hands into his hair, his face confused. "Then why—"

I cut him off again. I really needed him to listen. "Ian, I was with Cubby this summer because I wanted someone to *see* me. Really see me. And not just in comparison to you three." I took a deep breath. "I just wanted to be someone other than Bennett number four—the one who's just mediocre."

"Mediocre?" Ian's eyes widened in disbelief. "Why didn't you ever tell me you felt that way?"

"Why should I have to tell you? It's so embarrassingly

obvious." A bird hopped happily over, a french fry clamped in its beak. "And, Ian, I'm really sorry that I sent the photo, but—"

"Whoa, whoa, whoa. Back up." Ian's hands shot into the air. "You think I'm mad at you because you sent the photo?" He looked me square in the eye, his knee bouncing. "Addie, that's not what this is about. Sending a photo was your decision. It's your . . . body." We both grimaced. This was firmly out of the realm of brother-sister conversations. At least it was for us.

"Sorry," he said quickly, blush forming on his cheeks. "I don't know if I'm saying this the right way, but what I mean is that I wasn't mad that you sent the photo. Your picture getting passed around the team wasn't your fault—Cubby's the one who did that." He kicked at a loose pebble on the sidewalk. "I was mad that you didn't trust me when I told you to stay away from him. I've been around Cubby for years. I've seen how he's changed, and I just wanted to protect you."

Tears prickled my eyes, and I leaned over, resting my elbows on my knees. The knot in my chest felt like it would never unravel. "Ian, I'm so sorry about football," I whispered.

He exhaled slowly. "Okay, now it's my turn to come clean on something else. I didn't mean what I said back there in the room. I was just angry. And trying to make a point."

I shot up quickly. "You mean you're still on the team?"

He shook his head. "No, I am one hundred percent off the team. What I mean is that's on me, not you."

"So it wasn't about the photo?"

"Well . . ." He hesitated. "I wouldn't say that exactly. But more happened than just me confronting Cubby in the locker room. I mean, I definitely lost it that day. But it was all the other fights that put things over the edge."

"Fights?" My head snapped up. "As in plural? How many did you get into?"

He hesitated. "I'm not really sure. And I'll be honest, at first they were about you, guys making stupid comments to get under my skin. But then it was like I just snapped. I couldn't handle my teammates anymore, and everything set me off. Coach kept giving me warnings and then . . ."

He straightened up, throwing his shoulders back. "But it's okay that I got kicked off, because I hate football. Always have, always will."

"What?" I ripped my gaze from the ocean. Enjoying writing more than football was not the same as *hating* football. And he couldn't hate it, could he? Not when he was so talented. "Like you hate practice or . . . ?"

He shook his head, sending hair into his face. "No, I hate *football*. All of it." His eyes met mine. "I hate practice, I hate games, the pep rallies, the banquets, the uniforms . . . I hate how people treat me differently—like I'm special just because I'm good at this one thing. And it's been this way for so long. Once everyone figured out I was good, it was like someone threw this big football blanket over me—no one could see anything else. Everyone just wanted me to fall into this stereotype, and it just never . . . fit."

I had never even considered that Ian didn't like football. Suddenly, it all fell into place: the rush out of practices, the grumpiness before games, how hard he worked to not talk about football when it was all anyone else wanted to talk about. It had been right in front of me all along. "Ian, I had no idea. That must have been . . ."

"Awful?" he said, his eyebrows dropping.

"Awful," I repeated. "Why didn't you tell me?"

He shook his head. "I didn't want to disappoint you. Everyone gets so excited about me playing, and you were always at my games and . . ." He exhaled loudly. "I want to be like you and Archie and Walter. When you're on the field, it's like you turn into who you really are. You have so much fun. I've never felt that."

"But you feel that way with writing. And Titletrack," I said.

"Exactly," he said. "That's why this trip was so important to me. I thought that if I could maybe write something really incredible, maybe get it accepted into a large magazine, Mom and Dad would be less upset about my quitting football."

I pressed my lips together, barely containing my smile.

"So you're saying that you have something you need to tell Mom and Dad?"

He groaned, but a smile pierced his face too. "I know. Don't bug me about it, okay? I'm getting there."

"Are you kidding me? I am *definitely* going to bug you about it. At least as often as you bugged me."

"There you guys are!" Rowan suddenly appeared next to the bench, startling us. "I had no idea where you went. I ended up asking one of the bartenders, and he told me . . ." He stopped, his eyes drawn to my tearstained cheeks. "Wait, what's wrong? Did something happen?"

"You could say that." Rowan had the guidebook in his hand, and seeing it sparked an idea. "Hey, Ian, do you want to do the Cobh homework with us? I actually think it might help you."

"Good idea," Rowan said. "I bet you'll like this one."

Ian yanked his hair back, securing it with an elastic from his wrist. "I don't know. Do I have to talk to a tree? Or kiss something?"

I shook my head. "We're supposed to draw something that didn't work out the way we hoped it would. Then we're going to fold our papers into boats and send them out to sea."

"Hmmm," Ian said, but from the way his eyes landed on the book, I knew he was interested.

"I was looking for you because I wanted to do the homework before it gets dark. I even asked for paper back at the pub, but all they had were these." Rowan handed me a stack of old fliers advertising a show by a local violinist.

"Good enough for me." I handed them each a paper, and then we spread out, sitting on the ground with our drawings in front of us. Mine came easily. It was Cubby and me, walking down the hallway, his arm slung around me, admiring whispers coming from all directions.

The drawing itself was terrible, barely a level above stick figure, but getting it all out shifted something inside. Again, the pain was still there, but some of the weight traveled down through my pencil, solidified into something I could look at. Something I could let go of.

We gathered at the edge of the water, following Guidebook Lady's instructions for the Anti-Love Boat, and as I set my boat into the water, I let myself imagine for one more second what it would be like if things had gone differently. If Cubby had cared about me the way I'd cared about him. And then I let it go, watching as the waves carried it out to be dissolved by salt.

And when it was gone? Ian and Rowan were still beside me. Solid. It meant more to me than I'd thought it would.

* * *

There was a storm in the night, a gentle pattering that infiltrated my dreams and infused the late-morning sky with a bright peachy hue. Before getting out of bed, I rolled onto my back and stared up at the spiderweb cracks in the ceiling, testing out my new feeling of lightness.

The knot was still in my chest, but Ian and I being on the same team made everything seem easier.

I got dressed and then wandered into the boys' room to see them sprawled out on their beds, Rowan wearing a pink T-shirt depicting a cat riding an orca and Ian poring over his map.

I pointed to Rowan's shirt. "How many of those do you have?"

"Not nearly enough. And good morning to you, too," he said, his dimple making me smile.

I pointed to Ian's map. "One more stop before Electric Picnic?"

He grinned, bouncing off the bed. "Rock of Cashel. I can't believe the concert is *tonight.*"

"I can't believe *Lina* will be here tonight." I was still nervous, but now that the tension had eased between Ian and me, telling Lina suddenly felt much more doable.

Rowan lifted his phone. "Connor says we can pick up the car after ten. Anyone want to stop for breakfast first?"

"Me," Ian and I said in unison.

Miriam had left bright and early to drive to Dublin for a meeting, so after saying good-bye to the staff, we rolled our suitcases down to Main Street, stopping at a cobalt-blue coffee shop with BERTIE'S: FREE TEA WITH EVERY ORDER spelled out across the window in gold stick-on letters. Inside, a small bell jingled overhead, and we ordered eggs and toast from a woman standing behind the counter.

I wanted to watch the ocean for as long as possible, so while we waited for our toast and eggs, I chose a table near the window, wrapping my hands around my hot mug of mint tea.

Outside, tourists streamed past us on the sidewalk, and I watched them absentmindedly, spooning sugar into my cup and tuning out Rowan and Ian's conversation to think about Lina. I hadn't seen her in more than three months. What was tonight going to be like? Would we just pick up where we left off? Would we have to get used to each other again?

Our server had just set our plates in front of us when suddenly one of the passersby snapped me out of my peppermint-infused daze. He was tall with wide shoulders, a massive pair of headphones, and an undeniable swagger that reminded me of . . .

"Walter!" I squeaked. He glanced in the window and stopped dead, his gaze on Ian.

"NO." Ian dropped his spoon into his mug, sending hot water splattering. My instinct was to dive under the booth, but Walter's glare traveled from Ian straight down to me, and suddenly we were making eye contact. Furious eye contact.

"Is this seriously happening again?" Rowan groaned. "This island is way too small."

"Who is he?" our server asked, holding a pitcher of water in her hand. Walter pressed his face to the window, his breath steaming up the glass. "Is he dangerous?"

"Moderately," I muttered, jumping to my feet.

Walter pushed his headphones off and marched for the door, his lips already moving in an angry diatribe that we were privileged to be a part of the second he opened the door. "—two are the worst!" he yelled. "Here I am doing my best to forget that Addie appeared out of nowhere at Blarney Castle, and now you're here EATING BREAKFAST." He roared "eating breakfast" like it was at the top of a list of offenses people could commit against him. Secrets did not look good on Walt.

"Sir. Calm down," the server ordered, wielding her serving tray like a shield. "Can I interest you in a nice cup of tea? Maybe one of our soothing flavors? Chamomile? Lemon lavender? It's on the house."

"He's not a big tea drinker, but thanks," I said politely.

"Walt, stay calm," Ian commanded, edging away from the window. "Where's Mom?"

Walt yanked his headphones away from around his neck. "What are you even doing here?"

I gestured to Ian. "Rowan and I told you back at Blarney Castle. We're working on Ian's paper."

He shook his head disgustedly. "BS. I talked to Archie about it, and he thought it sounded made-up too. You don't need to go to a foreign country to do research for an admissions essay. Which makes you a liar," he said, thrusting his finger at Rowan. "Do you even wear John Varvatos cologne?" Rowan grimaced slightly but said nothing.

"You told Archie?" Ian demanded, bouncing to his feet. His map was on the table, and he quickly shuffled it aside.

Walter scowled. "Of course I did. I had to tell *someone*."

I shot a nervous look out the window. He hadn't answered Ian's question. "Where's Mom?" I repeated.

"At the cathedral. I talked her into letting me skip it."

The cathedral was only two blocks away. How close had we come to running into them?

Walt lasered in on Ian. "Now, for the last time, what are you doing in Ireland?" The server cowered at his tone, and I gazed longingly at my plate of fluffy eggs. Breakfast was not going to happen. And Walt wasn't going to believe any more of our lies. Time to come clean.

"Ian, just tell him." I sighed.

Ian grabbed a wad of napkins and mopped up the splattered tea. "We're going to a music festival called Electric Picnic to see my favorite band, Titletrack, do their final show. I had it planned all along. Addie intercepted me on the way out, so that's why she's here too."

Walt's eyebrows shot to the ceiling. "I knew it! I knew you were lying. So that makes international mentor here—"

"Ian's friend," Rowan piped up. "And fellow Titletrack fan. And I actually do wear John Varvatos. The Artisan Acqua scent is my favorite." Walt eyed him critically. He had to quit taking his scents so seriously.

Ian started again. "Walt, this is the plan. After the festival, we're going to meet you in Dublin to fly—"

"Just stop!" Walter threw his arms up and backed quickly toward the door. "Don't tell me any more. Just be safe and stop running into us."

"Deal," I said eagerly.

"You guys obviously aren't sticking to the itinerary," Ian pressed. "Where are you going next?"

"I don't know. Some rock place?"

"Rock of Cashel?" Ian slammed his fist onto the table. "But that's where we're going."

Rowan shook his head. "It's a really common tourist spot. I'm not surprised."

"Well, you're not going there anymore," Walt said, his Adam's apple protruding. "Because if you guys show up there, it's over. I'm barely keeping it together as is."

"Walt, please." I pressed my hands into a prayer. "You have to keep it together. I can't get kicked off the soccer team. Just don't tell anyone else." Out of all the siblings,

Walt and I were the ones who loved sports the most. He had to understand.

"What do you think I've been doing since Blarney Castle? I'm trying to help you guys out." He stumbled over to the door, looking out at the street before pushing it open. "They'll be at the cathedral for maybe twenty more minutes. You'd better get out of here. Fast." He shot out onto the sidewalk, the door slamming behind him.

"Now what do we do?" I asked, edging away from the window.

"Well, we're not going to Rock of Cashel." Ian's face fell in disappointment. "That was going to be a huge part of my article."

Rowan pushed his glasses up his nose. "Actually . . . I might have a place better than Rock of Cashel. It's a little bit of a detour, but it's close to Stradbally. And if the rumors are true, this place may have something to do with Titletrack."

"Really? What is it?" I asked.

He smiled at me. "It's a secret."

Secret Fairy Ring

I'm not exaggerating when I say "secret," pet. This next stop is pure off-the-beaten-path gold. An experience that you can stash in your carry-on and pull out when the jerk in 23A starts bragging about all the under-the-radar local places he visited on his trip. (Not that you asked.)

In general I'm all for the wander-till-you-find-it method of travel, but in this case, winging it just isn't going to cut it. Not when there's magic involved. Follow the map I've included on the next page to a T, then meet back here.

You make it? I knew you would. Such a capable duck.

Now, before you start slogging your way through that unassuming clump of trees on the east side of the road, I'm going to lay out a few ground rules. Fairy Etiquette 101. And I don't want to sound too dramatic, but your compliance or failure to follow these rules may alter your entire destiny.

So, you know. Comply.

Rule #1. Tread carefully.

Fairies need a place to dance their fairy dances and hold their fairy tea parties. And if they're Irish fairies, well, then they also need a place to plot the certain demise of anyone who has ever so much as looked at them cross-eyed. Which leads me to my next rule.

Rule #2. Don't make the fairies mad.

Irish fairies have the reputation of being just the teensiest bit vindictive. Like steal-your-baby, burn-your-barn-down vindictive. Irish fairies don't mess around, and you shouldn't either. Speak gently, don't tread on the flowers, and do your best to entertain only the kindest of thoughts.

Rule #3. Leave the fairies a gift.

I would suggest something tiny as well as either beautiful or delicious. Coins, honey, thimbles, fish tacos, your neighbor's firstborn . . . all excellent choices.

Rule #4. Make a wish.

Showing up to a fairy's home and not making a wish is like showing up to a junior high dance and refusing to do the Electric Slide. Not only is it unprecedented, but it's also rude. Also, be aware that real-life fairies act less as dream granters and more as dream *guiders*—helping you to figure out what it is your heart truly wants and then nudging you all along the way toward it. So listen closely, pet. You may hear something that surprises you.

HEARTACHE HOMEWORK: Fill in your wish here. I promise not to look.

____

____

____

____

—Excerpt from *Ireland for the Heartbroken: An Unconventional Guide to the Emerald Isle, third edition*

CLOVER'S ENGINE WAS COOL AS A MINT JULEP, HER tailpipe reattached with something a bit more trustworthy than a hanger. We'd sprinted for the mechanic shop, pooled our money to pay for the repairs, then torn out of Cobh like mobsters on a bootleg run. We'd been in such a rush that I'd even skipped the *I told you it was the radiator* gloat speech I'd mentally prepared for Connor.

After Walt run-in number two, it was becoming increasingly clear that Mom finding out was much less a question of *if*, but *when*. I held tight to my final sliver of hope. Maybe he wouldn't tell. But Walt had been on the verge of spontaneous combustion—anyone could see that. Every time a vehicle pulled onto the road behind us, I spun around, expecting to see Aunt Mel's tour bus bearing down on us, my infuriated mom in the driver's seat.

"Do you think Mom knows by now?" I asked, watching the trees whoosh by. "What about now?"

"Addie," Ian groaned, but a smile hovered just under the tension in his voice. Sometimes, joking was the only way to make it through. Particularly when you were about to get caught for sneaking away on a European road trip and in the process lose the thing you cared about the most. I glanced up at Ian's tangled hair. Well, maybe soccer didn't matter the *most*. But the fact remained, we'd begun the trip with the express hope that our parents would never find out, and now we were hoping to make it just a few more hours so we could go to the concert.

My, how the mighty had fallen.

It helped that Lina and Titletrack were already pinpoints of light on the road ahead. My stomach twisted in anticipation.

"I still say Walter isn't going to tell on you," Rowan offered. He was driving a solid twenty kilometers over the speed limit, cutting straight through turns, but now that we were on day three I didn't even bat an eye. He was actually a very alert driver, and the safe feelings I had around him transferred to being in his car. Ian, on the other hand, was channeling his inner Kermit the Frog, his face a dusky green.

I gestured to Ian. "Better ease up. This one isn't looking good."

"I'm fine," Ian insisted, but then in a rare moment of honesty he backtracked. "Nope, you're right. Not fine." He glanced over at Rowan. "I still don't get what this guidebook stop has to do with Titletrack."

Rowan beamed. "You'll see." Whatever the connection, he was very proud of himself over it. Sunlight kept blasting on and off and through our windows, and every time it hit his face, a constellation of freckles lit up on the bridge of his nose. It was oddly mesmerizing.

Finding the fairy ring was not a terribly straightforward process. Instead of regular directions, Guidebook Lady's map used landmarks like "rock that looks like David Bowie in 1998" and "barn the color of sin" to guide us. We had to circle around the road a few times and google David Bowie just to get within striking distance.

Finally, we pulled over, crossing the road to a clump of trees that looked incredibly unpromising. By this point, Ian was a bundle of nerves. Pukey nerves. Hopefully, all the U-turns would be worth it.

"What is a fairy ring anyway?" Ian asked, stepping off the road and into the mud.

"Fairy rings are actually ring forts," Rowan said. "They're the remains of medieval farms. People used to dig moats and then use the earth to make circular barriers. Their remains are all over Ireland. But for a long time people didn't know what they were, so they came up with magical explanations."

I didn't need any more convincing. "Let's go." I marched for the forest like I knew what I was doing. I hesitated for a moment before plunging into the mud. It had the consistency of extra-sloppy peanut butter. My Converse were not going to survive this trip. Ian groaned, sludging his way forward.

Rowan slogged up next to me. "You know what we're looking for, right? It's a raised circular wall, either made of stone or—"

"Like that?" I pointed to a rounded bank draped with patches of grass and moss, and we all hurried over.

But finding the fairy ring and getting into the fairy ring were two very different situations. The bank was about five feet tall and reminded me of a vertical Slip 'N Slide.

"How should we . . . ?" Rowan started, but Ian charged up behind us, summiting the ledge in four big steps. "I guess like that."

"Whoa. What is this place?" Ian shouted once he'd made it over the bank.

"Ian, no yelling!" I said, breaking my own rule. "You'll make the fairies mad."

"You think I'm scared of fairies when *Mom* is out there?" He hesitated, his voice settling reverently. "Seriously, though. What is this place?"

Rowan and I exchanged a look, then hauled ourselves up as quickly as possible. But as usual, Ian had made it look easier than it actually was. I fell backward twice, both times losing my balance and tumbling into the mud.

"Need a little help, Maeve?" I glanced up to see Rowan biting his cheeks.

"Are you *laughing*?" I demanded.

"No way. I'm much too scared of you for that. I was just standing here wondering if I've ever seen anyone fail so badly at climbing a five-foot hill."

"It's my shoes. I'm supposed to be riding around Italy on a scooter, not hiking through mud." I attacked the hill again, this time allowing Rowan to help haul me up.

Once I had my balance I leaned in close. "Okay, tell me the truth: Is this really a Titletrack site, or were you just trying ease Ian's devastation?"

"It really is." Rowan was one of those rare people who was even cuter up close. His gray eyes were flecked with blue, and a constellation of freckles danced across his nose, lit up by the sun.

"Guys! Look at this."

I tore my gaze from Rowan, instantly forgetting about the freckles. All around us, tall, beautiful trees echoed the circle, their branches reaching over to form a protective umbrella over the ring. But it was the light that got me. Sunlight had to filter through so many layers of leaves that by the time it reached the ring, it cast a warm, lucky glow.

If fairies lived anywhere, it had to be here.

Without breaking the silence, Rowan and I slipped carefully down the bank and into the ring. At ground level, everything was a notch or two quieter, the wind moving silkily through the grass. Small, shiny trinkets covered a gray stump in the circle's center: three gold thimbles, a silver lighter, two pearl-inlaid bobby pins, and a lot of coins.

"Wow," Rowan whispered quietly. He reached into his pocket, coming up with a handful of coins and a foil-wrapped stick of gum.

Real-life fairies act less as dream granters and more as dream guiders—*helping you to figure out what it is your heart truly wants and then nudging you all along the way toward it. So listen closely, pet. You may hear something that surprises you.*

I shuffled through my pocket, emerging with a handful of coins left over from paying for our spilled eggs at the coffee shop. I handed one to Ian. "We have to make wishes, and then place these on the stump as an offering."

"Just like Jared did," Rowan said triumphantly.

Ian's eyes grew wide, and not because Rowan's voice was over the fairy-approved decibels. "*Jared* came here?"

Rowan nodded, finally letting his smile break loose. "This morning I was reading more about Titletrack's early days, and I came across this old interview where Jared told a story about stopping at a fairy ring near Cobh. He was actually on his way to Kinsale, which is farther south, but he happened to stop at Au Bohair for lunch, and he met Miriam."

I bounced happily on my feet. "He stopped to make a

wish, and the rest is history. You really think this is the fairy ring he stopped at?"

Rowan shrugged. "I can't really know, but he said it was close to Cobh, and this is pretty much the only main road from Dublin. And here's the part I really liked about the story. Instead of wishing to become a famous musician, he said he asked the fairies for 'the next thing he needed.' A few hours later he met Miriam, and *then* the rest was history."

"Rowan, this is perfect!" Ian yelled, disregarding the fairies' delicate ears. He pointed to the stump. "This is the real beginning of Titletrack. Right here."

Rowan splayed his arms out proudly. "Didn't I say I'd deliver?"

I squeezed his arm. "Nice work, Rowan."

"All right, then, time for wishes," Ian announced. "If it worked for Jared, it'll work for us. Rowan, you found this place, so you go first."

Rowan strode over to the stump and carefully placed his gum next to a bobby pin. As he set it down, something about his posture changed. Opened up. There was a long, quiet pause, and when he spoke, his voice was quiet and clear. "I wish my mom and dad would let go of each other."

I suddenly felt like a trespasser, stumbling upon a private moment. Ian and I exchanged a quick glance. Did Rowan need a moment alone? I began edging backward, but Rowan's voice held me in place.

"My entire life they've always fought." He turned back toward us, his face even. "Bad fights. Even in public. Once we were out to dinner and their fighting got so bad that someone called the guards." He shuddered lightly. "I was so relieved on New Year's when they told me they were getting a divorce, because I thought, *Finally. It's over.*

"But it isn't over. They don't live in the same house anymore, but in some ways they're just as connected to each other by anger as they were by marriage. And now I'm always in the middle—I can't get away from it." He gestured toward the car. "They want me to choose who to live with for the school year. That's why all my stuff is packed into Clover. I still don't know which one. Both places sound miserable."

My heart thickened. "Rowan . . . ," I started, but I didn't know where to go from there. Sunlight spilled over him, highlighting all the layers of his sadness. I'd never thought of connection that way—that hatred could be just as binding as love. My chest ached for him.

"I'm so sorry," Ian said. "I didn't know you were going through all this. I would have tried to help."

"You did help; you just didn't know it." Rowan dug the toe of his sneaker into the ground. "I needed someone who knew me outside of my family context. And I'm sorry I kept harping on you guys about your arguing—it just kept triggering me. I know your mom can be hard on you, but you look out for each other, and I can tell your family is the real deal." He looked up, his eyes open and vulnerable. "I just wish I had what you have."

My feet carried me to him, my arm slipping around his back. "Rowan, you do have us. We're here with you, and we'll be here as long as you need us."

Ian flanked his other side, the three of us looking down at the stump. I carefully set a coin down. "My wish is for Rowan," I said, measuring my words. "I wish that Rowan will be happy, and that he'll know he's not alone."

"Me too," Ian said, setting his coin next to mine. "My wish is for Rowan."

Rowan didn't thank us. He didn't have to. Over the past three ridiculous days, Rowan had been carrying us, holding steady through our fights and bitter remarks. This was about thanking him.

Finally, Rowan broke the silence. "I think that helped. Anyone feel like going to Electric Picnic?"

"I guess," I said nonchalantly, and Ian grinned. "I don't really have any other plans."

We were exiting the muddy bank when my phone chimed. Ian stiffened. "Oh, no. Did Walt spill?"

I lifted the screen to my face. It was Olive.

ADDIE, ARE YOU OK? NOW EVERYONE IS TALKING ABOUT CUBBY AND A PHOTO OF YOU.

No. I froze, willing the letters to rearrange, willing the message to mean something other than what it meant. My breath turned shallow, my hands clammy.

Olive's "everyone" was bigger than most people's. She was one of those rare people who managed to fit in with every social group on the high school spectrum, as comfortable with the other soccer players as she was the debate team. If she said everyone, she meant *everyone*.

Ian's face flushed as he studied my expression. "Addie, what? Is it Mom?"

I managed to hand him the phone, and his face tightened as he read the text. "Oh, no."

* * *

I cried for a solid twenty-five minutes. The tears just wouldn't stop coming. Rowan and Ian took turns giving me concerned looks, but I could barely register them.

Everyone knew. *Everyone.*

Worse, what if everyone had seen?

Ian and Rowan kept trying to ask me if I was okay, but I was inside a bubble, completely separate from them.

Finally, Ian put his energy into texting one of his teammates.

"My coach found out, Addie," he said nervously. He was looking at me like I was something brittle. Breakable. Did he not realize I was already shattered?

"How?" My voice didn't sound like mine.

"I don't know how. *I* didn't tell him. Not even when he cornered Cubby and me about what the fight was about. But now he's found out. And . . ."

"And what?" My throat felt stuffed full of cotton. I couldn't even swallow.

Ian's knee ricocheted off the seat. "And there's talk that Cubby will be suspended from the team. Maybe more. It's still just rumors, but I think that's how this thing got out."

This thing.

This thing that was *me*. And my heart, and my *body*, all on display for anyone to throw rocks at. How big was it going to get? How long until Mom found out? Dad? I huddled in the corner of Clover, so miserable that my tears dried up. Both Ian and Rowan tried consoling me, but it was no use. I could already hear the whispers in the hallways. Feel the glances of boys who'd seen more of me than I'd ever show them. Teachers would know. My coaches would know. I wanted to throw up. Especially when my phone started dinging with messages from my teammates, some concerned, some just curious. **Did that really happen?**

Finally, I silenced my phone and stuffed it under Rowan's pile. What else could I do?

* * *

The closer we got to Stradbally, the tighter my body crunched into a ball. I knew we were just about there when traffic turned bumper-to-bumper and small white arrows directed us to a dirt road lit with fairy lights.

We filed slowly onto the fairgrounds in a long parade of cars, people yelling to one another and music pumping loudly from every car stereo. It reminded me of the high school parking lot every morning before the first bell rang. Home suddenly pressed in on me so tightly that I could barely breathe.

"We made it," Rowan said, meeting my eyes. His enthusiasm was a solid 98 percent lower than it should have been. Even Ian looked docile, his body remarkably still.

Ian glanced back at me and then pointed to an open field blooming with makeshift shelters—tents, caravans, teepees—all crammed together like one giant circus. "Pretty cool, right?" he asked, his voice soft. "And think, Lina will be here soon. It will all be better then."

Or worse, I silently added, my stomach twisting. Just a

couple of hours ago I'd felt good about telling Lina, but hearing from everyone back home had changed that.

Names of the designated camping sites glinted in the dimming sunlight. They were all accompanied by cartoon drawings of famous people: Oscar Wilde, Janis Joplin, Andy Warhol, and Jimi Hendrix. A man with a bright red vest ushered us into our parking spot, and Ian sprang out, stretching his arms. "I can't believe we're finally here."

"It does seem like it took us a lot longer than three days to get here," Rowan added. That I had to agree with. The Rainbow's End Hostel and Inch Beach felt like a lifetime ago.

I climbed out too and numbly followed the guys to the will call booth to pick up my ticket. Inside the gates, my first thought was *chaos*. The grounds were packed to the brim, people walking and riding and cruising around in some of the strangest outfits I'd ever seen. Lots of face paint and costumes ranging from leather capes to tutus. And music was everywhere, the separate melodies twisting together into a tight braid. Even the guys looked overwhelmed.

Finally, Ian turned to smile at us. "I say we do a big sweep, take it all in, and figure out where Titletrack is playing. Sound good?" He looked at me hopefully. What he was really saying was, *Let's distract Addie*.

"Sounds great," I said, attempting to match the glimmer

of hope in his voice. I'd been through a lot to get here; the least I could do was try to enjoy it.

Even with the costumes and overcrowding, Electric Picnic started out fairly normal, with all the usual festival ingredients: stages, food stands, eight billion porta-potties, kids screaming on carnival rides, tarot card readers . . . but the longer we walked, the more I began to feel like I'd stepped into a carnival fun house.

The first truly strange sight we stumbled upon was the sunken bus. A bright red double-decker bus angled into the mud, its bottom half almost completely submerged in a ditch. Next was a human jukebox, an elevator-size structure housing an entire band taking requests. Then a trio of college-age guys ran by wearing muddy sumo wrestler costumes.

"Did that just happen?" Rowan asked, watching them in disbelief. The one in the back wore a glittery tutu fastened around his waist.

"Did *that*?" Ian asked as a man rode by on a bicycle made out of a piano.

"I feel like I just fell down a rabbit hole," I said, wishing it were enough to distract me from the phone buzzing in my pocket.

The smell of cinnamon wafted over toward us, and Rowan sniffed the air. "I'm starving. Whatever that is, I want it. Anyone else hungry?"

"Me," I said, surprising myself. Normally, when I was this upset, I had no appetite, but carnival food did sound good. Plus, my mom claimed that most of life's struggles could be cured with butter and sugar. I was willing to give it a try.

"You guys go ahead and eat," Ian offered, pulling his notebook out of his backpack. "I'm going to try to find the stage Titletrack will be performing on. See if I can get some pictures."

"Want me to get you something?" I asked.

"Nah. Meet you back here," Ian hollered, taking off, he and his man bun blending in with the herd of music lovers.

Rowan and I wandered the food trucks, finally settling on a waffle truck that put my waffle attempts to shame. I ordered the Chocolate Cloud—a Belgian waffle drizzled with a mixture of white and dark chocolate—and Rowan ordered the Flying Pig, a combination involving bacon, caramel, and fluffy crème fraîche.

Our order took a long time, and when it was finally ready, we posted up at a mostly empty picnic table and ate slowly, in a silence that I was grateful for. Most people would probably try to talk me out of how bad I was feeling, but not Rowan; he just sat next to me, occasionally offering me bites of bacon. By the time our plates were scraped clean, the day was starting to look worn-out, the edges of the sky taking on a gold hue.

I drummed my fingers on the table. "Where is he?"

"Ian?" Rowan asked, licking some crème off his fingers.

"It's been a while. I thought he'd be back by now." I squinted into the crowd. The direction he'd gone in was dark and fairly empty, clearly not where Titletrack's stage would be.

"Probably lost track of time," Rowan said, leaning in. "I don't know if you know this about your brother, but he gets pretty excited about things he's passionate about."

A snort escaped my nose. "Really? I hadn't noticed."

His dimple appeared. "There it is, Maeve."

"There what is?" I assumed he was pointing out another weird costume, but when I looked up he was studying me.

"Your laugh." He glanced down, fiddling with his napkin. "Hey, Addie, I know what it's like to have the world fall down around you. . . ."

He trailed off, and I clutched my fork, hoping he was about to say something like, *Your friends will suffer from collective amnesia and no one will even remember the photo*, or *I'm actually a time traveler come to save you from your past*, but instead what he said was, "Today is a bad day, but it won't always be this bad. I promise."

I nodded, my eyes fogging up. I knew he was right, of course. Bad things knocked people off their feet all the time, and they got back up and kept moving. But right now I had a mountain in front of me, plus a whole pocketful of texts, and I had no idea how I'd reach the summit.

I shifted at the table, my eyes seconds away from giving the Irish rain a run for its money, but just then Rowan reached over, his hand as warm and comforting as it had been back at Inch Beach. "And what you said back at the fairy ring? About you and Ian standing next to me? That's true for you, too. I know I can't fix this, but I am here for you."

His eyes were earnest behind his glasses, and a pinpoint of calm suddenly dropped into my center, slowly rippling outward. Life could be so unexpected—I was supposed to be eating spaghetti in Italy, yet here I was, finishing up a waffle in the cold drizzle of Ireland, with a new friend I knew I could rely on. "Thanks, Rowan. That means a lot."

Rowan broke eye contact, his hand leaving mine as he looked over my shoulder. "Ian's back."

I stood up quickly, but before I could turn around, a hurricane of curly hair hit me so hard, I almost fell over.

"Lina!" I yelled, and in response she hugged me to the point of asphyxiation, my face planted in her lemon-scented curls. "Lina. I can't breathe," I managed.

"Oops. Sorry." She stumbled backward, and I laughed for no reason other than I was so relieved to see her, I almost couldn't stand it.

"Lina, you look amazing!" I said. She really did. Italy

looked good on her. Her skin was a dark olive color, and instead of her trying to tame her hair the way she always had, it fell loose around her face in bouncing, voluminous curls. Maybe it was the wild familiarity of her hair that got me, but suddenly I was blinking back tears. *Please don't let me start crying within the first few seconds of seeing her.*

"I can't believe I'm here. What *is* this place? Back at the entrance there were two guys running around inside a big rolling plastic ball." Lina stepped back, catching sight of Rowan. "Are you Rowan?"

"That's me," Rowan said, shaking her hand. I waited for him to do the Lina stare. All guys did it—between her hair and her big eyes, she was a lot to take in—but he just smiled politely and then glanced over at me. "I can see why you two are friends. You're both really good at making an entrance."

She grinned and put her arm around me. "We do our best."

Ian suddenly appeared, deep in conversation with a guy roughly Lina's height, a mess of dark, curly hair crowning his face. "Ian found us near the fairy woods," Lina explained.

"Ren?" I asked the curly-haired stranger. His nose was exceptionally Italian, and when he smiled, a small gap between his front teeth instantly put me at ease.

Ren yanked me in for a hug. "So nice to meet you. I've heard things."

I knew what he meant, but I still stiffened slightly. *Not*

those things, I instructed myself. He didn't mean the text messages, or Cubby. But it was too late; panic crept through my center, and suddenly my head spun. Telling Lina had been hypothetical for so long, and now the moment was here.

Of course, Lina zeroed in on my uneasiness. "Addie? Are you okay?"

I'd better just tell her now. Get it over with. I swallowed nervously. "Lina, can we talk in priv—"

"I just found a Titletrack museum in the woods," Ian interrupted, sidling up next to me. "I don't know who made it, but you guys *have* to see it." And before I could protest, he was suddenly dragging Lina and me in the direction he'd come from, Rowan and Ren trailing right behind.

I tried to dig my heels in, but his momentum was too much. "Ian, *stop*. I need to talk to Lina. I need to tell her about . . . ," I trailed off, hoping he'd take the hint.

Instead he sped up, taking us to a jog. "Sorry, but this really can't wait. The concert starts in less than an hour."

Lina's curls were bouncing in time with our pace, and she wrenched her neck back to look at the guys. "Everyone keeping up?"

"Ma certo," Ren answered affirmatively.

And that's when I realized that it wasn't just Ian pulling me along—it was Lina, too. She was just as intent on getting to the museum as Ian was.

"What is going on?" I demanded. "Why are we all running?"

"Just trust us," Lina said, squeezing my arm, and then all four of them looked at me with big Cheshire-cat smiles.

This was officially getting weird.

* * *

Ian finally stopped in a clearing underneath a canopy of decorated trees. Old CDs hung by strips of ribbon, swaying gently in the evening breeze, and fairy lights snaked around tree trunks and branches. A collection of candles sat flickering on an old tree stump that reminded me of the one in the fairy ring.

"What is this?" I asked, stopping in my tracks.

"Sorry, Addie. I know you were really looking forward to a Titletrack museum, but that's not what this is." Ian grinned at me, then turned to Lina. "Did you bring the ceremonial garb?"

"Of course." She unhooked her arm from mine and then dropped her overstuffed backpack to the ground, pulling out four long white pieces of fabric and tossing them to everyone.

I stared as everyone began twisting the fabric into haphazard togas. "Are those sheets? What's going on?"

Ian knotted his over his shoulder. "We're putting on our ceremonial garb."

"What ceremony?"

"And this is for you." Lina pulled a long, plum-colored

shawl from the bottom of her bag and draped it carefully around me, pulling my ponytail out from under it.

I grabbed the bottom edge and held it up to the light. Intricate mandalas swirled through the pattern. "Where have I seen this before?"

"It was my mom's. She wore it to all of her gallery nights; she said it made her feel royal."

My heart quickened. "Lina, this is special. You really want me to wear this?"

"No, I want you to keep it." She straightened the shawl so it sat evenly on my shoulders, and I bit the inside of my cheek, holding back my protest. Every bit of me wanted to refuse the gift, but I couldn't; it was too meaningful. "Thank you," I said, my voice wobbly.

"You're welcome. Now let's go. Attendant?" Lina gestured for Rowan, who quickly moved to my side, escorting me to the twinkling tree stump.

"Rowan, will you tell me what's going on?" I whispered. "Did you know about this?"

His dimple lit up in the twinkling lights. "Sorry, Maeve, but I was sworn to secrecy. What I can tell you is that this is not a Titletrack museum."

Ian gestured to the stump. "Everyone, grab a candle so Addie can stand up there." His hair looked extra tangly, the hood of his sweatshirt poking out over the top of his toga.

I shook my head quickly. "Oh, no. We are not re-creating Au Bohair." The stump was completely entrenched in lights, and even though we were on the edge of the grounds, plenty of festivalgoers still milled around us, a few already stopping to watch.

"Relax. You don't have to say anything. We'll be the ones doing the talking. So climb up," Ian said firmly.

"Why?"

He exhaled loudly. "Can you please not fight me for once? Please?"

It was the extra "please" that got me. I climbed up and then turned to face my friends. They'd formed a half circle around me, their candles casting strange shadows on their faces. It looked like I was about to be initiated into a cult. Or sacrificed. "What is going on?"

They shared a conspiratorial grin. Then Ian nodded at Ren. "Okay, master of ceremonies. Start us out."

Ren cleared his throat and then let loose, his voice booming through the trees. "Ladies and gentlemen. Stradballas and stradballees. We have before us a fair maiden—"

"Ren, don't improvise," Lina interrupted. "Just go with the script. What we talked about."

"Nessun problema." He cleared his throat again. "On this fine summer day, there was a group of people who loved someone and wanted her to know they had her back. And so they

held the first ceremony of Queen Maeve. Here at Stradbally, in full view of many."

"In full view of many" was right. The crowd was growing by the second, no doubt hoping for a show. Ren gestured theatrically, raising his voice to the tops of the trees. "And so, like Queen Maeve of old, we have put her in a high place and will honor her by building her up, one rock at a time."

Suddenly, I noticed a pile of fist-size rocks at their feet, and I realized what this was about. They were re-creating Queen Maeve's growing tomb—the one Rowan had told me about back when he first dubbed me Maeve. "Wait a minute. Whose idea was this?" I asked.

"Ian's," Lina said.

Ian shook his head. "We all get some credit. Rowan gave you the nickname, I came up with the ceremony, Lina brought all the supplies, and Ren is master of ceremonies."

"Ian called me right before we left for the airport," Lina filled in. "I only had fifteen minutes to prepare."

"My mom helped," Ren added. "She has a surprising number of fairy lights at her disposal."

"This is . . ." I bit my lower lip, not sure what to say. My eyes were already burning with tears. "So what do I do?" I managed.

"Just stand there." Ren turned to Lina. "You're up, *principessa*."

Lina picked up the rock closest to her, stumbling on her toga as she stepped forward.

"A good friend is like a four-leaf clover. Hard to find, lucky to have." She paused, weighing the rock in her hand. "I didn't make that up. I saw it on a T-shirt at the airport." She turned slightly, addressing the group. "For those of you who don't know, my mom died last year. Her illness was very sudden, and it took her much too fast." Her voice trembled, but she looked up, locking her eyes on mine and lowering her voice a bit. "Remember right at the end, when my mom couldn't breathe on her own anymore and they knew it was only going to be a few hours?"

I nodded. The memory was etched into my mind. I would never forget answering that phone call. Lina had been crying so hard that I couldn't understand her. All I knew was that I had to get to the hospital. Fast. The old familiar clamp moved over my throat.

Lina exhaled, making the flame on her candle jump. "It was four in the morning, and even though I'd known this was coming, I suddenly felt like it was all brand-new. Like the diagnosis and treatments and everything had just been some elaborate joke. My grandma was there—she was crying so hard, and my mom was hooked up to all these monitors. It was the first moment that I truly understood that I was going to lose her." Tears were running down her face, but she didn't bother to wipe them away. Ren slipped his hand onto her back. "But do you know what I remember most about that night?"

I shook my head, not trusting my voice.

"You. Less than ten minutes after I called you, you came running down the hallway to her room. All the nurses were yelling at you to stop, but you didn't care—you just came running straight up to me. And you'd left your house so fast, you hadn't even put on your shoes." She paused, her eyes glittering. "That's what I'll always remember. You running barefoot down the hall, the nurses yelling as they chased after you. That's who you really are, and I'll never forget that when I needed you the most, you literally didn't wait a single second. You just showed up." She stepped forward, placing the rock at the base of the stump. "All hail Queen Maeve. My best and fastest friend."

We were both crying, tears washing down our cheeks. I'd never considered that that terrible night could hold something other than just pain. Something that Lina would carry with her as a comfort.

"Me next." Ren picked up a rock and stepped forward, squeezing Lina's shoulder. "Has everyone tried Starbursts?"

The abrupt shift in subject made me laugh. There was some general nodding, most of it from outside our circle, and I kept my eyes on Ren, trying not to notice that the crowd was now three people deep. Lina had once confided in me that Ren had the kind of looks that grew on you—the longer you knew him, the cuter he got. I suddenly saw exactly what she meant.

He continued. "Well, I love Starbursts. Whenever I'm in the States, I eat them nonstop. And you know how there's a social order to them? Like you dump out a bag and you eat all the pinks first, then the reds and oranges, leaving the yellows for when you're really desperate?"

Where was he going with this? I glanced at Lina, but she just smiled.

"Anyway, the point is, Addie, you're a pink. Everyone knows you're a pink. Actually, scratch that. You're next-level. You're that limited-edition kind that had all pinks. And I know that because when Lina needed you, you were there." He set his rock down. "All hail Queen Maeve. The pinkest of pink Starbursts."

"Thanks, Ren," I whispered. My body didn't seem to know how to handle what was happening. Laugh? Cry? Enjoy? I was going to go with enjoy.

Next, Rowan stepped forward, his rock resting by his side. The stump made us almost eye-level, but he didn't meet my gaze, and his nervousness wafted onto me. My heart began pounding even harder.

He exhaled. "Okay. Pink Starburst is always tough to follow, but here goes." He rocked anxiously on his feet, a move that looked Ian-inspired. "Three days ago, I was sitting in my broken-down, crappy car when I saw this girl tackle her brother in a parking lot. I thought she was surprising. And different. So I talked her brother into letting her come with us, which ended up completely ruining her plans." He looked up guiltily, shuffling his feet.

"But then the next three days were incredible, because I found out she was more than just feisty. She was smart. And loyal. And completely incapable of dressing weather-appropriate. And we talked about things I'd never talked about with anyone. And even when our car flooded, and we got chased by guard dogs . . . I just kept thinking, *I wish this week would never end.*"

He lifted his chin, looking me straight in the eye. "And I wanted to tell you that you don't need that guy back home. You don't need anyone, unless you want them. You're enough all on your own. You're more than enough. You're Maeve."

A warm, peaceful feeling settled on my shoulders, light as a second shawl. This was the thing that I'd lost track of this summer. That being chosen—or not chosen—was not the thing that made me valuable. I was valuable regardless. I was enough, all on my own. I wanted to climb down and rest my head on his shoulder, but instead I just ducked my head. "Thank you, Rowan," I whispered.

"You're welcome. All hail Queen Maeve." He bent to lower the rock, softening his voice so only I could hear. "I wish I didn't have to say good-bye to you tomorrow."

"Me neither," I whispered back.

Lina met my eye gleefully over the top of Rowan's head, unable to contain her smile. I smiled back.

Rowan returned to his place, and Ian stepped forward, holding up his candle to his open notebook, a string of words marching across the page. He'd prepared something. I straightened up.

"You know that question Mr. Hummel likes to ask at the beginning of the semester? 'If a tree falls in the forest and no one is around to hear it, does it make a sound?'"

I nodded. It was one of those problems designed to make your brain run in circles.

His candle bobbed. "Well, the first time I heard that question it made me think of you. Because my whole life it's felt like unless you were there—helping me blow out my birthday candles, cheering me on in the stands, out on our field trips—whatever I did didn't actually matter. That it didn't count. You're the only person who knows my whole life—who's been there with me through everything. Which makes you my life's witness." He lowered his notebook to his side. "So what's the answer? If a tree falls in a forest and your little sister isn't there to hear it, did it make a sound? I'm not really sure. I'm just glad we're in the same forest." He set his rock down, then stepped back with the others. "All hail Queen Maeve, my best and oldest friend."

Tears puddled under my chin, and I stood looking at Ian,

his eyes forming a shiny mirror, reflecting all the things he saw in me. Then one more voice chimed in, this one in my mind. *What about you, buttercup? What do you see in yourself?*

I looked hard. I saw a lot of things: bravery, compassion, perseverance, insecurity, even fear. But rising out of all of it, I saw Maeve. Her hair shone, and she held a shield, her throne solid behind her. And suddenly it was me on the throne—my robe thick and soft around me.

The upcoming year was going to be hard, no doubt about it. And maybe even the year after it. But I was strong enough. And brave enough. I was Maeve, and I was going to make it.

I jumped off the stump and let my friends encircle me in a warm, tight cocoon.

* * *

Everyone who wasn't already on the lawn in front of Titletrack's stage was headed there, streaming from every possible crevice. It wasn't just our main event—it was everyone's main event.

A muffled, faraway noise sounded over a loudspeaker, instigating a dull roar from the crowd and making us all quicken our pace. Ian bounded ahead, his toga trailing in the mud. None of us had bothered to change out of our ceremonial garb; there wasn't time. It actually made us fit in more with the rest of the festivalgoers.

"I'm going to find us a spot." Ian disappeared into the crowd.

"I hope we can find him when we get there." I held tightly to Rowan's hand, partially to keep us from getting separated and partially because once the group hug had ended, it had just happened. I couldn't get over the way our hands fit together. Like they'd been sitting on opposite ends of the globe just waiting for the chance to meet.

The crowd was turning brutal, bordering on absurd. We'd just survived a near-collision with a man on a bike wearing a peacock costume when a high-pitched choking noise that sounded vaguely like *oh, no* erupted from behind me.

"Lina, what's wrong?" Ren asked.

"Addie." Lina put her hand on my back, her voice still choked. I turned to meet her wide eyes, but instead got snagged on something moving rocket-fast toward me through the crowd. Was that . . . ?

It was.

The rocket was my mother.

"Oh, no," I choked, echoing Lina. *Run*, my brain advised, but even in my panicked state I knew that was a terrible idea. Running would just mean pursuit.

My mom was next to me in a matter of milliseconds. "Hello, Addison. Lina." Her pitch had reached new and terrifying depths. "You'd better start talking. Fast."

"How did you . . . find us?" I stammered.

The answer to my question appeared to her left. Walter. Followed swiftly by Archie, who held a massive bag of cotton candy. "Walter, you told her?" I yelled.

He held his hands up in protest. "It wasn't me. It was Archie. He got the secret out of me, and then he told Mom."

"Hey!" Archie tried to hit Walter in the face with his cotton candy, but my mom grabbed it midswing. "Don't blame it on me."

"No more talking." Mom turned back to me, her face set in a hard stare. Not many people knew this, but back in her college days she'd been one of the top roller derby contenders in the state. It was times like this that I knew exactly why she'd skated under the name Medusa Damage.

"Addison, you are supposed to be in Italy. *Italy.*" While I fumbled for an answer, she turned to Lina. "Does Howard know you're here?"

"Rowan, go warn Ian!" I whispered, taking advantage of the momentary distraction. He nodded and then sprinted into the crowd, no doubt thrilled to escape Medusa.

Lina nodded, her head bobbing one too many times. "Nice to see you, Mrs. Bennett. And yes, he does know. He booked my ticket." She shoved Ren forward a few unwilling inches. "This is my boyfriend, Ren."

"Hello there," Ren managed. "Really great to meet you."

He withered under her gaze, and I jumped to the rescue. "Mom, I can explain. This concert is really important to Ian—"

She lifted her hand angrily, silencing me. "Where is Ian?"

Now what? The last thing I wanted to do was unleash Mom on Ian. What if she didn't let him see the concert? "Um . . . I'm not really sure."

"Boys!" My mom snapped her fingers, and Archie and Walt jumped to attention. "You two are the tallest people in this crowd. Find him."

Walt stood on his tiptoes, craning his neck over the crowd, and Archie ran over to a music speaker and began climbing.

"Yeah, I don't think that's allowed," Lina said, just as a security guard made a beeline for him.

"Man bun in a white toga. Straight ahead," Archie shouted as the security guard dragged him back to ground level.

"Why are you guys wearing togas anyway?" Walter asked.

Suddenly, a loud cheer erupted in the distance, followed by a jangling strain of music. My heart somersaulted. "Mom, the concert is starting. I don't have time to explain why, but this is the most important thing that has ever happened to Ian. You have to let him see it."

My intensity caught even me off guard. Catarina would be proud. *Rule number four: Be passionate. No one can argue with passion.*

My mom stepped back slightly, her perfectly shaped eyebrows lifting. "Sounds like you two are getting along again."

I nodded. "Better than ever."

She hesitated, then gestured to Archie and Walter. "Everyone, follow me." Needless to say, we all complied.

Even though Rowan had provided him with a few minutes of warning, the sight of our approaching mother drained all the blood from Ian's face. "Mom," he choked. It was the only way either of us could seem to greet her.

"Ian," she said coolly. "There are a lot of things I want to say to you right now, but your sister claims that this is the most important thing in the world to you. So I'm giving you tonight." She pointed one finger at his chest. "But after the concert? You will both undergo extensive questioning and will most likely be grounded for the rest of your lives. Understood?"

"Understood. Thank you, ma'am," Ian said, shooting me a grateful look. In our family, "ma'am" was code for *I know you're going to pummel me into a fine pulp, and I respect you for that*. My mom nodded approvingly.

Rowan stepped forward, wringing his hands nervously. "Mrs. Bennett? I'm Rowan. Nice to meet you."

She tilted her head. "Ah. The Irish tutor."

"He's my friend," Ian said.

"And mine," I added.

"So then tell me, friend Rowan, why are we standing here when Titletrack is about to perform onstage, all the way up there?" She lifted her chin toward the front of the writhing mass of bodies. "How are we going to even see?"

"That is a problem," Rowan said. "We probably should have arrived a lot earlier. Like, yesterday."

Ian bit his lower lip, his face clouding, and defiance rose in me. *Oh, no.* I had not been through everything I'd been through just to stand at the back of a concert watching my brother crumple into a ball of disappointment.

But before I could come up with a solution, my mom clapped her hands together. "All right, people. Form a chain. We're going in."

"Going in where?" Ian asked. "Those people look like they've been here all week."

"Ian, don't argue with me. For all you know this is your last living act, so you might as well enjoy it." A glimmer sparkled in her eye as she surveyed the crowd, and suddenly I remembered the stash of vintage records she'd kept in the attic for as long as I could remember. The proverbial apple had not fallen far from the tree.

"Do I need to speak louder?" she asked when none of us moved. "Form a chain."

All the non-Bennetts went wide-eyed with disbelief as we obediently grabbed one another's hands.

"Ready?" Mom turned resolutely to the wall of people in front of her, Medusa Damage revealing herself in all her terrifying splendor. "COMING THROUGH."

"Hey, watch it!" a guy in a blue hat yelled at her as she jammed her elbow into him.

"No, *you* watch it," she snapped. "I'm about to ground these children for the rest of their underage lives because of this concert. The least they can do is enjoy it."

"Damn," Blue Hat's friend said. "Carry on."

"Has anyone ever told you that you're your mother?" Rowan whispered, his hand tight in mine. "I don't know who's scarier, Maeve or Mother of Maeve."

"I'm going to take that as a compliment," I whispered back.

It took us nearly the entire opening act, but my mother and her elbows managed to get us near the front, even clearing out a small pocket of space for us to stand all together. Once she stopped assaulting them, people sealed in, cinching us tightly together.

"Mom, that was amazing," Ian said, his face rapturous. "Thank you."

"I'm not saying you're welcome, because that would sound like I'm condoning this," she snapped. But the glint was still in her eye.

I did my best to settle into the crowd. My entire body felt bruised and sticky from colliding with so many Titletrack fans. Everyone was sweating. The temperature inside the crowd was at least ten degrees higher than on the outskirts.

Laser lights spilled over the stage, bathing us in bright red, and then four silhouettes appeared onstage as if by magic.

"That's them!" Ian shouted, grabbing my arm as tightly as a tourniquet. "Rowan! Addie! That's them!"

"Ian, ease up!" I yelled, but my voice got sucked up into the vortex of screaming.

The first chords started up, and I recognized the song immediately. "Classic." The one that had been made into a music video at the Burren. At first Ian looked too stunned to react, and then instead of smiling, a large tear zigzagged down his red-lit cheek. "What's wrong?" I shouted.

He squeezed my arm again, his fingernails forming half-moons in my skin. "We're here," he said simply.

The rest of the band joined in with the song, filling my ears and anchoring me to Ian and this moment. And suddenly I was thinking about a different aspect of my future. In one year, my big brother would leave for college, and we'd be separated for the first time. What would life be like without Ian by my side?

I tried to picture it, but the only thing that sprang to mind was the road we'd followed to Electric Picnic, Ian singing along to Titletrack, Ireland green and mysterious outside our windows.

The only thing I really knew was what I had to do next.

Before I could lose my moment of certainty, I reached across Ian, tugging gently at my mom's sleeve. "Mom, after the concert is over, I need to tell you something. Something important." She swiveled her gaze from the stage just as Ian reached down to squeeze my hand.

The road narrowed and then got wider, then disappeared into the distance, too far for me to see what was ahead. And I just let it.

You've come a long way, pet. Pettest of pets. You can't imagine the pride that's swelling up in my considerable bosom right at this moment to know that you have not only explored the Emerald Isle, but your broken heart is now MENDED. You are completely better, over-the-moon, one-door-closes-ten-more-open, beauty-in-the-pain better.

Right?

Right?

Let's cut the crap, pet. Because now that we're reaching the end of our time together, I feel it's time for me to come clean. I don't want that heart of yours to mend. And I never did.

What? Was she actually evil this whole time? No, pet. Heavens, no. Stick with me for a moment.

Do you know what I love most about humans, pet? It's our utter, dogged stupidity. When it comes to love, we never learn. Ever. Even when we know the risks. Even when it makes much more sense to relocate to individualized climate-controlled caves where our hearts have at least a fighting chance at remaining intact. We know the risks of opening our hearts up, and yet we keep doing it anyway.

We keep falling in love and having babies and buying shoes that look incredible but feel like death. We keep adopting puppies and making friends and buying white sofas that we know we're going to drop a slice of pizza facedown on. We just keep doing it.

Is it ignorance? Amnesia? Or is it something else? Something braver?

You opened this book because your heart was broken and you wanted it fixed. But that was never the cosmic plan. Hell, it was never *my* plan. Hearts break open until they stay open. It's what they were made to do. The pain? It's part of the deal. A small exchange for the wild, joyful mess you'll be handed in return.

I hate good-byes, so instead, allow me to hand you one last thought, a small Irish charm to clip to your charm bracelet. Did you know that each leaf on a clover stands for something? They do, pet. Faith, hope, and love. And should you happen to find one with four leaves? Well, that's the one that stands for luck. So, my love, I wish you all of those things. Faith, hope, love, and luck. But mostly, I wish you love. It's its own form of luck.

—Excerpt from *Ireland for the Heartbroken: An Unconventional Guide to the Emerald Isle, third edition*

Epilogue

IAN PULLED SMOOTHLY INTO A PARKING SPOT, TURNING off the ignition but leaving the music on. It was Titletrack, of course. Ever since we'd gotten home we'd been playing it non-stop, the songs overlapping in the hallway between our bedrooms, sometimes competing, sometimes meshing together. It had made a hard week a lot more bearable.

There had been a lot of upset. I'd wanted everything out in the open, so as soon as everyone was reunited, I called for a family meeting, where I laid it all out. My brothers had to be forcibly held back from storming Cubby's house, and my dad was silent and teary for a terrible ten minutes, but they'd all stood by me. And one glimmer of benefit: my news had paved the way for Ian's. His quitting football was just a firework next to my atomic bomb.

I flipped down the visor to check out the dark rings under my eyes. Jet lag combined with nerves had made for a lot of sleepless nights. Last night I'd ended up calling Rowan and staying on the phone until two a.m. watching a terrible movie he'd found on YouTube about a Celtic warrior princess named Maeve, who slashed everyone who got in her way. I think he was trying to pump me up.

Ian lowered the volume. "So, Christmas, huh?"

My cheeks warmed. I swear he could read my thoughts sometimes. "What about it?"

"A certain Irishman told me there are only sixty-eight days until his Christmas break starts. We're good friends and all, but that countdown has nothing to do with me. It's about you."

"Stop. Now." Just like I'd thought, once the situation had been ironed out, my mom and Rowan had bonded almost instantaneously. And now he was coming to visit. Every time I thought about seeing him again, a small, careful butterfly fluttered its wings in the center of my chest.

We looked out the windshield, neither of us in a hurry to leave the car. Was it just me, or had the student body magically tripled? For a second my vision tilted. How many of them know about my photo?

Probably a lot of them.

"Maeve, you ready?" Ian finally asked, the sound of his drumming fingers breaking through my thoughts.

"Yes," I said, sounding surer than I felt. *Act in control.*

"Don't worry, Addie. I'm here for you," he said, like he

hadn't heard me. "I'm going to walk you to all your classes. I already checked your schedule. My homeroom is in B hall and yours is in C, so meet me at the front office. And if anyone says anything to you, you tell them—"

"Ian, I've got this," I said more forcefully. "We just survived a road trip across Ireland in a broken-down car. I think I can handle walking into high school."

"Okay." Ian went back to drumming, his eyes serious. "I know you've got this, but if there's ever a moment when you don't, you've got me. And it doesn't matter what anyone else says. You're Maeve."

"I'm Maeve," I repeated, allowing the nervousness in his voice to extinguish mine. Was it possible that he was more worried for me than I was worried for me? I leaned on that feeling.

Outside, we pulled on our backpacks. Mine was extra heavy, because along with my textbooks, it had rocks in it. Four of them to be exact. It had been a last-minute call, but I liked the way their weight pressed into my shoulders, grounding my feet into my sneakers, my sneakers into the ground. Plus, TSA had had a complete fit about my traveling with them. I might as well put them to use.

We started across the parking lot, Ian sweeping the crowd anxiously.

"Ian, relax." I broke into a jog and fell into step beside him.

"I'm completely relaxed," he protested, but a clump of

hair found its way into his mouth. That habit, unfortunately, looked like it was here to stay. We reached the bank of doors, and he stopped, ignoring the crush of students as he rocked nervously onto his heels. "Ready, Maeve?"

It was a good question. Was I ready?

This summer had shown me that I was a lot of things. I was messy, impulsive, occasionally insecure, and sometimes I did things that I regretted—things I couldn't undo. Like not listening to my brother. Or handing over my heart to someone who couldn't be trusted with it. But despite all those things—no, *alongside* all those things—I was Maeve. Which meant that regardless of how ready I did or did not feel, I was going in anyway. This was my life, after all.

You'll do it, buttercup. You really will.

"I'm ready," I said firmly. I looked into Ian's blue eyes, gathering one last shot of courage. Then we grabbed the door handles and pushed in. Together.

Acknowledgments

Nicole Ellul and Fiona Simpson. Did you all get that? NICOLE ELLUL AND FIONA SIMPSON. The timing of this book was just a hair shy of cataclysmic, and there were many, many moments when you threw me on your backs and carried me. Thank you for your graciousness, support, wisdom, and overall awesomeness. I consider you the Goddesses of Editing. (Would it be embarrassing if I had crowns made?)

Mara Anastas. Thank you for your patience, support, and enthusiasm. I dream of having Mara energy.

Simon Pulse. You are an exceptional group of people sending exceptional books out into the world, and it is a PRIVILEGE to publish with you. *Thank you.*

Sam. Somewhere in the tornado of 2016/2017, you marched up to me and said, "Mama, I see you. And I *like* you." Not only did that line inspire a major theme of this book, but it also struck me as one of the most profound things one person can say to another. To be seen in your messy hair in your messy kitchen, by a very small and very honest person, and be deemed *likable*? It's the entire point. I see you, Sammy. And man, do I ever like you.

Nora Jane. Every second you're here makes the world better. I could compare you to a pink frosted cupcake or a perfect chocolate éclair, but that would be silly. You're a little girl, not a confection! (Although it's easy to see why one would make the mistake.) Thank you for sharing your baby years with *Love & Luck*. And I cannot even begin to tell you how much it thrills me that 90 percent of your tantrums involve wanting to be read to. I love you, Bertie Blue.

Liss. Have I ever told you that you are in my top five women I look up to? You are. Sometimes when the world gets scary, I square my shoulders and march in, attempting that unique Liss combination of simultaneously loving hard and not giving a damn, which is exactly what I've watched you do for the past twenty years. Thank you for keeping me on track.

Ali Fife. This is where I should thank you for dropping everything to spend seventy-two hours on an Irish road listening to me attempt to swear, but I'm going to skip that and talk about another day. It was also in the 2016/2017 haze. Life had been uphill for such a tremendously long time, and

I was worn out in every possible way a person could be worn out. I found myself literally lying on the floor, with no idea how I was going to get up off it. And who walked through my door? You. I didn't even have to call. You just showed up, surveyed the mess my life was in, and *stayed*. For several days. Who does that? You. Thank you for doing that for me.

The women in my postpartum depression support group at the Healing Group. Even if I never run into any of you again, I will never, ever forget that rock-bottom morning when you surrounded me and gave me the strength I needed to walk out of the room and face being a mother for one more day. Thank you.

Mary Stanley. For providing wisdom and irreverence and large boxes of tissues. Also, for being the first person to whom I ever said the words "I am an artist."

The Children's Center. For giving me hope when mine had run out.

Preschool Moms Gone Wild. The friends I didn't know I needed until we crash-landed at the same picnic table. Thanks for making Motherhood 2.0 less lonely, and for making me laugh harder than just about anyone. I think you are all divine. (When are we getting our tattoos?)

Andrew Herbst. For knowing things about cars and patiently coming up with ways for me to ruin them. (Hey, we've been friends for a long time now!)

Eli Zeger. The inspiration for Indie Ian and his articles. Thanks for the phone call. You are *such* a good writer—I can't wait to see where your talent takes you. Everyone, look him up on Twitter, @elizeger.

Roisin & Ross. I think the flight attendant who switched our seats was acting under divine influence. Thank you for teaching me the ways of Irish teens and for being so eager to help! Also . . . congratuations on your engagement!

The Army of Nannies. Dana Snell, Hannah Williams, Sarah Adamson, and Malia Helbling. Thank you for carrying my babies when my arms weren't enough.

My family. Rick, Keri, Ally, Abi, Brit, McKenna, Michael. Thank you all for showing up in your own ways. I am so blessed.

DAVID. My love, my peace, my strength. For a year and a half, we had an ongoing conversation that consisted of me saying, "I can't—this is too much," and you responding with, "You can—this is what you're here for." You are *far* more than I deserve, and I'm hanging on tightly to you anyway.

And this last one's just for me, but it needs to be here. Thank you to the little girl on the raft. New deal: you lead, I follow. I can't wait to see where we go next.

Travel to Greece in Jenna Evans Welch's next romantic adventure!

All that Liv remembers about her estranged father is their shared love for the lost city of Atlantis. So when Liv suddenly receives a postcard from her father explaining that *National Geographic* is funding a documentary about his theories on Atlantis, Liv jumps at the opportunity to fly out to Greece and help.

But when she arrives to gorgeous Santorini, things are a little . . . tense. Yet Liv doesn't want anything to get in the way of a possible reconciliation with her dad. She also doesn't want Theo—her father's charismatic protégé—to witness her struggle.

And that means diving into Santorini's beautiful sunsets, hidden caves, and delicious cuisine. But not everything on the Greek island is as perfect as it seems as Liv begins to discover that her father may not have invited her to Greece for Atlantis, but for something much more important.

Read on for a sneak peek at Jenna Evans Welch's highly anticipated new novel!

THE VILLAGE OF OIA MANAGED TO SIMULTANEOUSLY look exactly like all the photos I'd seen online, and not like them at all, because photos just couldn't do it justice. The village felt grittier and prettier and smaller, and somehow even more charming than still images could capture. Or at least, that's the impression I was getting; I was mostly trying to keep my eyes on whatever scrap of Theo was still in my view, and that wasn't easy.

At first Oia all looked the same. The buildings all had a similar theme—low, white, and angular—but as we ran through the narrow corridors, the buildings began to distinguish themselves. We passed a small church with blue candy-striped poles out front, and then a grocery store full of things that I vaguely remembered my dad buying from the grocery stores in Chicago's Greektown: soft nougat, canned octopus, sun-dried figs, sesame bars, and jars of Nutella.

Tourist shops displayed their wares on open patios, everything from stuffed donkeys to original artwork. But most of all there was *white*. The buildings, churches, and walkways all glowed a stark white in the late evening sunlight, broken up by the occasional bursts of fuchsia bougainvillea flowers and the bright blue of Greek flags. There were no cars in Oia, and that was a good thing, because there were so many people.

Pedestrians—tourists, judging from their rapturous gazes—clogged up nearly every inch of walking room. Half of them were dressed stylishly in flowing dresses and summer suits, and the rest looked like they'd just climbed off the beach. They moved in slow, dazed clumps, cameras in hand, stopping to take photos of small churches and charming doorways and stepping over all the shaggy lumps of dogs lounging inconveniently in the middle of the sidewalks. They were unbelievably annoying—the people, I mean; the dogs, I wanted to scoop up and carry to wherever we were going—but I would be taking photos and staring too, if I weren't desperately trying not to get left behind.

Theo dodged down streets and careened up steps while I ran behind him, my sandals slippery on the marble walkway, my backpack bouncing heavily. And finally, *finally*, right at the moment when I felt like my heart might explode, Theo skidded to a halt. I attempted to stop, but my sandals were no match for the worn-down marble, and Theo caught me by the upper arm to keep me upright. I was a sweaty mess and was breathing like I was making a jailbreak.

"Welcome to Atlantis," Theo said.

"Atlantis?" I wheezed. This was the most exercise I'd had in . . . ever. I turned slowly, taking in this new set of surroundings. We'd run to what had to be the west side of the island and were now just a stone's throw away from the edge of the cliffs. The caldera—the bowl-shaped bay partially enclosed by the island—spread bold and glittery below us, a much smaller island bobbing in its center like a heavy rubber duck. To our left the rest of Santorini curved around into a backward *C*, and to our right the marble path extended a tad more, ending in what looked like the ruins of a castle. We were at the very top of Santorini, but it felt like we were on top of the world. No wonder this place was so crowded. *Welcome to Atlantis.*

I turned back to Theo. He didn't seem at all out of breath, just sort of glowy and healthy looking. "You mean because Santorini is the origin of the Atlantis myth?" I asked, finally catching my breath.

"Myth?" He squinted at me in amusement. "No, welcome to Atlantis *Bookstore*."

He pointed, and suddenly I became aware of a spit of a building sitting right in front of all that spectacular view. Not just any building—a *bookstore*. It was tiny, maybe about as wide as my bedroom back home, and looked like it had been carved into existing rock, its facade dominated by two whitewashed staircases, one leading up toward an open terrace overlooking the ocean, and another leading down to an arched entryway flanked by shuttered windows. Murals of books colored the external walls, and every possible nook and cranny was stuffed with shelves and books and quirky hand-lettered signs, all in English. CAT FOR RENT, 25 CENTS. And DINOSAURS DIDN'T READ, AND NOW THEY'RE EXTINCT. COINCIDENCE? An excellent, excellent point.

The mishmash of color and images and writing gave the whole bookstore the appearance of a life-size collage.

And then above the door, painted in gold and in handwriting I would have recognized anywhere:

WELCOME TO
ATLANTIS BOOKS.

WHAT WAS LOST IS NOW FOUND.

(Open Daily from First Coffee to Sunset)

The force of that handwriting knocked the breath out of me. Before I could stop myself, I hurried over and reached out to touch the letters, feeling the rough texture of the building under my fingertips. Underneath the words was a hand-painted map of Santorini—a shape I could have drawn in my sleep. And yes, I'd inherited drawing from my dad. I just didn't like to acknowledge that very often.

I looked up at the writing again. *What was lost is now found.* My breath caught in my throat. Was it that easy?

"First impression?" Theo said, his voice muffled. I turned to see he had the video camera out again, zoomed in way too close on me.

"Not again," I said, attempting to dodge out of the camera's view. If I had my back to the writing on the wall, then it didn't hurt as much.

Theo kept the camera trained on me, entirely unfazed. "Remind you of anyone?"

"Are you really asking me that?" I folded my arms self-consciously. With a camera on me, I had no idea where to put my hands or where to look. Besides, it was a question that obviously didn't need answering. The bookstore was whimsical and weird and so charming it sucked the breath straight out of you. This was the brick-and-mortar version of my dad. And by that, I mean it was sending me into spirals of panic.

I wanted to demand that Theo stop filming me, but instead I pointed to the bookstore's door. "Is he in there?"

"Yes, just give me a minute to prepare." Theo set his camera on the ground, fiddled with it for a moment, and then aimed it at me again. “Ready. I’ll stand here while you knock.”

He had to be joking. But when I turned to look at him the camera’s RECORD light was on, and he gave me a thumbs-up over the top of it. “Ready,” he said.

“Theo, *no*. This is not happening.” I tried to dart away, but several tourists on the walkway had taken notice of the camera, and now a small congestion of people blocked my escape.

“What do you mean?”

I hurried up next to him. “You aren’t *filming* our reunion.” It wasn’t a crowd exactly, but the knot of people standing behind Theo was starting to make me feel dizzy. “What are you, my paparazzi?”

“Paparazzo,” he corrected. “Olive, this is an important moment. You said it yourself. You haven’t seen him since you were eight.”

“*Liv*,” I reminded him. My voice was beginning to sound panicked.

“It’s important for the story,” he said.

So far, he hadn’t said the name Liv once. “This isn’t a *story*; this is me seeing my dad.”

“Everything’s a story. And you’re going to want this, believe me.” He adjusted his camera lens and moved in closer. “Okay, I’m ready. You go knock.”

“What? I’m not staging this—” But before I could fully

panic, there was fumbling at the door, and then there was no time. My breath came in hot and quick, a rushing filled my ears, and then the door flew open and . . .

Not my dad.

Not unless he'd aged a lifetime since I'd seen him last.

The man was bright-eyed and well dressed, with wrinkled cheeks, thinning hair combed carefully to the side, and this sort of overall dapperness that made me think of the Frank Sinatra vinyl record covers James had displayed on the wall in his home office. The man had the same thick eyebrows and large eyes that Theo had, and he was holding a small cake covered in white frosting petals.

"Kalispera!" I wasn't sure if I was relieved or disappointed. Was my dad ever going to show up?

"*Kalispera*," I said back. I'd said that word all the time as a child, but today it felt thick and too heavy on my tongue. *Good evening.*

The man let off a string of Greek, losing me instantly, and Theo answered, gesticulating toward me. The only thing I understood was *Olive.*

"Olive, this is my grandfather, but you can call him Papou—everyone does." He said it from behind his camera, which was still firmly aimed at me. "He wants me to tell you that he knows 'some' English. Proceed with caution."

Papou beamed at me, and I felt the full awkwardness of

the situation. “It’s nice to meet you, Papou,” I said uncertainly.

“Beautiful! Welcome to Santorini!” Papou yelled, jabbing one of his meaty fingers at me enthusiastically.

He was massively likable. “Thank you,” I said, trying to return a smile that was half as friendly as his. “That’s a beautiful cake.”

Papou scrunched up his face, and Theo translated, which earned me a dazzling Papou smile. Like grandfather, like grandson. Papou raised the cake toward me in a toast.

“Theo? Theo, is it you?” Suddenly the entrance was rushed by another person, and then there were two of them crowding the door.

Also not my father.

Most *definitely* not my father.

The woman was short and curvy, with golden-brown skin and dark hair pulled up into a topknot, with thick bangs fringing her dark eyes. She wore a vintage pair of dad-style Levi’s that had been cuffed at the ankles, a faded Rolling Stones T-shirt, no shoes, and a red lipstick the exact shade of firehouses and Red Hots candies. I was immediately obsessed with her.

“Olive!” she shouted, spreading her arms wide. “Welcome to Atlantis! I can’t tell you how happy I am to finally meet you.” Her voice was deep and throaty, and her accent was so similar to my father’s that my homesickness snowballed into something much bigger and more hollow-feeling. Longing? Pain?

"Call me Liv," I croaked.

She hurried up the stairs and gave my outfit a quick once-over. "Iconic," she breathed. "You have perfected the art of French makeup, my little Greek trickster! And I should know. I spent ten years in Paris."

Gulp. It was like she could see straight through me.

"Olive, this is my mother, Ana," Theo said from his camera.

"Your m-mother?" I stammered. Ana looked too young to be anyone's mother, much less Theo's. But now that he'd said it, I suddenly saw their matching big eyes and lips. "It's nice to meet you. Is my dad . . . ?" *Here? Ever going to show up*? I wasn't sure what to say. Luckily, Ana jumped in.

"Of course. Your father just stepped away to—" Ana caught sight of Theo's camera, and her expression turned sour. "Theo! Respect! I told you not to—" She finished her sentence in Greek, her tone sharp.

Theo half-heartedly lowered the camera, but it was up again the second she turned around. But whatever she said didn't have any impact on Theo, because the camera stayed firmly in my personal-space bubble, and Ana must have been fully aware of his stubbornness because she didn't push it.

"Olive, we must get you to the roof for your surprise.

Hurry, please. And I will meet you there." She rattled off something to Theo and he nodded; then she hurried back down the steps to the bookstore.

Finally, Theo dropped the camera to his side. His eyes were bright with excitement, just like his mom's, and without any consent on my part, my stomach twisted with excitement too. I knew my dad's surprises. Whatever this was, I knew it would be a big deal.

"They want you to close your eyes. I'm going to guide you up." Theo's voice was authoritative, this time not giving me a choice. I put my hand tentatively in his and he grinned, flipping my hand over to inspect my cuticles. "You bite your fingernails, just like your dad does."

"I don't," I said, pulling my hand back. Olive had been a consummate nail-biter; Liv was not. But when I inspected my nails, I saw that he was right. I'd chewed them to bits. When? On the plane?

"Is my dad up there?" I asked.

"No. Your hand, please, Olive," Theo said.

"Liv." I sighed, but it was entirely without hope. I put my hand in his, and once Theo was convinced that my eyes were closed, he led me stumbling up the terrace steps (was this really necessary?), walked me a few paces, and then turned me until I felt the breeze from the ocean wafting up the cliffs. Footsteps started up behind me, and my heart quickened until I heard Ana's voice. "Where is Nico? We can't wait any longer."

"Let's begin," Theo said to her. Then his voice was near my ear, sending a tickle down my spine. "Ready for your surprise? Open your eyes."

I opened my eyes, with no idea what to expect, and what I saw—

Well, it delivered.

The top level of the bookstore was a rooftop patio about the size of our dining room, with just a short ledge separating it from the cliff and the sprawling vastness of the caldera. Bookshelves lined the patio's perimeter, and strings of light bulbs snaked around and between them. Jewel-toned cushions lay scattered under a small wooden pergola, and flowers and plants blossomed from repurposed tomato cans all along the ledge. But all of that paled in comparison to what was happening just over the ocean.

While I'd been taking in the bookstore and Theo's family, the sun had dropped to just above the horizon and in the process transformed into something entirely different. Instead of a bright splash of yellow, it had condensed into a dense orange ball, its edges hot and defined. Sunlight splashed against the white cliffside buildings, reflecting in a spectrum of blazing oranges.

The sunset was too bright to look at directly, so I turned

my gaze to the caldera. The water was still, but several large boats were booking it toward the sun, leaving silvery snail trails in their wakes. One of them let off its horn, and the full, lonely noise reverberated around the caldera, culminating in a spot just below my rib cage. A chill moved through me, as sudden as a breeze.

I tried to say something, tried to react, but I couldn't. All I could do was stare, transfixed. The sun dropped slowly, elegantly, like a lady sinking into a curtsy, getting redder and denser as it sank inch by inch into the ocean. It was almost too beautiful. Behind me, the island was quiet, the crowds holding their breath, just like I was.

When the final pinprick of red had melted away, there was a large whoosh of cold, salty sea air that sent my hair flying, then one delicious moment of silence, followed by the entire island bursting into wild, unfettered applause.

It was the only appropriate response.

"Happy you trusted me?" Theo said. He'd put the camera down and was smiling at me like he was somehow responsible for the sunset. Which I guess he was, or at least for the fact that I'd seen it.

I was about to ask him if Santorini's sunsets looked like this every night, when a hushed voice carried up the steps, stopping me cold. "Ana! She's already here?"

"With Theo," Ana said.

I didn't just recognize that voice with my ears; my cells recognized it. I knew its weight and timbre. I could smell the cigarette smoke in it, hear the pop of the cinnamon gum. I had been unconsciously listening for that voice since I was eight years old.

My body turned without me having to tell it to, and then there he was. Flying up the stairs with a wrapped package tucked under one arm, a spray of fuchsia flowers in the other, out of breath from running, his eyes focused on me.

Nico Varanakis.

My dad.

FAMILY SECRETS.

UNEXPECTED ROMANCE.

THRILLING ADVENTURE.

Read on for a sneak peek into Jenna Evans Welch's *New York Times* bestseller, *Love & Gelato*.

Prologue

YOU'VE HAD BAD DAYS BEFORE, RIGHT? YOU KNOW, THE ones where your alarm doesn't go off, your toast practically catches on fire, and you remember way too late that every article of clothing you own is soaking wet in the bottom of the washer? So then you go hurtling into school fifteen minutes late, *praying* no one will notice that your hair looks like the Bride of Frankenstein's, but just as you slide into your desk your teacher booms, "Running late today, Ms. Emerson?" and everyone looks at you and notices?

I'm sure you've had those days. We all have. But what about really bad days? The kind that are so pumped up and awful that they chew up the things you care about just for the fun of spitting them back in your face?

The day my mom told me about Howard fell firmly in the *really bad* category. But at the time, he was the least of my worries.

It was two weeks into my sophomore year of high school

and my mom and I were driving home from her appointment. The car was silent except for a radio commercial narrated by two Arnold Schwarzenegger impersonators, and even though it was a hot day, I had goose bumps up and down my legs. Just that morning I'd placed second at my first-ever cross country meet and I couldn't believe how much that didn't matter anymore.

My mom switched off the radio. "Lina, what are you feeling?" Her voice was calm, and when I looked at her I teared up all over again. She was so pale and tiny. How had I not noticed how *tiny* she'd gotten?

"I don't know," I said, trying to keep my voice even. "I feel like I'm in shock."

She nodded, coming to a stop at a traffic light. The sun was doing its best to blind us, and I stared into it, my eyes scalding. *This is the day that changes everything*, I thought. *From here on out there will only be* before *and* after *today.*

My mom cleared her throat, and when I glanced at her, she straightened up like she had something important to tell me. "Lina, did I ever tell you about the time I was dared to swim in a fountain?"

I whipped around. "What?"

"Remember how I told you I spent a year studying in Florence? I was out photographing with my classmates, and it was such a hot day I thought I was going to melt. I had this friend—Howard—and he dared me to jump into a fountain."

Now, keep in mind, we'd just gotten the worst news of our lives. The *worst*.

". . . I scared a group of German tourists. They were posing for a photo, and when I popped out of the water, one of them lost her balance and almost fell back into the fountain with me. They were furious, so Howard yelled that I was drowning and jumped in after me."

I stared at her, and she turned and gave me a little smile.

"Uh . . . Mom? That's funny and everything, but why are you telling me this now?"

"I just wanted to tell you about Howard. He was really a lot of fun." The light changed and she hit the gas.

What? I thought. *What what what*?

At first I thought the fountain story was a coping mechanism, like maybe she thought a story about an old friend could distract us from the two blocks of granite hanging over our heads. *Inoperable. Incurable.* But then she told me another story. And another. It got to the point where she'd start talking and three words in I'd know she was going to bring up Howard. And then when she finally told me the reason for all the Howard stories, well . . . let's just say that ignorance is bliss.

"Lina, I want you to go to Italy."

It was mid-November and I was sitting next to her hospital bed with a stack of ancient *Cosmo* magazines I'd swiped from the waiting room. I'd spent the last ten minutes taking a quiz called "On a Scale of One to Sizzle: How Hot Are You?" (7/10).

"Italy?" I was kind of distracted. The person who'd taken the quiz before me had scored a 10/10 and I was trying to figure out how.

"I mean I want you to go live in Italy. After."

That got my attention. For one thing, I didn't believe in *after*. Yes, her cancer was progressing just the way her doctors said it would, but doctors didn't know everything. Just that morning I'd bookmarked a story on the Internet about a woman who'd beaten cancer and gone on to climb Mt. Kilimanjaro. And for another, *Italy*?

"Why would I do that?" I asked lightly. It was important to humor her. Avoiding stress is a big part of recovery.

"I want you to stay with Howard. The year I spent in Italy meant so much to me, and I want you to have that same experience."

I shot my eyes at the nurse's call button. *Stay with Howard in Italy?* Did they give her too much morphine?

"Lina, look at me," she said, in her bossiest I Am the Mother voice.

"Howard? You mean that guy you keep talking about?"

"Yes. He's the best man I've ever known. He'll keep you safe."

"Safe from *what*?" I looked into her eyes, and suddenly my breath started coming in short and fast. She was serious. Did hospital rooms stock paper bags?

She shook her head, her eyes shiny. "Things will be . . . hard. We don't have to talk about it now, but I wanted to make sure you heard my decision from me. You'll need some-one. After. And I think he's the best person."

"Mom, that doesn't even make sense. Why would I go live with a stranger?" I jumped up and started rifling through the drawers in her end table. There had to be a paper bag *some-where*.

"Lina, sit."

"But, Mom—"

"Sit. You're going to be fine. You're going to make it. Your life will go on, and it's going to be great."

"No," I said. "*You're* going to make it. Sometimes people recover."

"Lina, Howard's a wonderful friend. You'll really love him."

"I doubt it. And if he's that good of a friend, then why haven't I ever met him before?" I gave up on finding a bag, collapsing back into my chair and putting my head between my knees.

She struggled to sit up, then reached out, resting her hand

on my back. "Things were a little bit complicated between us, but he wants to get to know you. And he said he'd love to have you stay with him. Promise me you'll give it a try. A few months at least."

There was a knock on the door, and we both looked up to see a nurse dressed in baby blue scrubs. "Just checking in," she sang, either ignoring or not noticing the expression on my face. On a Scale of One to Tense, the room was at about 100/10.

"Morning. I was just telling my daughter she needs to go to Italy."

"Italy," the nurse said, clasping both hands to her chest. "I went there on my honeymoon. Gelato, the Leaning Tower of Pisa, gondolas in Venice . . . You'll love it."

My mom smiled at me triumphantly.

"Mom, *no*. There's no way I'm going to Italy."

"Oh, but, honey, you have to go," the nurse said. "It will be a once-in-a-lifetime experience."

The nurse ended up being right about one thing: I did have to go. But no one gave me even the tiniest hint about what I'd find once I got there.